KT-569-672

BOURNEMOUTH LIBRARIES
300010247

THE ROAR OF THE BUTTERFLIES

By the same author

Dalziel and Pascoe novels

A CLUBBABLE WOMAN
AN ADVANCEMENT OF LEARNING
RULING PASSION
AN APRIL SHROUD
A PINCH OF SNUFF
A KILLING KINDNESS
DEADHEADS
EXIT LINES
CHILD'S PLAY
UNDERWORLD
BONES AND SILENCE
ONE SMALL STEP
RECALLED TO LIFE
PICTURES OF PERFECTION
ASKING FOR THE MOON
THE WOOD BEYOND
ON BEULAH HEIGHT
ARMS AND THE WOMEN
DIALOGUES OF THE DEAD
DEATH'S JEST-BOOK
GOOD MORNING, MIDNIGHT
THE DEATH OF DALZIEL

Joe Sixsmith novels

BLOOD SYMPATHY
BORN GUILTY
KILLING THE LAWYERS
SINGING THE SADNESS

THE COLLABORATORS
FELL OF DARK
THE LONG KILL
DEATH OF A DORMOUSE
DREAM OF DARKNESS
THE ONLY GAME
THE STRANGER HOUSE

REGINALD HILL

The Roar of the Butterflies

Bournemouth Libraries **SP**	
300010247	
Askews	2008
AF	£10.00

hers

This novel is entirely a work of fiction. The names, characters and incidents portrayed in it are the work of the author's imagination. Any resemblance to actual persons, living or dead, events or localities is entirely coincidental.

HarperCollins*Publishers*
77–85 Fulham Palace Road, London W6 8JB

www.harpercollins.co.uk

Published by HarperCollins 2008

1

Copyright © Reginald Hill 2008

"Roar of the butterflies" extract copyright © P G Wodehouse
Reproduced by permission of the Estate of P G Wodehouse
c/o Rogers, Coleridge & White Ltd., 20 Powis Mews,
London W11 1JN

Reginald Hill asserts the moral right to
be identified as the author of this work

A catalogue record for this book
is available from the British Library

ISBN-10 0-00-725273-0
ISBN-13 978-0-00-725273-2

Set in New Baskerville by Palimpsest Book Production Limited,
Grangemouth, Stirlingshire

Printed in Great Britain by
Clays Ltd, St Ives plc

Mixed Sources
Product group from well-managed forests and other controlled sources
www.fsc.org Cert no. SW-COC-1806
© 1996 Forest Stewardship Council

FSC is a non-profit international organisation established to promote the responsible management of the world's forests. Products carrying the FSC label are independently certified to assure consumers that they come from forests that are managed to meet the social, economic and ecological needs of present and future generations.

Find out more about HarperCollins and the environment at
www.harpercollins.co.uk/green

All rights reserved. No part of this publication may be reproduced, stored in a retrieval system, or transmitted, in any form or by any means, electronic, mechanical, photocopying, recording or otherwise, without the prior written permission of the publishers.

This book is sold subject to the condition that it shall not, by way of trade or otherwise, be lent, re-sold, hired out or otherwise circulated without the publisher's prior consent in any form of binding or cover other than that in which it is published and without a similar condition including this condition being imposed on the subsequent purchaser.

For

WRECKING CREWS
the world over.

(You know who you are!)

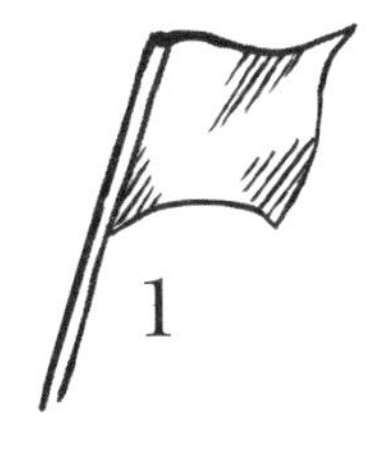

1
'Fonlies

Joe Sixsmith was adrift in space.

Light years beneath him gleamed the tiny orb he was supposed to make contact with, but he knew it was an impossible dream.

His muscles had melted, his lungs were starved of oxygen, and the only part of his mind not paralysed by terror was the bit that dealt with 'fonlies.

'fonly I'd done this . . .'fonly I'd done that . . .

'No use messing with 'fonlies,' Aunt Mirabelle used to say. ''fonlies don't get your homework done, Joseph. You miss your football Saturday morning, you've got no one to blame 'cept yourself.'

How right she was! No one to blame 'cept himself . . . except maybe Willie Woodbine for being such a social climber . . . and Beryl Boddington maybe for standing him up . . . and definitely Merv Golightly for having a mouth like the Channel Tunnel . . . but first and last and as usual, himself, Joseph Gaylord (even Mirabelle kept quiet about *that*) Sixsmith for always going boldly half-assed where nobody had ever come back from before!

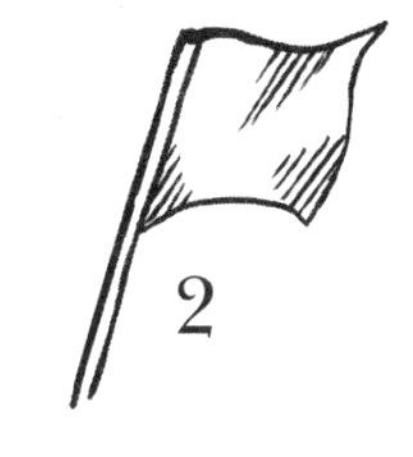

2

Enter a YFG

Way it started was this.

Monday afternoon, day before yesterday, though it seemed a lot longer ago, he'd been sitting in his office, minding his own business, which didn't take much minding this time of year. Summer had parked its anti-cyclone firmly over Luton and fused the days and nights of July together with a heat too enervating to start a race riot in, let alone perpetrate any of the crimes that might send the distressed citizenry in search of a PI. Ice creams melted before they could reach your mouth, birds huddled beneath cats for shade, and flies buzzed with relief into spiders' webs whose owners felt the tremor along the line and thought that maybe next Friday they'd stroll down there to take a look.

The plus side was that Joe too felt as energetic as a poached egg and couldn't whip up much concern at the lack of client incentive to head off down the mean streets.

So clad in an off-white singlet and Bermuda shorts patterned with scarlet parrots sinking their beaks into rainbow-striped pumpkins, Joe sat at his desk and relaxed with his favourite book, *Not So Private Eye,* the reminiscences of Endo Venera, the famous Mafia soldier turned gumshoe. This was Joe's bible. Everything you needed to know about being a PI was here, except maybe how to stay awake.

His head nodded, and he slipped into a dream in which he and Beryl Boddington were sliding naked down an iceberg, and he wasn't at all pleased to have his descent interrupted by a voice saying, 'Mr Sixsmith? Would you be Mr Sixsmith?'

He opened his eyes and found he was being addressed by a Young Fair God.

He was thirty at most, tall, boyishly handsome, with hair that shone pale gold against the darker gold of skin glowing with a proper expensive Mediterranean yacht kind of tan, not the russet-and-red skin-peeling version which made any large gathering of Lutonians look like Vermont in the Fall. His lean athletic frame was clad in a linen jacket, cream slacks and an open-necked shirt white enough to signal surrender at half a mile. He looked, thought Joe, just like one of those hunks you see in up-market mail-order catalogues where, despite the alleged cutting out of the middle man, the gear still costs three times what you'd expect to pay down Luton market.

But it wasn't this that caught and held Joe's attention. It was the fact that the guy looked cool. Not cool in the laid-back hey-man-how-you-doin'? kind of way, though that too. No, this guy looked like he was standing in some nice and easy air-conditioned zone of his own rather than the sauna of Joe's office. Perhaps this was a special deal available only to Young Fair Gods.

'Hope you don't mind. I just came in. The door was open,' said the YFG. He had a quails'-eggs-easy-over-on-cinnamon-toast kind of voice.

'Yeah, that's OK. Trying to get a through draught,' said Joe. Then repeated *trying* in ironic acknowledgement that not so much air was moving between the open window and door as would have fluttered a maidenhair fern.

'All right if I sit down?' said the YFG, sinking on to an old dining chair with the confidence of one whose creamy slacks have been treated with a dust-repellent potion unobtainable by the common herd. 'My name is Porphyry. Christian Porphyry.'

'U-huh,' said Joe, unsurprised. Creature like this wasn't going to be called Fred Jones, not if (as he firmly believed) there was an underlying order to things.

Also the name wasn't totally unfamiliar, at least the Porphyry bit. He'd seen it in the paper recently, but even memory found it hard to move back through this heat haze. He could check it out later if he had the energy, because he'd certainly not had the energy to dump any newspapers for the past week or so. In fact, come to think of it, he doubted if he'd had the energy to open one, so the Porphyry reference must have been front page or back page, i.e. headline news or sport. He realized that these thoughts had occupied rather more time than they would have done normally, and since his *u-huh* the sort of companionable silence had developed between them which was OK between a pair of buddies fishing off a river bank but didn't promise to move the PI/client relationship forward very far.

He said, 'Sixsmith. Joe Sixsmith.'

'Yes. I thought you must be,' said Porphyry with a pleasant smile.

Joe found himself smiling back. There was something very attractive about this guy. He felt really easy with him, which was not a good way to feel with someone who'd just strolled into your office. For all Joe knew, Porphyry could be a cop interested in the provenance of the six-pack of Guinness cooling in his washroom hand basin, which he'd got (plus another nineteen) from his taxi-driving friend Merv Golightly on the assurance that the fifty per cent discount Merv was offering derived from their being bankrupt stock. ('You mean,' Joe had enquired for the avoidance of doubt, 'that the guy these came from was bankrupt?' to which after a little thought Merv had replied, 'Well, yeah, I'd guess he is now.')

Or could be the YFG was a solicitor about to serve a writ

for non-payment of any of the things Joe had non-paid recently.

Or could even be he was a hit man on a contract taken out by one of the top criminals Joe had crossed in his unrelenting crusade for justice . . .

No, scrub that one. This guy didn't look like he'd slap your wrist for less than a grand, and in pay-back terms Joe's recent toe-treading didn't rate much more than a ten-quid kicking up an alley.

He realized another companionable silence was developing.

He said, 'How can I help you, Mr Porphyry?'

'I do hope so,' said Porphyry with such touching vulnerability of tone and expression that Joe hadn't the heart to point out this wasn't a helpful or even a possible reply to his question. But the YFG hadn't finished. Maybe divine revelation was on its way.

'Willie spoke very highly of you,' he said with the stress on *very* and a slight but emphatic nod of his beautiful head as if this testimonial from this source was confirmation absolute of Joe's competence.

'He did, huh?' said Joe, trying to identify his unexpected fan. Trouble was most of the Willies he could bring to mind failed on both counts – speaking highly of him or being on friendly terms with YFGs. He gave up and added, 'That would be Willie . . . ?'

'Woodbine,' said Porphyry.

'As in Detective Superintendent Woodbine?' said Joe disbelievingly.

'That's the chap. Done awfully well for himself, old Willie. Naturally I turned to him first. Not his line of country really, he said. But if I wanted to try the private sector, there's this chap, Joe Sixsmith. Cutting edge of investigation. He's your man.'

He smiled as he spoke, the happy smile of a voyager arrived at last in safe haven.

Another silence began. This time Joe didn't even disturb it with an *U-huh*. If the guy had been paying him, he might have felt different, but it was too hot for a man to exert himself with no certainty of reward, and besides he was wrestling with the problem of how come Willie Woodbine was pushing clients his way, particularly clients like this.

A phone rang. It wasn't Joe's. His desk phone had the harsh shriek of a crow just landed on an electrified fence and his mobile played the *Hallelujah* chorus. This one let out a soft yet firm double note, like the deferential cough of a butler wanting to catch master's attention.

'Sorry,' said Porphyry, producing the neatest mobile Joe had ever seen cased in what looked like old gold.

He put it to his ear and listened. Then he switched off, stood up and said, 'I'm afraid I have to go. Look, I'm tied up today, but can you do tomorrow morning? Let's meet at the club, how does that sound? I think it would be good for you to get a feel of the place. I can show you round. Scene of the crime, that sort of thing.'

What crime? wondered Joe. And which club? Time to get some sense into this interchange.

'Look, Mr Porphyry . . .' he began.

'Chris,' said the man. 'And I shall call you Joe. It will authenticate our cover, isn't that what you chaps say? You're interested in applying for membership, if anyone asks. Half ten all right for you? That gives us time for a look around, and we can have a spot of lunch after. OK?'

'I'm not sure,' said Joe, glad at last to have something concrete to get his teeth into, though, come to think of it, all that was likely to do was break your teeth. 'Look, I'm pretty busy just now and until I know . . .'

'Of course, I realize you're in great demand, Mr Sixsmith, Joe, and I certainly don't expect to take up your time for nothing.'

He produced a wallet, took out four fifties that looked like they'd just rolled off the press, and placed them on the desk.

'Will that cover today? Once you understand the fine details of the case, then we can regularize finances. So I'll see you at the club in the morning.'

'What details?' asked Joe, dragging his gaze from the money. 'Of what case? And what club?'

Experience should have taught him that if you ask more than one question at a time, you usually get an answer to the least important.

'The Who, of course,' said Porphyry, slightly puzzled as if this were not a question he expected to be asked.

His answer meant nothing to Joe. Luton wasn't short of clubs, and he'd expected something like Dirty Harry's, which was the hottest, or maybe Skimbleshanks, which was the classiest, except these weren't places people did much lunchtime rendezvousing in.

But whatever the time of day, the Who rang no bell. Presumably named after the famous seventies group – everything was retro these days – or maybe after Doctor Who, the TV space opera which was enjoying a revival. Either way, he didn't know the place. But for a PI to display ignorance of the club scene might finally begin to scratch the bright shiny image Willie Woodbine had created for him, so best to let it be and ask around.

'Till tomorrow then,' said Porphyry, heading for the door.

Here he paused and cast a speculative eye over Joe. He

seemed to be meditating a parting utterance. Joe paid close attention in case at last a clue was going to be offered.

But Young Fair Gods speak only in riddles.

'There's a shorts dispensation during the hot weather for those with the legs to stand it, but they have to be tailored, of course. Myself, I just love the parrots. Bye.'

And he was gone, leaving only a faint aroma of something too pleasant to be called aftershave in a slender zone of coolth, both of which the nuzzling heat gobbled up in a few seconds.

3

A Willie Day

Joe sat for a moment wondering if it had all been a desert mirage brought on by heat exhaustion. But the crisp notes remained on his desk, and now further confirmation burst into the office in the attractive shape of Beryl Boddington, his in-out girlfriend, one vision authenticating another.

'And who was *that* gorgeous creature?' she demanded, hurrying past Joe to peer out of the window. 'Saw the fancy wheels outside and soon as I clocked him on the stairs I thought, he's the man. Yeah, there he goes.'

Joe swept the money out of sight into his shorts pocket, then joined Beryl at the window.

Below, Porphyry was vaulting into an Aston DB9 Volante parked behind Joe's Morris Oxford. His golden hair bounced and shimmered in the midday sun. It was like looking down at a shampoo ad. As he pulled away he glanced up, smiled and waved.

Beryl waved back with huge enthusiasm.

'That's solved one problem,' she said. 'Now I know what I want for my birthday.'

'The car?' suggested Joe.

'That too,' she said. 'Come on. Tell me who he is. I'm sure I've seen him before. If he's not a movie star, he surely ought to be.'

'Oh, he's just a client,' said Joe negligently. 'If I take him on, that is.'

Maybe he should have felt jealous, but not in this weather. Anyway where was the harm in someone fantasizing about what was out of their reach, long as they stayed happy with what was in it? His trouble with Beryl was the way she hovered on the boundary of *out* and *in*. Sometimes she kept him at a distance, other times they were so close that if they'd been any closer they'd have fused. His mind drifted back to the last such occasion and he found as he studied her sturdy yet well shaped body in its very becoming blue-and-white nurse's uniform that this heat wasn't totally enervating after all.

'Don't I get a kiss then?' he said.

'Not in those shorts, you don't,' said Beryl. 'Surely you know the guy's name?'

'Porphyry,' said Joe, wishing she wouldn't go on about the YFG. 'I could always take them off.'

'Don't even dream about it. Porphyry. Of course! I

knew I'd seen him. His picture was on the front page of the *Bedfordshire Bugle* last week. He's just got engaged. Damn!'

'Maybe I can catch you on the rebound,' said Joe. 'So why's he important enough to get his picture on the front page just because he's got engaged?'

'Well, first, he's gorgeous; second, his family have been around the county for ever and a day; and third, he's got engaged to Tiff Emerson whose daddy owns nearly everything in the media that Rupert Murdoch doesn't, including the *Bugle*. Where you been, Joe?'

'Maybe I've got more important things than gossip columns to fill my mind.'

'Such as?' she demanded, looking around the office. 'So much dust on that filing cabinet, don't think it's been opened since Christmas.'

'So you're a detective now,' said Joe. 'First thing you should learn is, the real important cases, nothing goes down on paper.'

'What real important cases?' she laughed.

'Like the one I'm meeting Mr Porphyry, Chris, to discuss over lunch tomorrow,' he said triumphantly.

It worked. For a moment she looked impressed.

Then she shrugged and said, 'Well, that's a pity, 'cos that's why I dropped in to see you. I've got to break our date tonight. They're short-staffed at the hospital and need me to do an extra shift. I was going to suggest that maybe if you could find time in your busy schedule we could go somewhere nice and cool for a drink and a sandwich tomorrow lunch, but seeing as how you're engaged, I'd better look elsewhere. Bye, Joe.'

She headed for the door. He tried to think of something to say to halt her.

'I can always cancel,' he said.

'Let Chris Porphyry down? Don't be stupid, Joe.'

But she was obviously touched by the thought that he'd do this for her and when he moved forward to kiss her, she didn't back off even though she was right about the shorts. But her mind was still dwelling on the YFG.

'You must be on the up, Joe, getting clients like that. Where are you meeting him?'

'Some club I never heard of called the Who. You any idea where it is?'

She thought a moment then began to laugh.

'That's not a club like you think of a club, Joe. That will be the Hoo, aitch oh oh, the Royal Hoo Golf Club. That is seriously posh.'

'Yeah? A posh golf club?' He considered the idea dubiously. 'Any idea how I get there?'

'You could try bank robbery and a skin graft. Sorry. Head out on the Upleck road till you hit the bypass, then get off at the big roundabout; it's along one of those little roads no one ever uses, don't recollect which one, but you'll know you're getting close by the watch towers and the big signs saying *No Hawkers, Vendors or Racial Minorities.* They're particular what people wear too, I dare say.'

She glanced significantly at his shorts, which were resuming normal service.

'He said there was a dispensation in the hot weather,' protested Joe.

'For those you don't need a dispensation, more like a disposal unit,' said Beryl. 'You ever play golf, Joe?'

'May have done,' said Joe, reluctant to admit that what he knew about the game could have been written on the point of a tee peg. Football was the only sport he had any real interest in, and nowadays his active participation there consisted of shouting advice at his beloved Luton City FC and singing Songs from the Shows on Supporters' Club social nights.

'Oh yeah?' she said. 'So what's your handicap, Tiger? Apart from not being able to see the ball over your belly.'

She didn't wait for a response but ran laughing down the stairs.

'Why shouldn't I be a good golfer?' Joe called after her, stung by the reference to his waistline. 'Lot of things about me you don't know.'

Which, considering Beryl's intimacy with his Aunt Mirabelle, wasn't likely to be true, but a man was entitled to his dignity.

His musings were interrupted by the screech of the office phone.

He picked it up and said, 'Sixsmith Investigations. We're here to help you.'

'Today it's me helping you, Joe,' said a man's voice.

Joe recognized the voice, not because it was distinctive, but because it was Detective Superintendent Willie Woodbine's, which was a good voice to recognize. He hesitated a moment before he replied. His relationship with the Super was a bit like his relationship with Beryl. Not that he had any ambition to get in bed with the guy, but sometimes it was man to man, sometimes boss to man, sometimes first name, sometimes not. Trick was to read the signals and decide if this was a Willie day. Same with Beryl, if you thought about it.

He decided to sit on the fence.

'Hi there, how're you doing?' he said.

'That could depend on you, Joe. I was ringing to tell you that I've pushed a possible client your way. Christian Porphyry. You heard of him?'

'Didn't I see his picture in the paper recently?' said Joe. 'Got arrested or something?'

He didn't see the need to tell Woodbine Porphyry had been and gone. Might be some chance of getting a bit of info from the horse's mouth.

'Got engaged, Joe. Not the same thing. Though, come to think of it, maybe you're right.'

He chuckled. His voice was quite friendly. Looked like this might be a Willie day, which probably meant he wanted something. Woodbine was the kind of ambitious cop whose gaze was fixed on the high ground. He only glanced down in search of small change that someone else had dropped. In his mind, professional and social upward mobility marched hand in hand and he'd married accordingly. But popular judgement was that he'd need to become Lord High Executioner before his wife would reckon she'd been compensated for her noble condescension.

He stopped chuckling and went on, 'The thing is, Joe, I've given you a good write-up, and I just wanted to make sure you won't let me down.'

'Wouldn't dream of it, Willie, no sir, you can rely on good old Joe.'

He'd over-hammed it. Woodbine said sharply, 'This is serious, Joe. I hope you're going to take it seriously.'

'Of course I am,' said Joe in his serious voice. 'Might help, though, if you gave me a hint what it is I'm being serious about?'

'It's nothing, storm in a teacup, really. Mr Porphyry, Christian, has got himself a bit of bother at the golf club. He mentioned it to me, asked my advice. I gave it some thought, and I told him, Sorry, Chris, but this doesn't get close to being a police matter. You know me, Joe, always willing to stretch things a bit for a friend, but in this case I really couldn't see how anything in the official machinery could be of any use. But I hate to let a chum down. And it struck me, what he really needed was someone so unofficial, you'd pay him no heed. Someone so unlikely, no one would worry about him. Someone you'd not lay good money on to know his arse from his elbow. Someone like you, Joe.'

It wasn't exactly a glowing testimonial. But Joe knew that

he probably only survived in Luton because Willie Woodbine felt able to give it.

Very few cops like private eyes. Most view them with grave suspicion. And a few hate their guts and would love to put them out of business.

Not that Joe had looked like he needed much help in that line when he started. But somehow again and again after stumbling around like a short-sighted man in a close-planted pine forest on a dark night, he had emerged blinking with mild surprise into bright light and open country with everything lying clearly before him.

On more than one occasion Willie Woodbine had been nicely placed to take most of the credit. But the cop was clear-sighted enough to recognize it was Joe's success, not his own, and from time to time he reached out a protective hand, not so much to pay a debt as to protect an asset.

Reaching out the hand of patronage was something new.

'That what you told Mr Porphyry about me, Willie?'

'No,' sighed Woodbine. 'I told him that in something like this, despite appearances, if anyone could get the job done, it was likely to be you. So don't you go letting me down, Joe. Or else . . .'

'Yeah yeah,' said Joe, to whom a veiled threat was like a veiled exotic dancer. While you didn't know the exact proportions of what you were going to see when the veil came off, you knew you were unlikely to see anything you hadn't seen before. 'But just what is the job, Willie?'

There was another voice in the background now, saying something Joe couldn't make out, but the tone was urgent.

'Joe, got to go. Keep me posted, OK?'

The phone went dead.

'Shoot,' said Joe, draining his can of Guinness.

He hadn't got much further forward. What could a bit of bother at a golf club amount to? Taking a leak in a bunker, maybe. Or wearing shorts with parrots on.

There was mystery here, and maybe trouble. At least he had the consolation of knowing beneath the parrots he had two hundred quid of the YFG's money thawing in his pocket.

He looked at his watch. Just after three, but he might as well go home. He didn't anticipate getting any more business today.

He tossed the can towards the waste bin, missed, rose wearily and went out to brave the heat of the Luton dog days.

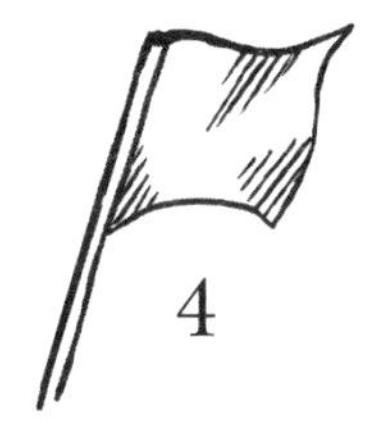

4

Blackball

As Joe drove the Morris through Bullpat Square, he saw a familiar figure coming out of the wide-open door of the Law Centre. Tiny enough for even a vertically challenged PI to loom over, from behind she could have been taken for a twelve-year-old, but that wasn't an error anyone persisted in once they'd looked into those steely eyes and even less after they'd listened to the words issuing out of that wide, determined mouth, usually borne on a jet of noxious smoke from a thin cheroot.

This was Cheryl Butcher, founder and leading lawyer of the Centre, which offered a pay-what-you-can-afford legal service to the disadvantaged of the city.

Joe slowed to walking pace and pulled into the kerb.

'Hey, Butcher,' he called. 'You looking for action?'

She didn't even glance his way.

'What the hell would you know about action, Sixsmith?'

'Enough to know you walk too far in this heat, you're going to melt away. Like a lift?'

Wise-cracking was an area of traditional gumshoe activity Joe didn't usually bother with. It required from-the-hip rapid-fire responses and he was honest enough to recognize himself as an old-fashioned muzzle-loader. But his relationship with Butcher somehow seemed to stimulate him to make the effort. Maybe it was the certainty that in their mutual mockery there was a lot of respect.

'You heading to Rasselas?'

The Rasselas Estate was a collection of sixties high-rise blocks which would probably have been demolished years ago if a determined Residents' Committee, led by Major Sholto Tweedie, ably assisted by such powerful personalities as Joe's Aunt Mirabelle, hadn't succeeded in making it a place fit for humans to live in.

'I surely am.'

'Then you can drop me at Hermsprong,' said Butcher, opening the car door and stepping in, which you could do with the old Morris Oxford if you were only as big as the lawyer.

Architecturally, Hermsprong was a mirror image of Rasselas built on the other side of the canal. And, like a mirror image, it showed everything back to front.

Unlike reconstructed Rasselas, every cliché of depressed urban high-rise living could be found on Hermsprong.

Crack-houses, corner dealers, lifts that were moving urinals when they moved at all, underpasses which were rats' alleys where you could lose more than your bones, the highest break-in rate, the lowest clear-up rate, more hoodies than a monastery, and so on, and so on. If ever a place should have been razed to the ground, Hermsprong was it. But paradoxically it survived because of Rasselas's success. How could you say an experiment had failed when you could produce evidence only a mile away that it could succeed? Or to put it another way, why should you demolish Hermsprong and relocate its inmates to the lovely new small well-planned developments the council was building to the east when the inhabitants of Rasselas were so much more deserving?

These were the arguments the sophists of the City Council produced in order to postpone a decision which was going to put an intolerable strain on their already overstretched budget.

Joe knew that to ask why Butcher was heading for Hermsprong would be like asking a bank robber why he robbed banks. *'Cos that's where my clients are, stupid.*

Instead he said, 'You're not going to light that thing in my car, are you?'

Referring to the cheroot which Butcher had inserted between her lips.

'Jesus, Sixsmith, you should watch more old movies. You can't be a proper PI unless you chain smoke!'

'Like you can't be a proper lawyer 'less you wear a wig and charge five hundred pounds a minute?'

'Don't insult me. I'm worth more than that.'

But she put the cheroot away then asked, 'So, business is so bad you've shut up shop and decided to spend the rest of the day watching mucky videos?'

'Wrong, as usual. Matter of fact, I'm going home to do some research on the very important client I'll be lunching with at his club tomorrow.'

'Oh yes? And I'm going to meet the Lord Chancellor to talk about becoming a High Court judge!'

This provoked Joe to telling her all about his encounter with the YFG.

She listened with interest. He tried to conceal his ignorance of what the case was all about by claiming client confidentiality but she saw through that straightaway.

'You mean you haven't got the faintest idea, don't you? How many times do I have to tell you, Sixsmith? Always find out what you're getting into before you get into it. Interesting though that the sun doesn't shine all the time, not even on Golden Boy.'

'You know Porphyry?'

'Not personally, but professionally I had occasion to do some research on the family three, four years back in connection with a compensation case.'

'Shoot. And that was against Porphyry?' said Joe, feeling illogically dismayed.

'Against the Porphyry Estate, which makes it the same thing. One of their employees died. Coroner said accident, no one to blame, but that's what they appoint coroners for, isn't it? To make sure the Porphyrys of this world never get blamed. There was a widow and a son. I reckoned they deserved better.'

'And did they get it?'

'Unhappily the mother didn't survive her husband long enough for things to run their course. If there is a God, he's a member at Royal Hoo and looks after His own.'

'I thought Chris was OK,' Joe protested.

'And you've got O-levels for character judgement, right? I'm sure he's a very likeable guy. In the class war, the ones that make you like them are the worst, Joe. He might seem to be trailing clouds of glory, but he's also trailing a couple of centuries of unearned privilege. And if you get to thinking he's different from the rest, remind yourself he's just got engaged to a fluff-head whose father runs some of the most fascist imprints of our mainly fascist press.'

To Joe this sounded a bit unfair on the *Bugle*, but political debate with Butcher was a waste of time.

'All I know is the guy's got some kind of trouble,' he said weakly.

'Yes, and that is good news,' said Butcher. 'But what's really puzzling is why he's looking for help from you of all people.'

Indignantly he retorted, ''Cos I was recommended, that's why?'

'Recommended?' she said incredulously. 'Who by? The Samaritans?'

'By Willie Woodbine, no less.'

Which meant he had to tell her all that part of the story too.

To his surprise she nodded as if it all made perfect sense.

'Poor Willie,' she said. 'Must be in a real tizz. And you're his last resort.'

'What's that mean?'

'You don't know anything, do you, Joe?' she said. He knew she was going to be really patronizing when she called him Joe, but he didn't mind. Folk could rarely be patronizing without telling you stuff you didn't know just to show how much more they knew than you did.

She said, 'Willie Woodbine's dad used to buttle for the Porphyrys . . .'

'Battle?' interrupted Joe. 'You mean, like he was a minder or something?'

'He was their butler, for God's sake. Willie must be three or four years older than Chris, just the age gap for a bit of hero worship, young master being shown the ropes by the butler's worldly-wise son. Boot on the other foot when they grew up, of course, but there's a relationship there which begins to assume at least the appearance of equality when Willie joins the police force and starts his rapid climb up the ladder. If he gets to be chief constable, he might even get invited round to dinner.'

'Miaow,' said Joe, who might have observed, had he been given to self-, social-, psycho-, or indeed any kind of analysis, how interesting it was that folk from nice bourgeois backgrounds like Butcher were much more inclined to get hot under the collar about the inequalities of class than natural-born plebs like himself.

She ignored him and went on, 'So it's not surprising that Willie, with his eyes on the top, should want to do the young master a service, particularly in this area.'

'You're losing me,' said Joe.

'It's finding you that's the problem,' she sighed. 'The golf club. The Royal Hoo. Getting into the Hoo is the ultimate accolade in Luton high society. If your face doesn't fit, you've more chance of getting into the Royal Enclosure at Ascot wearing shorts like yours!'

Now Joe did feel hurt. Class didn't bother him but snipes at his fashion sense did, 'less they came from a rich client or a gorgeous in-out girlfriend. He refused to let himself be diverted, however, and asked, 'So you don't just go along and pay your admission fee?'

'No! They need to look you over, check your family and friends then move on to your bank balance, your tailor and your table manners. After that if you've got someone to propose you, second you and probably third and fourth you, they take a vote . . .'

'Who's this they?'

'Some committee,' she said dismissively. 'And it just takes one blackball and you've had it.'

'Black ball?' said Joe. 'Don't like the sound of that.'

'Don't go vulgar on me, Joe,' she said.

'Sorry. So Chris is putting Willie up for membership, is that what you're saying?'

'So I'd guess. And of course if you want to get into the Hoo, then getting yourself proposed by Christian Porphyry is just about the closest thing you can get to a guarantee of success.'

'Because everybody likes him, you mean?' said Joe, who didn't find this hard to believe. One of the many perks of being a YFG had to be that everybody liked you.

'Don't be silly. What's liking got to do with it? Because the Royal Hoo more or less belongs to the Porphyry family, of course.'

'That more or less?' asked Joe.

'I don't know the precise details,' said Butcher. 'Just what I picked up when researching the family background. Know your enemy, Joe. You never can tell when some little detail might come in useful in court.'

Joe shuddered at the thought of finding himself on the wrong end of Butcher in a courtroom. Not even Young Fair Gods were safe.

He said, 'OK, give me the history lesson, long as you're not charging.'

'I'll put it on your slate,' she said. 'Back in the twenties, one of the Porphyrys was so hooked on golf he built a course on an outlying stretch of the family estate known as the Royal Hoo because, according to tradition, King Charles had been hidden there in a peasant's hut during the Civil War.'

'And he was anonymous, so they called it Hoo?'

'Funny. I hope. No, it's called Hoo because that's what

hoo means: a spur of land. At first it was for private use only, by invitation from the family. Then the war came and the course got ploughed up. When peace broke out, and the UK was once more a land fit for golfers, the old gang of chums and hangers on started pestering Porphyry to have the course refurbished. Only this was a new Porphyry, your boy's grandfather, I'd guess, and he was commercially a lot sharper and didn't see why he should pick up all the tabs. He insisted a proper company was formed and the Royal Hoo Golf Club as we know it – everyone, that is, except you – came into being.'

'With the Porphyrys still in control?'

'Don't know the contractual details, but I'd guess they kept a controlling interest. People like them don't give their land away, free gratis and for nothing,' she said grimly.

'So, with Christian's backing, Willie looks like a cert for membership? Good for him, if that's what he wants.'

'And good for you too, Joe. Maybe. I'd guess whatever trouble Porphyry's got, he did what the ruling classes always do and turned to his old butler for help. That's OK if you've got a Crichton or a Jeeves, but all he had was Woodbine, who felt he couldn't help officially but tried to keep his nose up master's bum by recommending you as a last resort.'

Joe tried not to show he was hurt but he wasn't very good at dissimulation, and Butcher, who was very fond of him, said placatingly, 'Look, I don't mean you don't get results. For God's sake, I've recommended you myself, haven't I?'

This was true, and the memory eased the smart a little.

'All I meant was, I mean, Jesus, what can you do in a set-up like the Hoo? You'll stick out like a . . .'

She seemed lost for a simile.

'Like a black ball,' completed Joe.

This time she didn't reprove his vulgarity.

'Something like that. When Porphyry met you, didn't he say anything?'

'Like, hey man, no one mentioned you were a short black balding no-hoper with parrots on his shorts? No, I don't recollect hearing anything like that. Unless giving me four fifties and saying come and have lunch with me at the club is posh shorthand for *I'd be crazy to hire a slob like you.*'

'Joe, don't go sensitive on me. It doesn't suit you.'

He consulted his feelings. She was right. And in any case, it was too much of an effort in this weather to keep it up.

'Apology accepted,' he said.

'Apology? You going deaf too?'

That was better. Now they were back on their proper footing.

They chatted about other things till Butcher told Joe to drop her in an area on the fringe of Hermsprong that even in the full brightness of a midsummer day had an aura of dark menace.

'You want I should come with you?' offered Joe, glancing uneasily at a group of young men who looked like they were planning to blow up Parliament.

'To do what?' she asked. Then, relenting, she added, 'No, I'll be OK, Joe, but thanks for the thought. It's you who needs protection. I'm just going among the poor and the disadvantaged. Tomorrow you'll be mixing with the rich and successful. That's where the sabre-toothed tigers roam. Take care of yourself there, Joe.'

She got out of the car, lit her cheroot, and set off along the pavement, pausing by the terrorists to say something that made them laugh and exchanging high fives with them before she moved on.

Sixsmith watched her vanish behind the graffti'd wall of a walkway, tracking her progress for a little while by the spoor of tobacco smoke which hung almost without motion in the lifeless air. She'd be OK, he guessed. She was worth more to these people alive than dead. This was her chosen world. People like Porphyry and the other members of the Royal Hoo were the enemy, which was why she knew so much about them, presumably.

Not that Butcher was the only one able to identify the enemy.

The terrorists had begun a slow drift towards the Morris.

He gave them a friendly wave and accelerated away towards the visible haven of Rasselas.

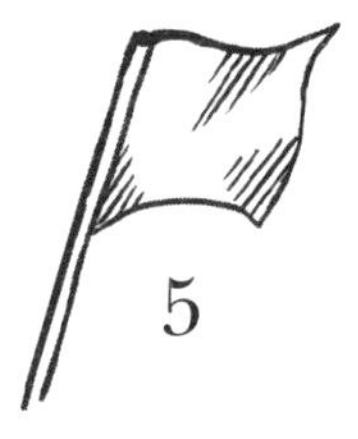

5

Tiger

That night, with Beryl working, nothing but repeats on the box, and his cat Whitey plunged deep into whatever the summer equivalent of hibernation was, Joe decided to wander round to the Luton City Supporters' Club bar in search of social solace.

To start with it seemed a good decision. He arrived just in time to get in on the end of a round that most democratic of club chairmen, Sir Monty Wright, was buying to celebrate the close-season signing of a sixteen-year-old Croatian *wunderkind*. Word was that Man U and Chelsea had both been sniffing around, but while they hesitated, Sir Monty, who hadn't got where he was by hesitating, had dipped his hand into his apparently bottomless purse and said to the manager, 'Go get him.'

Joe bore his pint of Guinness to a seat next to his friend, Merv Golightly, self-styled prince of Luton cabbies but known because of his exuberant driving style as the man who put the X in taxi.

'Good to see you, Joe,' he said. 'But I thought you was on a promise tonight. What happened? Beryl give you the elbow?'

'Something came up at the hospital,' said Joe.

'Better than washing her hair, I suppose,' laughed Merv. 'So how's business? Slow or stopped?'

The slur prompted Joe to tell Merv about Christian Porphyry. If he'd hoped to impress his friend he was disappointed.

'And this guy wants you to meet him at the Royal Hoo? And he's going to say you're applying for membership? Must be someone there he really wants to wind up! Give him the finger, Joe. He's using you. You don't believe me? Take a look at Sir Monty there.'

Joe, ever a literalist, turned to look towards the table where Sir Monty was holding court with some of his directors. He found Sir Monty was looking back. Joe gave him a cheerful wave and got a nod in return, which was not to be sneezed at from a man worth a couple of billion and rising.

The Wright-Price supermarket chain had started from a flourishing corner shop owned by the Wright family in a Luton suburb. When Monty was eighteen, one of the big supermarket chains looking to expand had approached

Wright senior with an offer for the business, while at the same time negotiating with the Council for the purchase of a small playing field adjacent to the shop. This looked a smart move, taking over a flourishing local business and acquiring enough land to expand it into a full-blooded hyper-market. With young Monty pulling his parents' strings, the sale of the shop was delayed and delayed until the day before the Council Planning Committee meeting which was expected to confirm the sale of the playing field on the nod. Fearing that if they went ahead with the land purchase before they'd got the shop, the Wrights would be in an even stronger bargaining position, the big chain caved in to most of their demands and ended up paying almost twice as much as their original offer.

The deal was signed.

Next day the Planning Committee voted to reject the chain's offer for the playing field, preferring, as it said, to put the needs of the local community first.

On the same day the bulldozers moved on to a piece of derelict land only half a mile away and, financed by the big chain's own money augmented by a large loan from a city bank whose CEO had long nursed a grudge against his opposite number on the chain's board, the first of Monty Wright's supermarkets was erected in record time.

Five years later even the City's most dedicated doubters had to accept that the Wright-Price chain was here to stay. By that time another dozen shops had gone up in the south-east and marketing whiz-kids were keen to climb aboard the bandwagon. The fact that an early appointee to the Board of Directors was a local businessman called Ratcliffe King who had happened to be Chairman of the Planning Committee which rejected the application to purchase the playing field was noted but not commented on. At least not by anyone with any sense. Ratcliffe King wasn't known as King Rat in Luton political circles without reason. No longer a councillor, he retained the title and still wielded much of the political power in his role as head of ProtoVision, the planning and development consultancy he had founded on retirement from public life. Officially his role on the Wright-Price board was and remained non-executive, but in the view of many he'd played a central strategic role in the campaign which twenty years on had led to Monty Wright being knighted for services to industry as head of a company no longer coveted by the market leaders as possible prey but feared by them as potential predator.

'What about Sir Monty?' asked Joe, turning back to Merv. 'And keep your voice down, I think he heard you talking about him.'

'What's wrong with that?' said Merv. 'Not saying anything everyone doesn't know.'

But he dropped his voice a little, or as much as he could, before he went on, 'Like I said, look at Monty. All that lolly plus the title – even got his teeth straightened to go to the Palace, I heard! – and what happens when he applies to join the Royal Hoo? They turn him down flat!'

'So what's your point?' asked Joe, who liked things spelt out.

'My point is, doesn't matter what this plonker Porphyry says. The only way they'll let you into the Royal Hoo is through the back door dressed as a waiter! Maybe that's it. Maybe they're short of staff. They ask to see your testimonials, just you be careful!'

Merv's difficulty in keeping his voice low even to share a confidence was compounded by a compulsion when uttering a *bon mot* to up the volume several decibels as if to make sure no one in the same building was deprived. Heads turned, and when a few moments later he went to the bar to get a round in, he was pressed to elaborate by several of the other drinkers.

The result was, for the rest of the evening Joe found himself the object of much cheerful waggery. Normally this was water off a duck's back, but even his good nature was finding it hard to raise a smile the tenth time someone tapped him on the shoulder and said, 'Pardon me, sir, aren't you the one they call Tiger?'

Rumours of the joke must have reached Sir Monty's table. After a visit to the Gents, Joe returned to see Merv sitting next to the baronet, talking expansively. At least he wasn't getting the easy laughs he'd wrung out of the rest of his audience. Indeed, Sir Monty, though listening attentively, had a deep frown on his face. Maybe after his own experience with the Royal Hoo he didn't reckon there was much to laugh at.

Serves Merv right, thought Joe.

'Fancy another one, Tiger?' called an acquaintance from the bar.

'No thanks. On my way home,' he replied.

It wasn't just the golf jokes that had got to him. He'd found himself thinking, what if Merv was right and this guy Porphyry was pulling his plonker by using him to get at some of his fellow members? He hadn't struck Joe as that kind of bean-head, but what did he know about the mind processes of Young Fair Gods? So tell him to take a jump. Except he didn't know how to contact him. OK, just don't turn up. Except he had two hundred quid of the guy's money in an envelope in his back pocket (somehow it hadn't seemed decent to put such lovely clean money in with the dirty old stuff in his wallet). Perhaps he should get there early, intercept him in the car park, hand back the cash and take off. But that would be hard.

'What would you do, Whitey?' he asked the cat, who'd woken up long enough to join him for a late supper after he got home.

For answer Whitey yawned, jumped up on the bed and closed his eyes.

'Good answer,' said Joe, who was blessed with the invaluable gift of rarely letting the troubles of the day spill over into his rest.

He lay down beside the cat and soon joined him in deep and dreamless sleep.

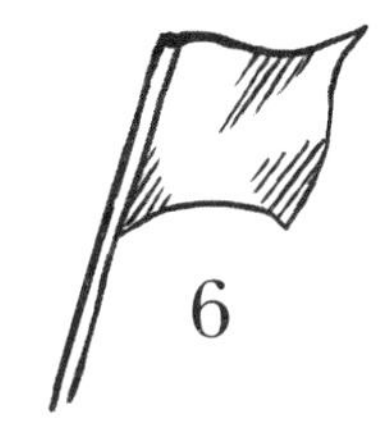

6

Pastures New

The Reverend Percy Potemkin, pastor of Boyling Corner Chapel, master of its famous choir, and known wherever song is sung or souls are saved as Rev Pot, preached a mean sermon.

Twice every Sunday he preached it, and with slight variations he made it do for weddings, funerals, christenings, and the opening of garden fêtes.

Any suggestion that a little variety might not come amiss was greeted with the response, 'If it's not broke, why fix it?' And if the doubter were foolish enough to persist in his doubt, perhaps educing in evidence the fact that most regular members of the congregation knew the words by heart, Rev Pot would reply, 'Now that is good, that's exactly what I want. I'm just a messenger, these are the words of the Lord, and He wants them to be burned on your soul so you never forget!'

A couple of lines from the mean sermon came into Joe's mind as he drove in search of the Royal Hoo Golf Club not long after ten o'clock the following sweltering morning.

Hell is a populous city a lot like Luton, and one of its suburbs is called Privilege and another is called Wealth. They look at things differently there.

Following Beryl's directions he found himself on the big roundabout which he sent the Morris round three times before opting for the only exit that didn't have a signpost. Soon he found himself driving along narrow country roads, not much more than lanes really, winding between high hedgerows. To make matters worse he got stuck behind a tractor for half a mile. Finally it turned into a gateway. When the driver stopped to open the gate Joe drew up alongside.

'All right for the Royal Hoo, am I?' he asked.

The man, who looked like a farmer in every respect except that his expression was happy, said, 'Oh yes, another mile or so, and there you are. Lovely day for golf.'

At least he doesn't assume I'm a delivery man, thought Joe.

Leaning over the gate he saw a possible explanation of the man's demeanour in the shape of an estate agent's sale board across which was plastered SOLD.

'Selling up then?' he said. 'Expect you'll miss it.'

'Miss drought, and drench, and interfering bastards from

DEFRA? Oh yes, I'll miss them, right enough! I'll lie in bed on a cold wet winter's morning and think of some other poor sod getting up to milk his beasts! It's a mug's game these days, farming.'

'Lucky you found a mug then,' said Joe lightly.

'Not really. Some so-called agri-conglomerate with a fancy name. "New Pastures", would you believe? Pastures! They'll likely cover the place in polytunnels and grow soft fruit. Me, I'll be long gone. Cheers now. Enjoy your game.'

'You too,' said Joe.

He drove on, smiling.

After perhaps a mile the high hedgerows gave way to an even higher wall, topped with shards of champagne-bottle glass that signalled clearer than billboards he was getting near one or both of Rev Pot's suburbs.

One thing you couldn't say about the Royal Hoo, however, was that it was ostentatious.

Joe had once been retained to look into a suspected fiddle in the kitchen of a very exclusive restaurant. He had walked by it three times before spotting the entrance. When he'd suggested to the owner that a sign invisible till you got within six feet wasn't going to bring in much passing trade, the man had winced and replied, 'The kind of people who don't know where we are, why would I want to tell them?'

The Hoo clearly worked on the same principle. Not that the entrance itself was understated. Eventually the wall was interrupted by a massive granite archway on which he wouldn't have been surprised to find listed the dead of both world wars.

Instead all he found after getting out of the car to do a recce was a sign as discreet as that of a Harley Street pox doctor. It didn't declare but rather murmured that this was indeed the Royal Hoo Golf Club.

Slightly more prominent on the left-hand pillar was a notice suggesting that tradesmen and others of the ilk might care to continue another half-mile till they encountered a lane on the left which would take them to the rear of the clubhouse. Joe was momentarily tempted. But he hadn't changed into his best blue slacks and yellow polo shirt for nothing, so he boldly sent the Morris rolling between a pair of gates containing enough wrought iron to make a small battleship.

Instantly he knew he was in a different country. Luton might be only fifteen minutes drive away, but this was somewhere else.

The driveway wound along an avenue of tall and probably ancient trees. Horticulture wasn't one of Joe's areas of expertise and the best he could say about them was that they weren't silver birches, palms, or monkey puzzles. Between their huge trunks he could see sweeping lengths of manicured greensward and from time to time he got glimpses ahead of what looked like the kind of stately home the proles were permitted to rubberneck around for a substantial fee a couple of days a week during the summer. Presumably this was the clubhouse. Eventually as he got closer, the driveway forked. Another of those signs so discreet he'd have missed it if he'd been doing more than five mph indicated that cars should bear to the right.

The car park, screened from the house by a colourful shrubbery, was full of serious machinery. You parked a Beamer here, you were anonymous. Couple of Rollers, lovely old Daimler, a vintage Bugatti, at least three autograph Range Rovers, Jags across the spectrum, a scarlet Ferrari that you tiptoed round in case you woke it up, several other sports jobs of varying degrees of flashness. But nowhere any sign of Porphyry's Volante.

Not surprising. He was deliberately early. It was something he'd read in *Not So Private Eye,* his PI Bible. When a meet's been set up on ground you don't know, get there first to suss things out.

He got out of his car and strolled over to the Bugati to take a closer look.

'Morning, sir? That your Morris?'

He turned to see a fresh-faced youngster of eighteen or nineteen coming towards him. At least it wasn't a heavy in a security uniform alerted by CCTV that a dodgy-looking character was prowling round the car park, but it probably amounted to the same thing.

'That's right,' said Joe. 'Not in the wrong car park, am I?'

Maybe at the Hoo they had auto-apartheid.

'Oh no, this is fine. Nice motor, but I think you could do with a bit of air in your front offside.'

‘Could all do with a bit of air,’ said Joe, checking it out. The kid was right.

‘Wouldn’t be Mr Sixsmith by any chance, would it, sir?’

‘That’s me, yeah.’

‘Mr Porphyry mentioned you might be coming,’ said the youth. ‘I’m Chip Harvey, assistant pro.’

He held out his hand. Joe shook it. The kid seemed genuinely pleased to see him.

‘First time here, is it, sir?’ he said. ‘I hope you like the look of us. It’s a lovely course. It would make a marvellous championship venue, but as I’m sure you know if you’re looking to join us, the membership here doesn’t care for that sort of public exposure. Let me show you to the clubhouse.’

If you’re looking to join us, thought Joe. Said without the slightest hint of *some hope!* In the light of morning, the doubts sown by Merv had withered considerably. Porphyry had struck him as straight and he was used to backing his own judgement. However daft the membership story might play to outsiders, what was the guy supposed to say? That he was bringing a PI to lunch with a view to casing the joint!

Really he would have preferred to hang around the car park till Porphyry appeared, but that would have looked a bit odd, so he let himself be guided through the shrubbery.

Close up, the clubhouse had even more of the feel of a stately home about it. French windows opened on to a long terrace spotted with parosoled tables. No plastic DIY superstore stuff these, but the kind of old-fashioned, twisty wrought-iron jobs you'd look to find in the gardens of folk who didn't have to buy their own furniture. Not that Joe spent much time among such people, but he was a great fan of heritage movies. Come to think of it, the scatter of people drinking coffee or long fruit drinks in elegant glasses could have been carefully arranged there by Messrs Merchant and Ivory. Of course these days, when class can be cloned as easy as sheep, anyone could buy the gear and walk the walk and talk the talk. But there's always a pea under the mattress, and to Joe's keen eye, where real kiss-my-ass class showed through was in the way your born-to-its sat easy. Folk like him either slumped or, at best, lolled. Somewhere towards the top of the heap you learned the art of reclining gracefully. Most of these folk here either had it, or were working very hard at getting it.

One end of the terrace overlooked a huge circle of lawn only slightly smaller than Kensington Gardens. From the numbered flag at its centre he deduced it was the eighteenth green. Green was the right word. It was so green it could have played for Ireland. Considering there'd been a hosepipe ban in the Luton area for a fortnight, reducing most gardens and public parks to dustbowls that would have made a dromedary cough, Joe couldn't understand why everyone here wasn't under arrest. And it wasn't just the actual green. The undulating crescent of tree-lined fairway stretching into the distance didn't look like it was dying of thirst either. Maybe here at Royal Hoo they had their own special cloud which sprinkled a little rain during the hours of darkness.

Chip Harvey sat him at a table and said, 'This do you, sir?'

'Yeah, this is fine,' said Joe. 'You don't have Mr Porphyry's – Chris's – number, do you? I could give him a bell, see if there's a hold up?'

He pulled out his mobile. The young man grimaced and said, 'No can do, I'm afraid, sir. Use of mobiles is strictly forbidden on the course or in the clubhouse. Heavy fine even if it just rings! You'd need to go back to your car to use it, but I'm sure Mr Porphyry will be here soon. Relax, have a drink. The steward will be along in a minute. Enjoy your day, sir.'

Nice boy, thought Joe, taking in his surroundings. This was OK, this was the real deal. Comfy seat under a parasol, lovely view, four crisp new monkeys in his pocket, steward would be along in a moment, even a breath of what must be the only breeze in the whole county, what more could a man ask? Envy and resentment didn't play a large part in Joe's outlook. Social injustices and inequalities had to be personalized before they hit his indignation button. If as he sat here he saw another black, balding, middling aged, vertically challenged, slightly overweight, redundant lathe-operator being given the runaround because of all or any one of these conditions, he would have groaned regretfully, stood up, and taken sides with the guy. But long as these folk didn't mind him, he certainly wasn't going to mind them. He'd learned his Bible the hard way, meaning Aunt Mirabelle's way, and that meant it stuck, especially her favourite bits, one of which was what Paul wrote to them Ephesians, whoever they were. *For we wrestle not against flesh and blood, but against principalities, against powers, against the rulers of the darkness of this world, against spiritual wickedness in high places.* Well, that was OK for Paul and Rev Pot, and good luck to them. Let all them preachers and politicians and newspaper columnists and such sort out the principalities and powers. Joe was happy to restrict his wrestling to good old-fashioned flesh and blood.

Out of the corner of his eye, he observed that one of a trio of men sitting a couple of tables away had caught Chip Harvey's attention as he passed and seemed to be questioning him closely. Oh shoot, thought Joe. Is good old-fashioned flesh and blood going to get to me before I can order a drink?

It looked like it. The man stood up. He was maybe forty, solidly built but mostly muscle, little flab. He was wearing a pale brown sports shirt and matching tailored shorts which made Joe glad he'd grounded the Technicolor parrots. His vigorous dark brown hair was rather becomingly tipped with grey and he had the kind of square open face which gets people buying double glazing or giving cash advances to jobbing builders. He was smiling but Joe didn't let this lull his fears. Places he did most of his drinking in, if a guy came at you with intent to smash your face in, he usually had the decency to look like a guy whose intent this was. Here, he guessed, different conventions might apply.

But it seemed he was wrong.

'Mr Sixsmith, I believe? I'm Tom Latimer, club vice-captain. Young Chip tells me you're waiting for Chris Porphyry.'

'That's right,' said Joe, taking the outstretched hand and returning the warm handshake. 'Nice boy, that Chip.'

'Yes, we have high hopes of him. Think he might make it on the tour. He'll need backing, of course, but we've got big hearts as well as deep pockets here at the Hoo.'

This didn't mean a lot to Joe, who in any case was preoccupied by the fact that the handshake had become a tow rope drawing him out of his seat as Latimer continued, 'Wonder if you'd care to join us? Chris isn't the best of timekeepers, I'm afraid. Always hits the first tee at a run!'

Unable to think of a good way to say, *No, thanks, I'd rather sit here by myself,* Joe found himself moving towards the other two men who were also brushing up the welcoming smiles.

One was less successful than the other. His name was Arthur Surtees, thirty something, his head close shaven presumably to hide the fact that he was bald anyway, and his deep sunken watchful eyes giving the lie to his wide stretched mouth, like a poorly put-together police photofit.

The other was Colin Rowe, in his fifties, grey-haired, with a lean intelligent face which would have looked well on a college professor. His smile was perfectly natural, nothing exaggerated about it, the kind of wryly sympathetic expression which would, Joe imagined, encourage an errant student to admit he hadn't done his homework.

But why do I get the feeling these guys know exactly who I am? thought Joe. That was impossible. Had to be his own sense of being out of place talking.

The steward, wearing a linen jacket as white and crisp as a hoar-frost, appeared as Joe sat down. Thinking that maybe a pint of cold Guinness might strike a wrong note, Joe asked for coffee.

'Hot or iced, sir?' the steward enquired. He had a lovely

voice, like an old-fashioned actor's. You probably needed a public school education just to get a job keeping bar at places like Royal Hoo.

Joe hesitated. Cold coffee? You got that down at Dot's Diner, you sent it back to be put in the microwave.

'Iced, I think, Bert,' said Latimer. 'And the same again for the rest of us. Well, Joe – all right if I call you Joe? We don't stand on ceremony here – how do you like the look of us so far?'

Joe had no natural talent to deceive, which could be a bit of a drawback in his chosen profession. He was working on it, but on the whole he made do in most situations by looking for straws of truth to get a firm hold of.

'I'm impressed,' he said. 'Weather like this, it beats sitting in my office.'

'We all know the feeling,' said Surtees. 'So where do you play, Joe?'

Why the shoot can't folk make conversation without asking direct questions? Joe wondered, as he marshalled the few facts he knew about golf to ascertain if there was an answer like 'left wing' or 'in goal'. Didn't seem likely, so presumably they were into geography. Could tell them Luton Municipal Pitch'n'Putt and watch their faces, but that two hundred nestling against his left buttock was beginning to feel very much at home there.

He said, 'I travel around a lot, so anywhere I can, really.'

'And welcome wherever you go, I'm sure,' said Latimer heartily.

A silence. With a bit of luck, thought Joe, it might turn into a siesta and stretch to fill the minutes till Porphyry appeared.

But luck wasn't on offer.

'So how's your game, Joe?' said Colin Rowe.

'Well, you know what it's like, up and down,' said Joe.

Rowe laughed and said, 'Part of its charm, eh? Pity they didn't build its fluctuations into the handicap system. Doesn't matter if I feel like crap, when I step on that first tee, I'm playing off 5. Arthur here's a bandit 7. And Tom's 9.'

'On a good day with the wind behind me,' said Latimer lightly. 'So how about you, Joe?'

'Sorry?' said Joe.

'Just wondering what your handicap was,' said Latimer.

Joe found a dozen smart answers crowding his tongue. He guessed a couple of them might be floating around Latimer's mind too. So don't give him the satisfaction, just play it straight. Which sounded a lot easier than it was. That golf had a handicap system he knew, but how it worked he had no idea. The only other game he knew that used handicaps was polo, and that was only because it had come up on *Who Wants to Be a Millionaire?* Joe, who was quite keen to be a millionaire, had been trying to improve his general knowledge by making a note of all the correct answers till Beryl had screamed with laughter and said, 'Joe, this stuff you're trying to learn is exactly the stuff you don't need to know, 'cos they've asked it already!' But the polo question had stuck.

What is the best handicap a top-class polo player can have?

The four alternatives had been 0, 10, 24, 36.

The answer had been 10. Seemed that beginners started at 0 or even minus something, and 24 and 36 didn't exist.

Which fitted very well here. Rowe had said he was 7 and Surtees was 5 while Latimer, the club vice-captain and therefore presumably one of its best players, was 9.

So play it safe.

'Oh pretty low, you know,' he said vaguely.

'Pretty low? Come on, Joe, don't be modest!' said Surtees with just the hint of a sneer.

He's trying to provoke me! thought Joe. Wants me to claim I'm a top gun, then he'll look for a way to show me up. Well, hard luck, mate. One thing I've learned is if you have to lie, keep it in bounds of reason.

'No, really,' he said. 'My handicap's nothing. A big 0.'

In other words I'm a rank beginner. Put that in your pipe!

'Scratch, eh? Thought as much,' said Rowe. 'Soon as I set eyes on you, I thought, there's a scratch man if ever I saw one!'

Scratch man. Now that sounded really offensive, but Rowe didn't say it in a particularly offensive way, and in any case a guy who was actually boasting when he said he was a lousy golfer didn't ought to get hot and bothered when he was told that's just what he looked like.

'Yeah? Well, like the man said, what you see is what you get,' said Joe pleasantly.

Rowe smiled but the other two were looking at him

speculatively and he began to wonder if maybe Porphyry had told Chip Harvey something different and he'd passed it on to these guys. Well, if he had, that was Porphyry's problem. Where was the man anyway? He didn't like to look at his own watch but he managed to cop a glance at the chunky gold Rolex on Latimer's wrist and saw that it was after ten thirty.

Bert, the steward, materialized at the table bearing a laden tray. He set it down and began distributing the drinks.

'Your iced coffee, Mr Sixsmith,' he said.

'Right,' said Joe, thinking, I'm only here five minutes and already the staff know my name.

He sipped the coffee. It was delicious. This was the sort of thing people who joined the Royal Hoo knew from birth, he guessed. Luke-warm coffee tastes like ditchwater but, lose a few more degrees and you get this nectar.

Latimer glanced at his watch.

'What time are you meeting Chris?' he asked.

'Ten thirty.'

'Passed that now. Bad form keeping a guest waiting, but Chris is always a bit of a law unto himself.'

'In more ways than one,' said Surtees shortly.

'Now, now, Arthur,' reproved Latimer. 'But not to worry, Joe. Even if Chris does stand you up, we'll see you don't have a wasted journey. We were just trying to work up enough energy to play a couple of holes before lunch. We could do with a fourth. What do you say, fellows? Shall we persuade Joe to join us and show us his style?'

'Only if he gives us half a dozen gotchas,' said Surtees.

This was evidently a joke. They all laughed immoderately and Joe joined in, partly to give the impression he knew what they were laughing about, but also because, as a naturally sociable man, he always found mirth infectious.

But when the laughs died away, Latimer returned to the attack, 'So that's agreed. You'll do us the honour then, Joe? If Chris doesn't show?'

They were all regarding him expectantly.

'Love to,' said Joe. 'Only I haven't brought my gear.'

His long experience of trying to get out of Aunt Mirabelle's arrangements, which usually involved meeting homely spinsters who'd reached the age where hope's allegedly eternal springs were drying to a trickle, should have taught him that any excuse that wasn't rock solid was tissue paper to a determined arranger.

'No problem. Young Chip will fit you up in two minutes in the pro's shop.'

The rock-solid excuse produced after the sandy-based one has collapsed rarely sounds totally convincing, but Joe didn't let such a consideration bother him. He hesitated only to decide between the urgent hospital appointment to discover if his recently diagnosed brain tumour was operable and the need to meet his wife and seven children who were arriving at Heathrow from Barbados mid afternoon.

Then over Latimer's shoulder he saw the air shimmer as if at the flutter of an angel's wings and a moment later salvation appeared in the form of a YFG.

'That's most kind of you,' he said. 'I'd really love to play with you guys . . .'

He paused to enjoy the shadow of surprise which ran across each of their faces, then he said, 'But, hey, it will have to be some other time. Sorry. Here's Chris now. Thanks for your hospitality.'

He stood up as Porphyry reached the table.

'Joe,' he said. 'So sorry I'm late.'

'No problem,' said Joe. 'Your friends have been making me really welcome.'

'That's kind of them. We're a welcoming club. Catch you later, Tom.'

'Why don't you and Joe join us?' said Latimer pleasantly.

'Thanks, but no. We're a bit pressed for time and I wanted to show Joe round.'

'Well, I hope you like what you see, Joe. And don't forget. You've promised us a game so we can see your style.'

Joe gave him the big grin.

'No problem, Tom,' he said. 'That's one promise I definitely won't forget.'

Meaning, if ever I come here again which at this moment don't feel likely, I'm going to buy me a plaster cast from the Plastic Poo Joke Shop and wrap it round my leg!

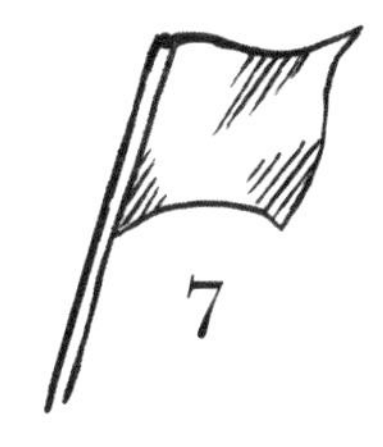

A Fortunate Lie

As they descended the flight of stairs which led down from the terrace on to the course Christian Porphyry apologized again for his lateness, adding, 'Still, you seemed to be managing very well on your own.'

'Yeah,' said Joe negligently. 'Undercover work hones you up for pretty well every extremity, even sitting around drinking iced coffee on a hot day. Seemed nice guys, your three friends.'

'The Bermuda Triangle?' Porphyry laughed. 'Yes, they're very good company.'

'So why do you call them that then?'

'Well, Colin runs Rowe Estates, you've probably seen their boards. And Arthur's a lawyer, while Tom is the boss of Latimer Trust, financial services and investment, that sort of thing. So, property, finance and the law – some members say if they suck you in, when you come out the other side, you don't know which way's up or down! Just a club joke. Means nothing.'

They were walking along the side of a fairway. A buggy came towards them, pulling a small trailer. The driver brought it to a halt and got out.

'I'd like a word, Mr Porphyry,' he said.

He was a small red-headed man with a face so savagely assaulted by the sun that it looked like a baked potato just plucked from the embers. He spoke with the kind of Scottish accent that Joe could only localize as more Glasgow Rangers than Edinburgh Festival.

'What is it, Davie?'

'It's about a replacement for Steve Waring. It's getting urgent.'

'He still hasn't shown up then?'

'No, he hasna, and it means the rest of us are working like blacks to keep the course in nick.'

Porphyry shook his head doubtfully. Maybe, thought Joe, he's going to tell the guy that anyone who talks like he does should go easy on the racism. But all the YFG said was, 'It's really Mr Rowe you should be talking to, Davie. He's chairman of the Greens Committee.'

'Aye, I know and I've tried that, but he says that when it came up, you said let's wait a wee while longer to see if Steve shows up.'

'Did I? Yes, I believe I did. I mean, it's only been . . . how long?'

'A week.'

'There you are then. Hardly any time. I know this job means a lot to Steve, and you yourself say he's been a good worker. Probably something's come up that he had to sort out, and he'll show up again any time now. I'd just hate for him to come back and find his job had gone.'

'It's a credit to your hairt, Mr Porphyry,' said Davie with only a small amount of discernible irony. 'But I called round at his digs last night and there's been no sign of him or word from him since last week. Landlady says he owes a month's back rent. I reckon he's done a runner and we won't be seeing hide nor hair of him this side of Christmas. We need another pair of hands now, else things will start slipping.'

'All right, Davie. I understand. I'll have a word with Mr Rowe.'

The man got back in his buggy and drove on.

'Head greenkeeper,' said Porphyry. 'Bit rough-edged, but the salt of the earth.'

Which was a good thing to have with a baked potato, thought Joe.

'Davie what?' he asked.

'Well, Davie actually. David Davie. Never sure whether it's his first or second name I'm using. Still, doesn't seem to trouble him.'

'And is he any part of your trouble?' asked Joe, keen to get down to cases.

'On no. Not at all. Definitely not.'

As if provoked by the question, Porphyry now strode forward at a pace which in Joe's case came close to a trot. It was very hot and though there were plenty of trees to their right, unfortunately the sun was in the wrong quarter of the sky to afford them any shade.

Suddenly Porphyry came to a halt.

'Stand still, Joe,' he commanded.

Though only too pleased to obey, Joe's natural curiosity still made him gasp, 'What for?'

'Chaps on the tee. Best be careful.'

Joe followed the YFG's gaze back down the fairway. Some figures had appeared at a distance so great he had to screw up his eyes to work out there were four of them.

'You think those guys could reach us here?' he asked doubtingly.

'Probably not, but what I meant was, we don't want to disturb their concentration by movement. And best keep your voice down too.'

'My voice? You're joking, yeah? I'd need a bullhorn before they could hear me!'

Porphyry smiled and said, or rather whispered, 'Normally, yes, Joe. But golf sensitizes the hearing remarkably. You know the great Wodehouse, of course?'

'Woodhouse? Played for the Posh and Grimsby then went into the fight game?' hazarded Joe.

'Don't recollect that, though he was a man of great and varied talent. In particular he loved his golf and of course he wrote some of the funniest books in the language. In one of them he talks about a golfer so sensitive, he could be put off his stroke by the roaring of butterflies in the adjacent meadow.'

The YFG chuckled as he spoke, but more as if appreciating a point well made than simply laughing at a bit of daftness. Joe was getting the impression that, apart from being stellar rich, you also needed a sense of humour from outer space to qualify for the Hoo. What was it the Bermuda Triangle had found so funny? Oh yes, the notion of him giving them something called *gotchas.*

Reckoning he wasn't going to get much further with roaring butterflies, he asked, 'What's a gotcha?'

'In golf, you mean?'

'Yeah. In golf.'

'Well, it has no official standing, you understand? Though I have known occasions when some of the chaps have had a couple too many before a game and have actually put it into practice.'

Did this guy know how to give a straight answer?

'But what is it?' demanded Joe.

'It means if, say, you agreed to have three gotchas each at the start of the game, on three occasions as your opponent was playing his shot you would be entitled to reach between his legs from behind, seize his testicles and cry *Gotcha!* I think we can move on now, Joe.'

It seemed a good idea, and the further the better.

Not that any of the golfers' drives had come within fifty yards of them, but that didn't make Joe feel any safer. OK, in his game of choice, football, you could get a smack in the goolies, but if the ref noticed, then it was a red-card job for the offender. But here in crazy Hoo-land, they built it into the rules!

It was time for some straight talking. The two hundred in his back pocket no longer seemed an issue. In fact it felt earned out already.

He put on a sprint and caught up with the YFG.

'Mr Porphyry . . .' he gasped.

'Chris.'

Joe took a deep breath. It felt like it might be his last but he wanted to be sure he got out everything he wanted to say in a form which even a Young Fair God could not misunderstand.

'Chris. In case you haven't noticed, Chris, it's so hot that I'd jump in a pond full of alligators if one happened to be handy. I'm out of breath, and there's a bunch of guys behind us drilling little white balls through the air at a hundred miles an hour. And even if they ain't disturbed by the rumpus all them butterflies is kicking up, I guess any control over direction they've got won't hold up much if someone grabs their family jewels just as they're making their shot. So unless what you want to hire me for is to guess what you want to hire me for, I'd appreciate it if you could get to the point and tell me just what it is you want to hire me for!'

That made things clear, he reckoned. In fact, he doubted if he could have made things clearer without adding semaphore.

'Point taken, Joe,' said Porphyry. 'I'm sorry. I suppose there are some things a chap just doesn't like to talk about.'

This took what little remained of Joe's breath away. The guy really didn't want to tell him what he wanted to hire him for!

He said, 'Look, I've worked on all kinds of cases, stuff you wouldn't imagine. And, long as it don't involve interfering with kids or farm animals, I'm cool, OK?'

'Yes, I see. Well, it's nothing like that, thank God, but it's bad. Really bad.' He took a deep breath and blurted out, 'The thing is, I've been accused of cheating.'

'Cheating?' echoed Joe. 'You mean like cheating on Miss Emerson, your fiancée?'

'No! Worse than that. Cheating at golf.'

'At golf? During a game, you mean?' Joe liked to get things absolutely straight, especially when dealing with an alien being. 'You've been accused of cheating at a game of golf?'

'That's it. Yes. Ghastly, isn't it? A really filthy thing to have laid on you. Filthy.'

His expression turned haunted and gloomy. It was like the sun going down, though, oddly, distress didn't age his features. On the contrary, he looked even younger, a young fair child now rather than a young fair god.

Joe felt his own spirits sink in sympathy. It hurt him to see the young man so unhappy, even though for the life of him he couldn't work out the cause of such unhappiness. Yeah, cheating in sport was bad, but this day and age, it was part of the game. Guy you were marking tried to give you the slip, you pulled his shirt. He got by you and posed a real danger to your goal, you took his legs out. You got tackled in your opponents' penalty area, you went down hard, holding your knee and screaming. OK, if the ref was a drama critic, he might award a free kick against you, maybe even give you a yellow card, in the very worst cases a red. But it was all in a day's work, no one thought any the worse of you for it, whether you were playing five-a-side in the park or earning a hundred grand a week in the Premiership. In fact, if you got a reputation in the pro game, it could be a nice little earner after you'd left the game with articles on *My Fifty Favourite Fouls* or *How to Be a Hard Man.* You might even do a movie or get a TV show.

So how was golf different?

He said, 'How serious is this?'

Porphyry said, 'If proven, I could be chucked out of the club.'

'Must be lots of other clubs,' said Joe consolingly.

'Not if you've been chucked out of the Hoo,' said Porphyry.

Joe doubted if it would make much difference down at the Municipal Pitch'n'Putt, but was sensitive enough to see this might be only a limited consolation.

'So what kind of case can they put together?' he said.

To his surprise, Porphyry reached out and squeezed his hand.

'Thank you,' he said.

'For what?' said Joe in some alarm.

'For not needing to ask if I'm innocent.'

He's missing the point, thought Joe. In life there was right and wrong. During his long childhood tuition at the hands of Aunt Mirabelle, that had been drummed into him by example, precept, and punishment. But in law there was only what could or couldn't be proved. But he hadn't got the heart to tell Porphyry he was misinterpreting a simple practical question as a wholehearted vote of confidence.

Porphyry, to his relief, had removed his hand.

Joe said, 'Yeah, but like I said, can they make a case?'

'Oh yes, I'm afraid so. Not much point in bringing an accusation otherwise.'

This at least was pragmatic. Eventually he didn't doubt he was going to have to ask, So what exactly do you imagine I can do to help you? without any expectation of a satisfactory answer. It might be kinder to ask it now and get the disappointment over.

Instead he heard himself saying, 'This cheating, just what are you supposed to have done?'

'That's what I was going to show you,' said Porphyry. 'Scene of the crime, or rather scene of the non-crime. I knew you'd want to see it.'

His face was back to full radiance. Oh shoot! thought Joe. He imagines I'm going to pull out my magnifying glass, crawl around the undergrowth for a bit, then stand up with an instant solution.

At least they'd turned off now under the shade of the

trees. A couple of minutes later they emerged on an elevated ridge of land which a sign told Joe was the sixteenth tee.

'It was exactly a week ago, Tuesday,' said Porphyry. 'I was playing Syd Cockernhoe in a singles. Second round of the Vardon Cup, that's the club's annual knock-out. I was lying dormy three down when we got here . . .'

'Lying what?' interrupted Joe, trying to translate this into English as he listened but unable to come up with anything beyond lying bastard, which didn't make sense.

'I was three holes down with only three to play. I needed to win every hole to halve the match.'

'To get a draw, you mean?'

'That's right. Now, the sixteenth's a real challenge, Shot hole one . . .'

'Sorry?' said Joe. It was like talking to a foreigner who knew enough of the language to sound fluent but who kept on getting words and phrases in the wrong place.

'Most difficult hole on the course. It's a par five, four ninety-eight yards, so it's not the distance. What makes it hard is that sharp dog-leg right you see up ahead at two hundred yards. Then another hundred yards on the fairway curves away to the left. Not a right-angle bend like the dog-leg, but a distinct change of direction. Once round that you can see the green way ahead, slightly elevated and protected by the Elephant Trap, that's the deepest bunker on the course.'

'Chris,' said Joe. 'I don't play golf and, up till now, I thought what I knew about golf you could write on a matchbox, but now I see I wouldn't need all that space. Could we maybe try basic English?'

'Sorry. I really don't know how else to explain things. But I'll try.'

He took a deep breath then he resumed.

'The fewer shots you take to reach the green the better. You follow that?'

Joe nodded.

'Good. Now the conventional way of playing this hole would be to hit your first shot from the tee, that's where we are, straight up to the dog-leg, that's the bend. Then you would hit your second shot to the next bend, hopefully with a bit of draw, that means making it curl to the left so that it actually goes around the second bend as far as you can get it, to lessen the distance of your third shot. OK?'

'Yes,' lied Joe.

'But what long hitters, and desperate idiots who are three down with three to play do is try to cut the first corner by hitting a drive straight over the trees on the right there, and hoping it takes a hop round the second bend and brings the green in sight.'

'So you can get there in two shots?'

'That's right!' said Porphyry, delighted. 'I'm both a reasonably long hitter and a very dedicated idiot. Also I was dormy three, so I really let one go, didn't quite catch it perfectly, and produced a slice. That means the ball started bending right. It wasn't a huge slice but it was enough. I heard the ball rattling among the trees. All I could hope was that I was lucky and had a decent lie so that I could chip out. Of course I played a provisional . . .'

He had started walking forward as he talked and Joe was once more trotting slightly behind.

'A Provisional?' he gasped, wondering how the IRA had got into things.

'I hit a second ball in case the first were lost,' explained Porphyry. 'You get a penalty shot for a lost ball, so if I didn't find the first one, that would mean I'd played three with my second.'

'Even though you'd only hit it once?' said Joe.

'Right! You're beginning to get it, Joe,' said the YFG with a confidence which was totally misplaced. 'Syd was up by the dog-leg but had drifted into the short rough on the left. My provisional was up there too. He went forward to locate his ball while I shot off into the woods hoping to spot my first.'

They were in the woods in question now. Again the shade was welcome. As they followed a diagonal line towards the stretch of fairway out of sight from the tee, Joe glimpsed a house through the trees, set well back.

As if answering a question, Porphyry said, 'That's Penley Farm where Jimmy Postgate lives. One of our founder members. In fact, come to think of it, the only one still with us. In his eighties, but still manages nine now and then. Lost distance, of course, but he's never lost the ability to hit a straight ball. Dead straight in everything,

Jimmy. True English gentleman, which is what makes it so difficult.'

'Sorry?' said Joe, thinking, here we go! Back to round-the-houses land.

'But I'd better stick to the proper sequence so's not to confuse you,' said Porphyry. 'I was poking around pretty aimlessly. To tell the truth, I hadn't much hope, when you hear a ball clatter like that, you know it could have gone anywhere. Then I glimpsed something white up ahead towards the fairway there. Thought it was probably a mushroom at first, but when I went up to it, lo and behold, it was my ball! Here it was, right here. A truly fortunate lie.'

They came almost to the edge of the trees. Here the ground was free of undergrowth, bare earth mainly with a bit of scrubby grass.

'How did you know it was your ball?' wondered Joe.

'Chap always knows what ball he's playing with, otherwise there could be all kinds of confusion. I'm a Titleist man myself, always Number 1, and just to make assurance doubly sure, I have them personalized.'

He pulled a ball out of his pocket and handed it to Joe. On it in purple was stamped a small seahorse with the initials *CP*.

'Family coat of arms. Three seahorses rampant, and a dolphin couchant.'

Joe listened uncomprehendingly, but once the bit was between his teeth, he wasn't a man to let himself be led astray, especially not by seahorses.

He said, 'So you found your first ball. What about the other one you hit?'

'Oh, I gave Syd a wave to show him I was all right, and he played his second shot, then picked up my provisional and brought it with him. No use for it, you see, not once I'd found the first one.'

Joe was still a bit bewildered by all this two-ball stuff. The same with tennis where if you missed your first serve, they let you have another. Imagine trying that in footie. *Oh sorry, ref,* says Beckham. *I didn't mean to blaze that one over the bar, can I have another go?*

But it was too hot for diversion.

He said, 'Any chance of getting to the cheating bit?'

'Yes, I'm getting there,' said Porphyry with just the faintest hint of irritation. Even gods don't care to be hurried. 'Syd's shot was pretty good, he drew it round the bend nicely, leaving himself a medium iron to reach the green in regulation. Now a half was no good to me – you recall I was dormy three. So I took out my three wood. As you'll have noticed, I didn't have a view of the green. I was going to need to get not only the distance but put enough draw on the ball to take it round the bend and up to the green. As if to make up for my drive, I hit a cracker. Off it went and when we got to the green it was lying four feet from the flag and I knocked it in for an eagle. That means two under par. Three shots on this hole. So even though Syd got a birdie, that's four shots on this hole, I won.'

Joe said, 'My head's hurting.'

Porphyry said anxiously, 'It must be the sun. You should have worn a hat. Would you like to sit down for a minute?'

'No, I'm fine. We any nearer the cheating?'

'Nearly there,' said the YFG, heading back into the woods in the direction of the house. 'What happened was that Syd was a bit demoralized. Getting a birdie and still losing the hole can do that. I won the next two holes so we ended up all square.'

'Like a draw?'

'That's it. But you can't have a draw in a knock-out competition, so we went down the first again.'

'To play another eighteen holes, you mean?' said Joe aghast.

'Oh no. First man to win a hole wins the match,' said Porphyry.

'Like a penalty shoot-out?'

'Yes, I suppose so. I won that hole too, so we headed back to the clubhouse for a drink. My treat, of course, being the winner. We were standing at the bar. Syd was telling everyone who came in that I must have sacrificed a virgin to the devil or something, coming back from dormy three to win. He was particularly eloquent on my incredible luck on the sixteenth, clattering my drive into the woods, and yet still somehow managing to come up with an eagle to beat his birdie. He'd just repeated the story for the third or fourth time when Jimmy Postgate came in. That's Jimmy from Penley Farm, the house I showed you on the far edge of these woods. He speaks quite loudly,

Jimmy, because he's a touch deaf. So everyone in the bar heard it loud and clear when he took a golf ball out of his pocket and tossed it to me, saying, "Here's the one you lost at the sixteenth, Chris. Plopped right into my swimming pool! Good job there was no one in there or it might have been a burial-at-sea job!"'

8

Trust

Now the Young Fair God fell silent, clearly reliving what even Joe with his weak grasp on the finer points of the game could see must have been a devastating moment.

But just to be quite sure he said, 'So if that was your ball went into the swimming pool, no way you could have found it sitting nice and handy right at the edge of the fairway. No way except one, that is?'

'Except one?'

The YFG was regarding him with hope brightening his face. Poor sod thinks I'm going to pull a rabbit out of the hat, thought Joe. Willie Woodbine must really have sold him the notion I'm some kind of voodoo priest. Well, it was disillusion time.

He said, 'The *except* one being that you put it there.'

The light died.

'Of course. That's the obvious conclusion everyone reached.'

'Not everyone, surely?'

'Oh, one or two like Jimmy tell me they find it impossible to believe, but I wouldn't blame them if even they had doubts. Let's face it, what other explanation can there be?'

'Only that you were fitted up,' said Joe.

'Fitted up?'

It was hard to believe in this wall-to-wall TV cop-show age that anybody could still be ignorant of the jargon.

'That it's a fix,' said Joe. 'That someone wants you to be accused of cheating.'

'Oh,' said the YFG, sounding disappointed again. 'That's what Willie suggested.'

'Willie Woodbine? You called in the police?'

'Good lord, no. I didn't do anything. I really thought it was so absurd it would just go away, some simple explanation would present itself, we'd all have a laugh and that would be that. But as the days went by, it became clear it wasn't going away.'

'People were accusing you, you mean?'

'Of course not. No, it was people coming up to me and assuring me they didn't believe a word of it that made me realize how much everyone was talking. I'd invited Willie along for a game on Saturday – I'm putting him up for membership, you know – and while we were playing, it just sort of came up. I suppose I was hoping his professional expertise might be able to show me a way out. He was very sympathetic, but didn't see how he could help officially. That was when he recommended you, Joe. So that's why I came to see you yesterday.'

'Yeah. Great. But Willie did reckon it might be an attempt to frame you?'

'Or a bad joke, perhaps, that went wrong. That's what he said. Told me to ask myself who might be capable of doing such a thing.'

'And?'

'I haven't been able to think of a soul.'

'You got no enemies then?' said Joe doubtfully.

'Not that I know of.'

That figured. Joe too had once had a similar sunny confidence in human kind, till his chosen profession showed him flaws in his argument. Now he knew, sadly, that the fact that Porphyry thought everyone loved him would be enough to make those who didn't hate him even more.

So no help with *who?* Which meant that the poor sod wasn't going to be much help with *why?* either. *How?* was the easy one. Porphyry hit his ball into the wood. A lurking plotter hurled a similar ball into Postgate's swimming pool, then placed the original one, or a third ball, if he couldn't find the original, on the fringe of the fairway.

Or maybe this guy Postgate himself had orchestrated the whole thing. That would make life a lot simpler.

A few minutes later Joe was scrubbing this particular theory.

Porphyry now led him to Penley Farm, entering the long rear garden by a wicket gate. A man was dozing on a cane chair by a small swimming pool. He had a mop of vigorous white hair and a sun-browned complexion. As they got near, Porphyry called out, 'Hello, Jimmy,' and the man opened his eyes, looking rather disorientated and extremely ancient. But when he saw who it was, a smile lit up his face, reducing him to a healthy eighty-year-old, and he rose to greet them.

'Chris, good to see you,' he said, shaking the YFG's hand vigorously.

'You too, you're looking well, Jimmy. This is Joe Sixsmith. He's a private detective. Joe, meet Jimmy Postgate, last of his kind – more's the pity.'

Joe, who'd been expecting his role as prospective member to be maintained everywhere in the club, was a bit taken aback by Porphyry's sudden attack of directness, but Postgate seemed to take it in his stride.

'Private detective, eh?' he said. 'Never met one of them before. You look a bit overheated to me, Joe. Fancy a glass of lemonade? Or do you chaps only drink straight bourbon?'

'Lemonade would be great,' said Joe.

They sat by the pool and drank their lemonade which was home-made and delicious, but it soon became apparent to Joe that it was going to be the only profitable part of the visit, unless you could count Postgate's uncompromising assertion of his undentable belief in Porphyry's innocence. Coming from a man who had inadvertently provided the cornerstone of the case against him, this struck Joe as a bit of a paradox, which he defined as something that didn't make sense or made more sense than at first appeared, but whether it helped or hindered him he couldn't say so he sent it to the Recycle Bin.

Invited to offer an alternative explanation of events, Postgate just shook his head and repeated, 'No, it beats me. Beats me. All I know is that young Chris here doesn't have a dishonest bone in him. Now, what can I do to help?'

Change your story, thought Joe. Though it was probably too late for even that to help.

He said, 'Could you explain exactly what happened?'

'I was sitting in my chair here, reading my evening paper, when there was a splash, and when I looked into the pool I saw a ball. Fished it out and recognized it as one of Chris's. No surprise there.'

'You weren't surprised?' said Joe, puzzled.

'No! Takes a big hitter and Chris is one of the longest hitters in the club. It's a carry of at least three hundred yards. Even though it was well off line, I thought Chris would be quite chuffed to hear he'd got that distance when I tossed the ball back to him in the clubhouse. If I'd known the bother it was going to cause, I'd have kept my mouth shut!'

Joe studied the pool then looked up at the trees towering high around the level lawns of the garden. He turned to

Porphyry, who was enjoying his lemonade as if he hadn't a care in the world, and said, 'Thought you heard your ball clattering among the trees?'

'Yes, I did.'

'You hear that?' he asked Postgate.

'No, but I'm a little deaf these days,' said the man cheerfully. 'OK up to a dozen or so yards, but after that it's the silent land.'

There seemed little else to learn here and Joe was beginning to find his host's cheery demeanour and his client's hopeful gaze equally oppressive.

'I'm done here,' he said, adding without any great conviction, 'for now.'

They took their leave of Postgate and headed round the front of the house. Joe was quite lost by now but Porphyry told him they were walking back towards the clubhouse up the third fairway. Then he added, 'So, Joe, now you know as much about the business as I know, what do you think?'

I think you're in freefall, mate, and the only way you're going to stop is when you hit the ground, thought Joe.

'I'm pondering it,' he said. 'Ponder first, speak last, that's my rule.'

The truth was that, despite his earlier resolution that just coming out here and seeing how the other one per cent lived had earned him the money in his back pocket, he was beginning to feel bad about it again. There was nothing he could even pretend to be doing. It wasn't a question of Porphyry's guilt or innocence, though the notion had crept into his mind that maybe when it came to golf the guy was so focused on winning that it blinded him to the truth of his own behaviour. Games could do this to people. Joe's taxi-driving buddy, Merv Golightly, was a case in point. A lovely guy, loyal in friendship, generous and kind in nature, a total sweetie – till you came up against him competitively, that was. Then he couldn't lose. He would cheat his young nephew at snap. Snooker balls rearranged themselves to give him an easier pot. Needing a double to win at darts, he would follow his arrow to the board and pluck it out with a cry of triumph before you could see for sure which side of the wire it had clipped. And if challenged, his protestations of innocence were so clearly genuine that Joe had long since concluded he really believed them!

No, the trouble was Joe couldn't see anywhere else to go, even to pretend he was doing something. Time to break away. The only question was, how much of the two hundred did he feel he could legitimately take with him.

'You earned any of it, Joseph?' he could hear Aunt Mirabelle asking.

'Not exactly.'

'Then you give it all back, boy,' she said sternly. 'You know I'm right.'

The Bermuda Triangle were still sitting on the terrace. As they passed their table, Latimer waved a glass and called, 'Chris, why don't you and Joe join us?'

Not waiting for Porphyry to reply, Joe said, 'Look, I need

to get back to town. Got an urgent appointment, running late already.'

'Pity,' said Porphyry. 'Thanks anyway, Tom. Oh, Colin . . . something I had to tell you . . . what was it? Sorry . . . a bit distracted lately . . .'

Impatient to be away, Joe chipped in. 'Wasn't it about some worker who's gone missing? Waring or something?'

'Well remembered, Joe,' said Porphyry, regarding him proudly. 'Only here two minutes and you know more about things than I do. Colin. I've just been talking to Davie. He reckons Steve Waring's bilked his landlady and done a runner. Can't believe it of the lad myself, but Davie's really keen to get a replacement.'

'OK, I'll give him the go-ahead, though where we'll get someone any good in the middle of the summer, heaven knows,' said Rowe.

'Bye, Joe,' said Latimer. 'Don't forget that game you've promised us.'

'You bet I won't. Keep listening for them butterflies, boys,' said Joe, light-hearted at the thought that this was probably the last time he'd see the Triangle.

His attempt at a golfing joke produced only polite smiles, but what the shoot did he care? He was out of here. But he soon found his sense of finality wasn't shared.

As they made their way towards the car park, Porphyry said, 'Sorry you have to go, Joe. Hoped you'd stay for a spot of lunch. But Willie warned me you were in great demand. So, what's our next move?'

His tone held nothing of despondence. It was the voice of a man confident in the expertise of the man he'd hired to help him.

Joe sighed. It was beginning to feel like disillusioning this guy would involve a full refund after all. And Willie Woodbine wouldn't be pleased. Presumably his application for membership would be buried in blackballs if his sponsor got done for cheating.

But it wasn't the anticipated wrath of the policeman that bothered Joe most, it was the look of bewildered disappointment that his turn-down would probably bring to the Young Fair God's young fair features.

Best to do it when he was already in his car, ready for a quick take-off before he could weaken.

To pass the time till he did the deed, he said, 'So what happens now?'

'It's in the hands of the Four Just Men – that's what we call our Rules Committee. They'll consider the evidence at their next meeting in a fortnight's time, then hand down their vedict. I know I'll get a fair hearing, but as things stand . . .'

That note of uncertainty caught at Joe's heart, but his mind was made up. He'd got a plan and he was going to stick to it. In the car, hand back the money, say sorry, and off! It was the best thing for all concerned.

But like a lot of Joe's plans, it didn't turn out as easy as that.

The Morris's resemblance to a tramp who had strayed

into the Royal Enclosure at Ascot was now underscored by the fact that its front offside tyre was completely flat.

'Oh shoot,' said Joe, not realizing he was on the edge of another 'fonly or he might have set off walking down the drive.

'Oh dear,' said Porphyry. 'How long have you got, Joe?'

'What?'

It took a moment to work out this wasn't an enquiry about his general state of health but a reference to his mythical urgent appointment.

He made a show of looking at his watch and said, 'Five minutes. I'm going to be late.'

'No problem,' said Porphyry. 'Here, take mine.'

Again it required a little time to grasp his precise meaning, which not even the sight of the car keys in Porphyry's outstretched hand could affirm absolutely.

'You mean,' said Joe turning his gaze to rest on the Volante, 'you mean, like, I should drive your car?'

'Yes. I'll get yours sorted, we can meet and exchange later.'

Joe's heart was full. This was like the moment when Rev Pot asked him to sing the Priest in *Gerontius*, or the first time Beryl Boddington asked him to babysit her young son. This was big trust time. OK, so Porphyry must be loaded to afford such wheels, but he didn't seem the kind of plonker who drove a Volante just to tell the world how rich he was. He'd bought the car because he loved it, and Joe didn't doubt for a moment that the club terrace was full of folk the YFG wouldn't have dreamt of offering his keys.

It was certainly full of folk who wouldn't dream of offering their keys to Joe Sixsmith!

How could he tell a guy like this there was no way to prove he wasn't a lousy cheat?

His other equally urgent problem was to resist the temptation to accept the loan of the Aston. He could see himself driving slowly round the streets of Luton, waving casually to his jaw-dropped acquaintance, letting Merv check out the engine, inviting Beryl out for a spin . . .

Then as on a split screen his mental projector ran parallel footage of him crushing one of those immaculate wings against a concrete bollard, or coming out of his office to find that some lowlife had scratched his envy across the bonnet with a Stanley knife.

His mind said *No* but his hand was stretched to receive the keys when Chip appeared pushing a mobile hydraulic jack before him.

'Hi, Mr Sixsmith,' he said cheerily. 'Checked back to see how that tyre was doing and when I saw it had really gone, I looked for you on the terrace to get your key so that I could put your spare on. No sign of you, so I thought I'd make a start anyway and get the wheel off.'

'Hey, man, this is real service,' said Joe.

'That's what we aim to give our members, right, Mr Porphyry?'

'That's right, Chip. Well done,' said the YFG. 'Joe, if five minutes is going to make a difference, my offer still stands.'

'No thanks, Chris,' said Joe reluctantly. 'It'll be fine.'

'If you're sure. I'll leave you in Chip's safe hands then. By the by, Chip, you've not seen anything of Steve Waring recently, have you? Not round here – he hasn't shown for work since last week – I meant in one of those clubs or pubs you wild young things frequent, maybe?'

'No, sorry, Mr Porphyry. I'll keep my eyes open though.'

'Thanks, Chip.'

He put his arm round Joe's shoulder and led him a few steps away.

'You'll ring me later, let me know how things are going, Joe? It's such a load off my mind, knowing I've got you on the case.'

He smiled as he spoke. Now was the moment to put him straight. But it would have been like telling the sun not to rise.

He turned back to the young assistant pro who already had the wheel off.

As he helped Chip manoeuvre the spare into place, Joe said, 'Nice chap.'

'Mr Porphyry? Oh yes, one of the best.'

'Yeah. Pity about this bother . . .'

'Bother?' said Chip. 'Oh, *that.* Nothing to worry about there, Mr Sixsmith. Anyone who knows Mr Porphyry knows there's as much chance of him cheating as there is of Ian Paisley becoming Pope. But I don't need to tell a close friend that, do I?'

'No, well, there's close and close,' bumbled Joe. 'I mean, we're pretty close, I suppose . . .'

'He was going to let you drive his car, wasn't he?' laughed Chip. 'Now that's what I call close.'

'He's a generous man,' said Joe.

'You don't need to tell me,' said Chip. 'He's really pushing the boat out on my tour fund and where he goes, the rest will follow.'

'Must like you.'

'Yeah, but he's like that with all the staff.'

'Certainly seems bothered about this guy, Waring,' said Joe. 'What's all that about?'

Before Chip could answer, a voice said, 'Hi there, Joe. Need any help?'

He turned to see Colin Rowe had come up behind him, his open friendly face wreathed in smiles.

'No. Chip here's doing a grand job.'

'Glad to hear it. We have high hopes of young Chip, but you don't get to be Open champion without being willing to get your hands dirty, right, Chip?'

'Right, Mr Rowe.'

'You go in for vintage, do you, Joe?' said Rowe, examining the Morris. 'Lovely old girl, this. Grand for running around locally, eh? Means you can save the big gas-guzzler for the motorway.'

'Yeah, that's right,' agreed Joe.

Rowe moved away and got into a silver Audi A8 Quattro. He'd evidently come out to make a phone call. Good rule that, thought Joe. All the big money people who were members of the Hoo, it could be like the belfry at St

Monkeys if they didn't make them switch their phones off.

He stood and watched as the young assistant pro completed the job with graceful efficiency and placed the wheel with the flat in the boot.

'There you go, Mr Sixsmith. Done and dusted,' said Chip.

Joe said, 'Thanks a lot. That's real service.'

'That's what Hoo members pay for,' grinned the youth.

'Yeah, but I'm not a member.'

'Anyone with Mr Porphyry behind them can order his tie straightaway,' said Chip confidently.

Rowe had finished his call and got out of the Audi.

'All done? Good. Chip, any word on that new travel case I ordered?'

'Should be here tomorrow, Mr Rowe.'

'Why don't we go up to the shop and you can check with the suppliers?'

He began to walk away with the youngster, then glanced back over his shoulder and called, 'Don't forget that game you promised us, Joe. Look forward to seeing you again soon.'

'Who can tell?' said Joe.

And as he drove away he heard Aunt Mirabelle's usual response to that question.

Only the Lord, and sometimes He speaks awful soft and low.

9

A Royal Summons

Aunt Mirabelle had imprinted in Joe's heart a faith in a benevolent deity that it would have taken surgery to remove, but when it came to everyday practicalities, he paid as much attention to Sod's as God's Law.

All that stuff about the lilies of the field and taking no thought for the morrow was fine, but any fool knew that a man driving around with a flat in his boot was bound to have another blow-out pretty damn quick, so on his way back to town he pulled into Ram Ray's garage on the ring road. Ram wasn't around, and he had to deal with the head mechanic, Scrapyard Eddie, who'd got his nickname because it was said that if you fell out with him, that was where your vehicle was likely to end up. Joe had recently been foolish enough to second-guess Eddie on a fuel pump fault in the old Morris, and now the mechanic seemed disinclined to admit the possibility of fixing the spare before the weekend.

Fortunately Ram's highly efficient and very desirable secretary, Eloise, who had a soft spot for Joe, came out to say hello. When she heard his problem she said, 'Do it, Eddie,' in a tone which reduced the mechanic to fawning co-operation, and invited Joe into the office for a cool cola.

'Don't you just love this weather, Joe?' she asked, leaning back in her chair and crossing her legs, a manoeuvre which made Joe glad he already had an excuse for sweating.

'Yeah, it's got its attractions,' he said. High among which was Eloise's abandonment of outerwear just this side of decency, or a long way that side if you were Aunt Mirabelle.

'So how's business?' she asked.

'So so. And how's George? Saw him demolish Ernie Jagger last month. He's on a real winning streak!'

George was Eloise's boyfriend. A rising star in the boxing world, he stood two metres high, about the same across the shoulders, with fists like bunches of petrified bananas. Known in the sporting columns as Jurassic, the image of George was a good thing to keep in mind when talking to Eloise.

'Not with me, he ain't,' said Eloise. 'All that training, he takes it so seriously. Me, I like a sporting guy, but not when it turns him into a monk. No, George is out. Got myself a new sport, only Chip don't let it interfere with his time off.'

'Chip?' said Joe. 'So what's his game?'

'Golf, among other things,' laughed Eloise. 'He's assistant pro out at the Royal Hoo.'

Joe wasn't particularly surprised. Coincidences that would have had others running to the parapsychologists he took in his stride. Butcher had once said to him, 'Sixsmith, you're in a job you've got no particular talent for, and you go at it in a half-assed way, but you've got a strike rate Willie Woodbine would die for. Serendipity, that's what it's called. That's what you've got, Joe.'

'Can I get treatment on the NHS?' he'd asked.

'Don't joke about it!' she'd retorted sternly. 'It's probably the only thing keeping you alive!'

Joe had thought about it later, then he'd sent it to the Recycle Bin to join all the other stuff that looked likely to stretch the period between his head hitting the pillow and sleep hitting his head by more than five seconds.

'Chip Harvey,' he said. 'I've just been talking to him. Nice lad.'

'You've been to the Royal Hoo?' said Eloise. She was too nice to make cracks about getting a job in the kitchen or sweeping up leaves from the course, but Joe's musical ear detected the harmonics of surprise in her tone.

It occurred to him he'd have done better to keep his mouth shut. But no point crying over spilt milk, said Mirabelle.

Anyway, as Whitey added, may be spilt milk to you, but it's manna from heaven to me.

'Yeah. I'm on a case. Working for a member called Porphyry. Look, he's told people he was showing me around with a view to applying for membership, so that's what Chip thinks. When you talk to him, make sure he keeps it to himself, OK?'

A lesser man might have tried to swear Eloise to secrecy, but Joe had had it drummed into him as a child, never ask for what you know you can't get!

The young woman didn't seem to have heard his plea.

'Christian Porphyry? You're working for Christian Porphyry?'

Here we go, thought Joe, recalling Beryl's reaction to the Young Fair God.

'That's right.'

'I met him couple of days back,' she said, dreamy eyed. 'First time I went out with Chip. He took me back to his flat out at the Hoo. He was showing me round, shouldn't have been, really, but it was a dead quiet time, then we bumped into Mr Porphyry. He was just so nice! Anyone else and Chip might have been in bother. He says some of the members there act around him like he was invisible, like a footman in one of those big old houses you see on the telly. But not Mr Porphyry. What are you doing for him, Joe?'

'Sorry, can't tell you that, El,' said Joe. 'Mr Porphyry wants it kept confidential. You'll make sure Chip understands that, won't you?'

This got through.

'Sure, Joe. Chip thinks he's great. If that's what Mr Porphyry wants, you can rely on Chip.'

Whereas if it's just what I want . . .

Joe pushed the unhelpful thought away and looked for upsides.

Some of them act around him like he was invisible . . .

He said, 'Yeah, Mr Porphyry's having a spot of trouble at the club. Chip knows all about it and, from what he said, he's very much on Mr Porphyry's side. In fact, it might help Mr Porphyry a lot if I could have a quiet word with Chip away from the club . . .'

Eloise knew a hint when she heard one.

'I'm meeting him down the Hole tonight, half seven, if you want to catch him before we go clubbing.'

'Might just do that,' said Joe. 'Sorry.'

His mobile was ringing. He didn't recognize the number in the display nor the voice that said, 'May I speak to Mr Sixsmith?' in response to his noncommittal, 'Yo?'

The voice was a woman's, young, confident, educated but not posh, and above all friendly rather than menacing.

'That's me,' he admitted.

'Oh good. Tried your office number but just got your answer service. My name's Mimi, Mr Sixsmith. I'm Mr Ratcliffe King's PA. He would like to see you with a view to employing the services of your agency. Would it be possible to make an appointment?'

Sam Spade might have growled, 'Why not? I'll be in my office about four if he wants to drop round.'

But Joe was a pragmatist.

He said, 'Sure. What time would be convenient for Mr King to see me?'

'Three o'clock this afternoon?'

He liked the question mark. It could have come out as a statement or even a command.

He said, 'That's fine.'

'You know where we are?' Mimi asked.

Which, considering how ProtoVision House dominated the north end of the High Street, was like asking if he knew where the Queen lived in London.

'I can always ask a policeman if I get lost,' he replied, risking a joke.

Mimi laughed a bubbly genuine kind of laugh.

'See you at three then,' she said. 'Bye.'

'Bye,' said Joe.

He looked at Eloise, who was busy scrolling incomprehensible spreadsheets down her computer screen.

He said, 'You know someone called Mimi, PA to Ratcliffe King?'

'Maggie Hardacre? Yeah, we went to school together. That her you were talking to?'

'Yeah. Her boss wants to hire me.'

'King Rat? Get yourself a watertight contract then, Joe, and a couple of good witnesses to his signature.'

'Why do you say that?'

'I've seen the kind of discount he gets from Ram.'

Her boss, Ram Ray, was rated one of Luton's sharpest in a commercial deal.

'So this Mimi . . .'

'Maggie's OK,' said Eloise. 'Went off to secretarial college in London, turned herself into Mimi and a top-flight PA, but she hasn't lost herself, know what I mean? Never wanted to come back here, but King made her an offer she couldn't refuse, so they say, and every time she gets restless, he makes her a better one. That's one thing about King Rat; he's a bastard, but if he really wants you, he doesn't count the pennies.'

'I'll remember that,' said Joe.

The door opened and the head mechanic said, 'Tyre's done and back on your car, Mr Sixsmith.'

'Thanks,' said Joe.

'I'll come out with you and make sure the job's been done up to Ram Ray standards,' said Eloise.

They walked out to the car together. Across the road from the garage Joe noticed a Chrysler PT Cruiser. Leaning against its bonnet with a mobile in his hand was a skinny guy who either had a nervous twitch of the head or was being bothered by flies. Joe was sure he'd been there when he got out of the Morris. Maybe his car had broken down and he was trying to contact the AA rather than stroll over the road and pay Ram Ray's charges.

Not only was the repaired tyre back on the Morris and the spare locked back in position, but the layer of dust and dead insects had been scraped off the windscreen.

'Nice one, Eddie,' said Eloise, smiling at the mechanic. 'Ram will be pleased you looked after Mr Sixsmith so well.'

She knows how to pour the oil after stirring up the water, thought Joe. Those women who went around moaning they didn't get a fair shake at power should spend more time in Luton.

He started pulling his billfold out of his back pocket.

'That's OK, Joe,' said Eloise. 'This one's on Ram.'

'Tell him I'm grateful.'

'You are? Well, this one's on me.'

She leaned forward and gave him a kiss. It was deep and delicious and lingering and he might have encouraged it to linger even longer if he hadn't been so surprised.

'See you tonight then,' she murmured.

'Look forward to it,' said Joe rather hoarsely.

As he drove away he put the lid on the fantasies bubbling up in the wake of Eloise's kiss by pondering on the royal summons from King Ratcliffe. Could there possibly be a connection with his employment in the Porphyry affair? OK, the links were at best tenuous. He'd told Merv about it at the Supporters' Club last night. He'd seen Merv engaged in deep conversation with Monty Wright before he left. Monty Wright had been turned down by the Royal Hoo. And Sir Monty and Ratcliffe King were closely allied . . .

Not much there, certainly nothing worth getting your thoughts in a tangle over. Maybe Merv and Sir Monty had been discussing City's prospects for next season. Or haggling over the taxi fare from the club to the millionaire's mansion at Whipsnade. The lucky discoveries that often moved his investigations along their meandering road to conclusion he took in his stride, but attempting to find shortcuts by studying some kind of mental map got the mist rising from the fields in about two minutes flat.

Anyway, a PI's place was out there where the action was. Deep thought was for professors, and master criminals, and lawyers.

He was on speaking terms with only one person in any of these categories. He drove to Bullpat Square, parked on a double yellow in the confident belief that no traffic warden who had any sense would be pounding the pavement in this heat, and went into Butcher's Law Centre.

The outer office which doubled as reception and waiting room was usually packed with Luton's indigent, eager to have their wounds healed, their enemies destroyed and their rights protected, but the weather seemed to have taken its toll here too and there was only one seat occupied.

'Hi, Joe,' said the youth on reception, one of a whole bunch of law students who helped out at the Centre, usually, Butcher had once said to Joe in a bout of alcohol induced cynicism, so that in later life whenever the moral burden of charging a thousand quid an hour for their services got a little too heavy, they could ease it by remembering that time in their salad days when they worked for free.

Joe distinguished them only by gender, and he didn't always get that right, but they all seemed to know him. He sometimes fantasized turning up at the Court of Appeal and the judicial trio all giving him high fives and saying, 'Hi Joe!' but he hadn't yet put it to the test.

He said, 'Hi. Like a word with Butcher, if she can fit me in.'

'Take a seat, you're next but one,' said the young man, whose voice was deep enough and chin shadowy enough for Joe to be fairly confident he was a man.

He took a chair opposite the solitary client, a woman of middle age who sat with head bowed and eyes closed. There was something vaguely familiar about her, but what really bothered Joe was she was sitting so still, he began to worry she might just have come in here to die.

He was about to share his anxiety with the receptionist when Butcher's door opened to let out a young woman with a tiny infant suspended round her neck in a sling, another two crowded before her in a push-chair, and a trio of older kids, from four to seven perhaps, bringing up the rear. If they were all hers, Joe's heart ached to think of the age she must have been when she first gave birth.

But the mother seemed happy enough, calling a cheerful 'Thank you' to Butcher, who appeared in the doorway behind her, and flashing Joe a brilliant smile as he leapt to the outer door and opened it.

The lawyer's gaze registered Joe without any sign of enthusiasm then moved on to the still figure in the chair.

'OK, Betty, you can come through now,' said Butcher, and to Joe's relief the woman rose instantly and vanished into the office.

Joe sat down again, took out his mobile and speed-dialled Merv.

'Hi there. Merv's taxis. If you want to go fast, Golightly.'

'It's me, Joe.'

'Joe, my main man! That antique heap of yours broken down again and you want picking up?'

'No thanks. That vintage vehicle I drive will be cruising round Luton long after that paddy wagon you call a taxi is taking up valuable space in Pinkie's Scrapyard. Listen, Merv, something I need to know, no bull now; when I left the club last night you were sitting beating Sir Monty's ear like you were trying to sell him some of that dodgy booze of yours.'

'Dodgy? Hey, Joe, I told you: bankrupt stock.'

'Yeah yeah. Anyway, what I want to know is, what were you talking about?'

'With Monty, you mean?'

'Of course with Monty! Come on, Merv. Don't play for time 'cos there ain't enough time for you to think up a lie would fool me.'

'That must mean you know what we were talking about already, so why're you asking?'

'You were talking about me, right? Come on, Merv, I'm not pissed, this is business.'

'OK, if it's business, yeah, he'd heard some of the guys joking about you being put up for membership at the Royal Hoo and he wondered what that was all about, so I told him the tale. Hey, it wasn't a secret, was it? Everybody in the club knew.'

'Only because you told them,' grumbled Joe. 'But never mind that. So you told him the story, and . . . ?'

'Well, he wanted to know all the whys and whens and whatfors.'

'Which you supplied, right? Even though what you really knew you could write on the point of a pin, which is about the size of your brain!'

'Hang about, Joe. You said this was business,' said Merv indignantly. 'Last time I try telling you the truth if all I'm going to get is abused for my openness.'

'Only thing open about you is your mouth,' declared Joe. 'So what exactly did you say?'

'Nothing you could deny wasn't true.'

'Try me,' said Joe.

'I said this guy Porphyry had put you on a big retainer for the duration 'cos there was something dodgy going off down the Hoo and being the guy who pretty well owns the place he's determined to get to the bottom of it, no expenses spared. I said you'd been cagey about the details because of client confidentiality, all that shit, but it was definitely something that could really drop some big-name people in it.'

'Yeah? And what part of what I told you gets within free-kick distance of making that true?' demanded Joe.

'Well, I may have done a bit of tweaking here and there, Joe. That's a fault of yours, ruining a good story by dwelling on the dull bits. And I thought that Sir Monty, after him getting the elbow there, would be bum-chuffed to hear something bad might be happening to the Hoo, 'specially as the word is it was your main man, Porphyry, who put the black spot on him.'

'Blackball,' said Joe. 'And was Sir Monty chuffed?'

'Not so's you'd notice. In fact, all he did was ask questions about you. Whether you were any kop, that sort of stuff.'

'So what did you do? Rubbish me?'

'Joe! How long we been friends? People ask you to recommend a taxi driver, do you say, "Stay away from that Merv Golightly, he's death on wheels and will rip you off into the bargain"? Of course you don't! No, I said what I always say. That Joe Sixsmith may not be much to look at and I don't know how he does it, but when he gets his teeth into a case, the bad guy may as well put his hand up straightaway because Joe won't let go till he's got him by the short and curlies. That's what I said and that's the God's honest truth, Joe.'

'Yeah. Well, thanks Merv,' said Joe, touched.

'Think nothing of it. We OK now, Joe?'

'Buy me a pint at the club and we're fine.'

'You got it. Now I'm on my way to pick up a wealthy widow who likes a drive out into the country now and then so she can exercise her dog, only she don't have no dog, know what I mean? See you, Joe!'

He switched off. With perfect timing, the door opened and the moribund woman emerged. She looked more lively now and the increase in animation was matched by an increase in familiarity, but not to the point of recognition.

The lawyer shook hands with her client in the doorway then turned and disappeared back into her office without a glance at Joe. But she left the door wide open.

He went in. She was sitting behind her desk lighting a thin cheroot. On the scuffed and ink-stained leather of the desktop in a silver frame stood a notice which read *You are in a smoking zone. If you don't like it, feel free to leave.* If asked about the new smoking ban in public places, she would reply, 'This is my private office, not a public place. I don't have staff because no one who works here gets paid. And I don't have customers because people who show up here give whatever they can afford, which in many cases is nothing, so any money that comes my way is a donation not a fee.'

From a cloud of smoke she said, 'This visit social or professional, Joe?'

'What's the difference?'

'If it's social, it's not convenient. I've a stack of work to get through. If it's professional and you're in work, I'll expect a contribution.'

'OK.' Joe pulled the YFG's roll out of his back pocket. It had to be his imagination but it still felt crisp and cool. He peeled off a fifty and dropped the note on to the desk.

Butcher looked at it then said, 'How much time do you expect for that?'

'Well, it was yesterday afternoon I got the money, two hundred, let's call it a day's fee, and let's say a day is twelve working hours, so I reckon that's three hours' worth there.'

'You work short hours,' she said. 'I'll give you till I finish this cheroot.'

She took a long drag and said, 'Better start talking, Sixsmith. And talking fast.'

10

Favours

Joe talked as fast as he could. Even so, by the time he got everything in – and he knew it was important with Butcher to give her every detail – the narrow fuse of tobacco had burnt within an inch of her lips.

She interrupted only once, when he mentioned his encounter with the Bermuda Triangle, letting out a *hrmph!* on a jet of noxious smoke on hearing Arthur Surtees' name.

'You know him?' said Joe. 'Served on the lawyers' charity committee together or something?'

'I know of him,' she said. 'They say if you're crossing a desert and stop to take a rest, after a couple of minutes there'll be a black speck way up in the sky and that will be Arthur Surtees. Go on, Joe. I don't intend blistering my lips.'

When he finished she said, 'So let me get this straight. You got yourself a client you can't see any way to help, but you don't want to step away because (a) the guy offered to loan you his car and (b) the money's good.'

Joe didn't argue. He hadn't come here for comfort but for clarity.

'That's about it,' he said. 'Also I reckon he's got a bad deal.'

'Evidence?'

'Don't have no evidence, else I wouldn't be here, would I?'

She stubbed the cheroot out in a cracked soup plate. This is where she pockets the fifty and tells me to refund the rest, thought Joe.

Instead she said, 'OK. I'll poke around a bit. Let me know how you get on with King Rat.'

He said, 'You think there could be a connection then?'

'I don't think anything, Sixsmith, not till I've got the facts,' she said negligently. 'It was you who suggested the possibility.'

'Yeah, but I was reaching. Like I said, I got this feeling those guys at the Hoo knew what I was doing there, and the only way I could see them knowing that was someone hearing Merv shooting his mouth off down the Supporters', and the guy who seemed most interested was Monty Wright . . .'

'Who as everyone knows scratches when King Rat itches. Yes, I followed the line of reasoning, but seeing where it starts at, to wit, you, I'm not going to lean on it too heavily. Now get out of here. Can't waste any more time doing favours when I've got real work to do. Close the door behind you.'

It wasn't a big room and even with Joe's smallish step it only took three of them to reach the doorway.

As he took the first he thought, she's doing me a favour? So how come that's my fifty lying on her desk?

As he took the second he recalled Aunt Mirabelle saying something like, lawyers do favours like cats take mice for a walk.

And as he reached the doorway the sight of the empty chair in which the woman, Betty, had been sitting gave him a flash of where he'd seen her sitting before.

He turned round and said, 'Butcher, you being so nice to me wouldn't have anything to do with that Betty being a checkout girl at Wright-Price, would it?'

For a second the lawyer blanked him out. Then suddenly she relaxed and grinned.

'Sixsmith, you never cease to amaze me, which is why I put up with you, I suppose. All right, once again you've taken a blind swing and hit the right button.'

'So she's been giving you some bad stuff about Wright-Price, is that it?'

'Don't get your hopes up, Joe. Yes, Betty Bradshaw lost her job there, but she didn't come to me to complain. What she wants is help dealing with all the obstacles our beloved leaders put in the way of needy folk getting their hands on the benefits they're entitled to at the time they most need them, which is usually yesterday.'

Joe digested this then said, 'But you know better, Butcher.'

'Now why do you say that, Joe?'

'Because you always do,' said Joe. 'Specially where big business is concerned. You think maybe there's something dodgy about the way she got fired and you're looking for a hook to hang your suspicions on but you've not found anything, and when I come along with Mr Porphyry's case and you hear me mention Sir Monty's name, you think, likely this is just another bunch of old Joe's squashy bananas, but just in case he does stumble across something you could rattle Monty's cage with, you'll string him along.'

She didn't blush. Butcher didn't do blushing. But she did wrinkle her lips into a rueful smile.

'Something like that, Joe, maybe. Hey, what are you doing?'

Joe had moved rapidly back to the desk and retrieved the fifty-pound note.

'First, you do a friend a favour, you don't charge money,' he said. 'And second, it seems like it could be me doing you the favour, right?'

One thing about Butcher, she knew how to lose.

She nodded and said, 'Could be. So long as you don't expect me to pay you money.'

'Like I say, I don't charge friends for favours,' said Joe.

'OK, OK,' she said. 'You've made me feel bad so I suppose

I'd better atone. You said you were seeing this young fellow, Chip, in the Hole in the Wall tonight? Why don't I come along? You can tell me what King Rat wants with you and I can stop you looking like a dirty old man come to eye up the young talent.'

'We go Dutch?' said Joe.

Butcher laughed.

'Joe, the way your aunt brought you up, there's no way you'll sit on your bum while the lady you're with goes to the bar to buy her own drink.'

'Yeah,' said Joe, heading for the door. 'But that only works when I'm with a lady.'

11

Knobbly Scones and Lipton's Tea

It wasn't often Joe got away from Butcher on a good line so as he stepped out into the cauldron of Bullpat Square, he felt so full of bounce that he greeted the heat with a spirited rendition of the opening lines of 'Mad Dogs and Englishmen'.

Then the words dried up on his lips and his mood deflated as he saw that he and Noël had got it wrong together. It was mad dogs and English traffic wardens that went out in the midday sun. One of them was just about to stick a ticket on the Morris.

The guy looked very hot and very ill-tempered so Joe aborted his instinctive friendly how're-you-doing-let's-talk-about-this approach. Instead he held out his hand for the ticket and said, 'Thanks. I'll see Mr King gets it.'

'Uh?' said the warden, squinting malevolently through a fringe of sweat.

'Mr Ratcliffe King. It's his car.'

The warden looked doubtfully at the Morris.

'He collects vintage,' said Joe. 'I'm delivering it to him. Here, let me take a note of your number. You know Mr King, he likes to keep things close up and personal.'

The warden snatched back the ticket.

'Piss off out of here,' he growled and shambled on his way.

As Joe got into the car he should have felt triumphant that his ruse had worked. Instead he found himself thinking, if King Rat's name's enough to send an overheated traffic warden into retreat, better watch how you go, Joe Sixsmith!

ProtoVision House was Luton's Trump Tower, on a more modest scale perhaps, but in proportion to the buildings that surrounded it, just as dominating. Its golden obelisk arrowed into the sky a good thirty metres above its nearest rival and it was said that at certain times of day the sun striking back from its reflective surface caused the pilots descending towards Luton Airport to put on their Ray-Bans. The architect had been not unsuccessful in realizing his client's vision of a building that would convey the power and the feel of a newly launched space rocket, and it was the generally unspoken hope of many Lutonians that they would wake up one morning and find it was actually going boldly where no building had gone before. Certainly it had been born in fire, the much loved if rather dilapidated old theatre that had previously occupied the site going up in flames one night. There had been talk of replacing it with a new modern arts centre, then suddenly, no one quite knew how, it emerged that King Rat already owned the site and had somehow got planning permission to build an office block there. The sop to civic pride was that the bottom floor contained a small concert hall and studio theatre, enabling King to present himself as a local benefactor.

The next five floors were prestigious office space, soon taken over by Luton's premier commercial organizations who paid a price for the privilege that, combined with the grants obtained for the ground-floor arts area and the insurance pay-out for the burnt theatre, meant that the ProtoVision Consultancy got the top three floors pretty well free gratis and for nothing.

King Rat himself had established his throne room in the obelisk's apex or the rocket's nose-cone, depending how you looked at it. Joe had never been in the building before and he entered the reception area at street level half expecting to be subjected to the kind of intimidatory security checks which were now the norm for anyone crazy enough to go near an airport. Instead as he made his way towards the desk a small but perfectly formed young woman with a smile which could have lit up a prison cell on a cold winter's morning intercepted him and said, 'It's Mr Sixsmith, isn't it? Hi, I'm Mimi.'

He took her offered hand. It was far from frozen, but if he'd been a young romantic tenor he might have burst into song. From a middling aged, middling bald, middling middled baritone it would just be embarrassing. Anyway, she'd probably had to endure the joke a thousand times before.

He said, 'Pleased to meet you. Sorry, I'm a bit early.'

The wall clock behind the desk read ten to three.

'That's good. Mr King likes early,' said Mimi. 'Over here.'

Taking his arm, which was nice because you could feel the animal energy surging through her gorgeous frame, she steered him past the main lifts to a narrower rather anonymous-looking door with a key pad on the wall beside it. She punched in a code and the door opened to reveal a mahogany-panelled lift with a deep-piled carpet.

'In you go, Joe – may I call you Joe?'

'Oh yes,' said Joe.

She followed him in and waved up at a discreet camera set in a corner of the ceiling.

The door closed and the lift began to ascend so smoothly the motion was almost imperceptible.

'You don't press any buttons then?' he said.

'Oh no. If you're not who you should be, you stay down below.'

She laughed as she spoke and he found himself laughing with her. She wasn't conventionally beautiful; in fact she had what Aunt Mirabelle would have called a good old-fashioned homely sort of face. But she radiated so much vitality and merriment that it was a pleasure to be in her company.

'You worked for Mr King long?' he asked.

She thought about it then said, 'Four years,' as if slightly surprised.

He recalled what Eloise had said about King's powers of retention.

'Was talking to an old school mate of yours when you rang,' he said. 'Eloise Bracewell.'

'Oh, *Edith,'* she said. 'Haven't seen her for ages, How is she?'

'She's fine. Sends her best. Edith, you say? You all change your names?'

'A few of us. Why not? Like clothes. Up till nine or ten you wear what your mum buys, after that you choose your own, right?'

'Right,' he said, thinking that he was nearer twenty before he finally convinced Aunt Mirabelle he could buy his own gear. As for turning up one day and saying, from now on in I want to be called Brad, the simple thought made him shudder!

'Good boss, is he, Mr King?' he ventured.

Again she had to think.

'Fine,' she said, a slight frown momentarily darkening her face. But it was only the shadow of a summer cloud cast by the bright sun which now came out again as she smiled and said, 'Four years working for the one guy has to mean something, right?'

But what? wondered Joe.

He'd never met King face to face but, like most

Lutonians, he'd heard a lot about him. Nothing to look at, was the general verdict. In fact so inconspicuous you could meet him then forget all about him when you turned your back. Until you felt the pain.

Only child of middle-class parents who were willing and able to send him to university, instead he had opted to remain in Luton, working as a clerk and getting involved in local politics as a ward councillor. In the eyes of old school friends who were forging ahead in the rat race, he appeared as a stick-in-the-mud they'd left far behind. In council circles, his apparent lack of interest in money won him the reputation of being rather unworldly, and as he never appeared a threat to anyone, he was everyone's compromise candidate when positions of power were wrangled over.

And then gradually it began to dawn on his fellow councillors that all lines of power led to Ratcliffe King, and on his rat-racing school friends that, far from sticking in the mud behind them, King Rat was already breasting the tape some distance ahead.

It was said that it only took one meeting for King Rat to suss out your talents and your weaknesses. He could then, if it seemed worthwhile, show you how to channel the former to achieve your aspirations, at the same time using the latter to bind you close to him for ever.

The lift came to a jerk-free halt and the inner door opened, but their exit was barred, literally, by a curlicued lattice in gold metal through which Joe could see a man seated at a desk behind a bank of security screens.

The man studied them for a moment. He had the sleek muscularity of a killer shark, the kind of no-expression face you don't want to see on your doctor coming to give you your X-ray results, and his eyes were so cold they froze you where they touched.

It wasn't a long moment but long enough for Mimi to say with good-natured patience, 'Hey, come on Stephen! You going to keep us waiting all day?'

The man called Stephen looked like he might be considering the possibility. Then he smiled a smile which hardly made even a token effort to get a grip on his features and pressed a button that opened the lattice.

Joe knew for sure that if he hadn't passed the cold-eye test, there was another button alongside it that would have vaporized him.

Mimi's warm hand on his back broke his chilly paralysis and he stepped into the room. Cold-Eye said, 'Welcome, Mr Sixsmith.' Joe recalled how flattered and impressed he'd been at the Hoo steward's almost instantaneous use of his name. Hearing it from this hard mouth, it felt like a menace.

Mimi said, 'Joe, this is Stephen Hardman, Mr King's other personal assistant.'

She said it slightly sniffily, but Joe was too busy registering *Hardman.* Had to be a joke. Didn't it?

He didn't feel inclined to ask.

His feet made no sound on the deep-piled carpet. In fact he'd been in noisier chapels of rest. There wasn't even that tell-tale hum you got from an air-conditioning system, but this beautifully cool atmosphere with its faint tang of ocean breeze certainly didn't come from downtown Luton. A door opened and a plumpish man of about fifty with a round, pink instantly forgettable face emerged. Assuming he was making for the lift to go down, Joe gave him a nod and stood aside, but he felt his hand seized and a pleasant light voice said, 'Mr Sixsmith, good of you to come.'

Oh shoot! thought Joe. This was him! King Rat himself. He'd seen his photo in the local paper, of course, but he'd still blanked the guy in his own office!

'Mr King, hi,' he said. 'Nice place you've got.'

Mimi giggled and said, 'You ain't seen nothing yet, Joe. Can I get you a cool drink?'

'Thank you, Mimi. Mr Sixsmith would prefer tea, I think. Stephen, will you see to it?'

Joe, rather to his surprise, found King was right. Since the heatwave hit the eighties, he'd generally been panting like the hart for cooling streams of extra-cold Guinness, but up here in this temperate mini climate, a cup of tea sounded very nice.

King led the way through a door behind the desk into a larger office which, with its bright colours, pop-art paintings, vigorous houseplants and a trace of freesia on the air alongside the ocean breeze, had to be Mimi's. Then through another door into King Rat's throne room.

The girl was right. He hadn't seen nothing yet!

He was on top of the world here. Two huge windows gave him a view of Luton which previously he'd only glimpsed from a holiday charter dropping towards the airport, and then his aesthetic appreciation had been considerably inhibited by the sheer terror he always felt on take off and landing. Now he could study at his leisure the bones and arteries of his beloved city. He let his gaze move round from the floodlights of the soccer stadium, across the drooping flags of the Wright-Price Superstore and the golden cross on the dome of St Monkey's, to the Clint Eastwood dirigible anchored to the roof of Dirty Harry's. The glass had to be that fancy light-reactive stuff you got in expensive sunglasses because it darkened where the sun hit it directly so you could look the old boy straight in the eye. As for heat, there was no competition with the ProtoVision air-conditioning system.

'Have a seat, Mr Sixsmith.'

Reluctantly he channelled his attention from outside to in. The room was sparsely furnished with four easy chairs round a glass table. With a view like that you didn't need a desk the size of a football pitch to show you were boss.

At the same time he'd have expected something more to confirm you were in King Rat's lair. The colour scheme of the décor and furnishings was a restful blend of browns and beiges and ochres repeated in the linen jacket and slacks that Ratcliffe King wore.

More King Hamster than King Rat! thought Joe.

Then Hardman came in with a silver tea tray and his sense of relaxed complacency vanished.

On it was a small wicker basket piled high with the unmistakable knobbly currant scones from the Billabong Bakery which were his favourites. Alongside it was a plateful of the delicious apple tartlets which he always had at Charmaine's Olde Worlde Tea Shoppe. He did not doubt that the jam in the jam dish was Baxter's Raspberry, the butter Irish unsalted, and the tea Lipton's.

Mimi poured his tea. She didn't ask him how he liked it but stirred in three spoonfuls of sugar before adding the milk.

Suddenly Joe was wanting to be out of here.

He said, 'So what did you want to see me about, Mr King?'

'Straight down to business? I like that,' said King. 'Here then is the situation, Mr Sixsmith. I have a client who has been relying on my advice in a large-scale development project. His role in it is mainly financial and the moment is fast approaching when he must decide whether or not to commit a considerable sum of money to the scheme. On the surface there are large profits to be made which he is eager to share in. In matters of large profit, of course, there are always attendant risks and our main task at ProtoVision is to assess those risks and advise accordingly. You follow me so far?'

'No problem,' said Joe, sinking his teeth into a scone which he'd coated liberally with butter and jam. As he'd expected, Baxter's raspberry and Irish unsalted. Wasn't it Georgie Best who said, if you're drowning in Guinness, might as well drink deep?

'Excellent. Now my main concern is with another member of the consortium behind this development, a man called Brian Tomlin. His contribution is more in terms of commercial expertise and contacts than hard cash. Basically, he is the one tying everything together. To be honest, I suspect a sting may be planned. I have absolutely no evidence to back my feelings, and I may be wrong. But if I'm not, then there is no way Tomlin cannot be deeply involved.'

'You'll have had him checked out, surely?' said Joe through his second scone.

'Naturally. Everything holds up. But I need to be absolutely sure. There are three days left till D-Day, D standing for delivery of money. During that period I want his movements and his contacts observed and analysed every waking hour of his day.'

'So it's a surveillance job?' said Joe, turning his attention to the apple tarts. He was seeing his way out of this and thought he might as well tuck in while the tuck was there.

'That's right.'

'And a blanket surveillance job, from the sound of it,' said Joe. 'Well, I'm sorry, Mr King, but for that kind of operation you need a team and I'm just a one-man band. It can't be done. You need one of the bigger outfits.'

'None of whom come as highly recommended as you,' said King. 'I foresaw the problem, of course. You would need at least one other person, I imagine, to give you cover for rest, refreshment, and calls of nature. Mimi here has volunteered to be your assistant.'

'Mimi?' said Joe, almost choking on his tartlet.

The young woman who'd perched on the arm of one of the chairs smiled at him, her eyes shining with excitement.

'Yes!' she exclaimed. 'I know I've got no experience and I'd just be along to fetch and carry. But I'm a fast learner, Joe. It would be real fun!'

'And Mimi would bring a different kind of expertise to the surveillance, I believe,' said King. 'One based on her work with me.'

'But doesn't this guy know her?' objected Joe.

'In fact, no. They've never met, though Mimi is fully au fait with the file I have put together on him. So your task would be simply to observe and record while Mimi filters out anything she thinks may be pertinent to the business in hand and alerts me. I understand your usual hourly fee is thirty pounds. As this would require your round-the-clock commitment for three, let's call it four days, why don't we bypass the arithmetic and call it a straight four thousand? Plus, of course, expenses.'

Oh dear, oh dear, thought Joe. He saw that the apple tartlets had almost vanished. Could he decently return to the knobbly scones? Such a U-turn would in Aunt Mirabelle's eyes demonstrate the kind of ill-breeding you might expect from rough-edged Johnny-come-latelys but not from a born-and-bred Lutonian.

He said, 'Who was it recommended me so high, Mr King?'

'Now let me see. I know Detective Superintendent Woodbine thinks very well of you. And Ms Butcher of the Bullpat Square Law Centre is a fan, I believe. And the Reverend Potemkin of the Boyling Corner Chapel, a fine judge of character as well as of choristers, acknowledges your excellence in both fields.'

For the first time Joe really focused on Ratcliffe King, trying to get beyond the courteous manner, the soft brown eyes, the amiably undistinguished features, to King Rat who knew everybody and everything. But it was impossible, and that was truly frightening.

He looked from King to his PA. This was better. Mimi's eyes were shining with excitement, like a kid who's been promised a fun outing with a favourite uncle. How could he disappoint her? And surely her involvement confirmed this was a genuine job. He must be crazy to think anyone would go to this trouble just to divert his attention from a case that only his soft heart had prevented him from giving up already.

His soft heart and Porphyry's hard cash, he corrected

himself. Which he could now afford to refund in full and hardly feel any pain at all.

He said, 'When would you want me to start?'

'Your fee-payment meter started ticking at three o'clock, or perhaps we should more strictly say five to three when you turned up here,' said King. 'But you need not bother with hands-on involvement till tomorrow morning. That will give you time to clear your decks, so to speak, and of course to pack.'

'Pack?'

'Oh yes. Didn't I say? Our man is flying out to Spain in the morning. Hopefully he'll feel relaxed enough there to drop his guard and give himself away, if there is anything to give away. Mimi . . .'

Mimi handed him a pale green plastic file smart enough to deserve a Gucci label.

'You'll find your ticket and hotel reservation in there, along with photographs and a full briefing,' she said. 'Plus a small float to cover initial expenses. It's an early start, I'm afraid. Plane leaves at seven a.m., so we need to check in by five thirty. Any queries and you can get me on my mobile. The number's in there.'

'Goodbye, Mr Sixsmith. I'm so glad you are able to help me out here. And believe me, if in the end your report is completely negative, I shall be very pleased to hear that too. Goodbye now.'

Joe shook hands. As he and Mimi headed for the lift, Hardman said, 'Nice to have you on board, Joe.'

He was Joe now. Should have come over real friendly, but the message Joe got from those cold eyes was that the alternative to coming on board was being tossed over the side with an anchor chain round your neck.

In the lift he said to Mimi, 'That guy Hardman, is that really his name?'

'Never seen his birth certificate, Joe,' she said. Again he caught a note of dislike which emboldened him to say, 'He ain't the same sort of PA as you, I'd guess.'

'What sort is that, Joe?'

'Sort of gorgeous.'

She laughed her champagne bubbly laugh and said, 'I can see I'm going to have to watch you. And if you see Stephen coming, maybe you'd better watch him, Joe. I don't know exactly how he assists Mr King, and I don't want to know.'

The lift door opened. Joe stepped out. Mimi stayed where she was and said, 'See you tomorrow, Joe. I'll pick you up, shall I? I've got to pass Rasselas on my way to the airport. Five o'clock, OK? I can't wait!'

Then the door closed and she was gone. And if it hadn't been for the elegant pale green file in his hand, Joe might have thought it was all a dream. He opened the file as he made his way out of ProtoVision House. It was all there as Mimi had itemized with the small expense float consisting of an envelope containing five hundred euros.

Outside the hot air of Luton's long summer hit him like a barber's towel.

But the euros didn't dissolve.

So definitely not a dream.

Which didn't necessarily mean it might not be a nightmare.

12 The Hole

The Hole in the Wall pub was a popular trysting point for Luton's wild young things looking to tread the primrose paths to clubbing pleasure. Here they met old friends, discussed new plans, and took on board the liquids and medicaments necessary to keep them going during the long night's journey into day ahead.

As Joe entered the cavernous bar, his mind went back to a time when the pub had had four separate rooms distinguished by décor, size and function as indicated by their names, which were the Public, the Snug, the Mixed, and the Snooker. Then the sign above the entrance had read the Jolly Sailor. Later it changed to Finbar McCool's and the room names changed also to the Shebeen, the Crack, the Céilidh and the Aitch-Block. That experiment had ended in tears and a riot, the damage caused by which had probably given the next owner the idea of knocking down what remained of the interior walls, putting in a central round bar, and rechristening it the Hole in the Wall.

In another hour you would need a shovel to dig your way through to the bar. At seven thirty it was just beginning to fill and he had no problem spotting Eloise and Chip. The former was wearing a halter and skirt that made the office wear that had so affected Joe's blood pressure look like a burqa.

The latter was wearing a puzzled frown, which meant that Eloise had forgotten to mention that Joe might be showing up.

'Mr Sixsmith,' said Chip. 'Hello again.'

Joe didn't blame him for being puzzled. The Hole was not the kind of place you expected to encounter prospective members of the Royal Hoo. The parrot shorts which Joe was wearing once more probably didn't help either.

He sat down and said, 'Hi, Chip. Hi, Eloise.'

'You two know each other?' said Chip.

'Long time,' said Eloise.

Then, perhaps to compensate for not preparing the ground, or more likely because she reckoned if she let a pair of men enter the mazy paths of explanation, they'd never get out, she reduced the situation to its basics.

'Joe's a PI. He's been hired by Mr Porphyry to look into something at the golf club. I said being as it's Mr Porphyry, you might like to help.'

Chip Harvey looked far from enthusiastic at the prospect.

In fact he looked seriously pissed, but before he could respond, Eloise leaned forward to give him a long and breathtaking kiss, and Joe a long and breathtaking view down her halter, then said, 'I'll get some booze while you two talk. Guinness, Joe. Right?'

The kiss was the kind of incentive to co-operation Joe couldn't match so he didn't bother with his prepared line about knowing Chip was a loyal and discreet employee of the Hoo but sometimes a guy had to choose between loyalties and anything said here and now was in absolute confidence etc etc.

Instead he said, 'In the car park you were definite Chris Porphyry couldn't have cheated. Was that you being polite 'cos you thought I was his friend?'

Still feeling the intoxication of that promissory kiss, Chip said emphatically, 'No way!'

'So what do you think's going on?'

'Has to be a mistake, doesn't it?'

'Like a coincidence, you mean? He hits a ball into the wood just at the same time as a passing sparrow drops an identical ball into Mr Postgate's swimming pool? You get a lot of trouble with sparrows stealing balls at the Hoo?'

'No. Sometimes a dog . . .'

'A flying dog? Flying pigs more likely, Chip. Come on. What's the crack? You must have talked it over with friends on the staff. And I dare say you've heard some of the members talking about it, too.'

'Yeah, maybe.'

The tone had changed to cautious. He was coming out of his kiss-trance. Time to remind him.

'Look, Chip, I don't want to harass you, OK? Only Eloise seemed to think you liked Mr Porphyry enough to want to help him. I know he'd be very grateful. Eloise too. She thinks you're pretty special. But I can see this bothers you. Look, best I just head on out of here. Tell Eloise I'm sorry she got stung for a Guinness. You like Guinness, Chip? Maybe she'll give it to you.'

It was hardly fair, but as Merv Golightly was wont to say, fair doesn't get you rich and it doesn't get you laid.

Chip said, 'No, it's OK. Look, I'd like to help Mr Porphyry, only there's some of the others who'd get me sent down the road if they knew I'd been talking to you.'

'Because they wouldn't want to help Mr Porphyry, you mean? Who's got it in for him then? You can talk to me, Chip. This is off the record, won't go no further.'

Even with this reassurance it was clearly going to be hard to get names out of the young man.

'Everyone likes Mr Porphyry,' he insisted. 'He's very popular. Only some of the members worry about what it might be like if he wasn't such a nice guy . . .'

'Sorry? You mean they're worried about a personality change?'

'More like a personnel change, I think,' said a new voice.

Joe had been aware of the Hole filling up in the last few minutes but hadn't noticed that one of the new arrivals standing close to their table was Butcher. The background music, which was background like the sound of falling water at Niagara, and the general chatter level had seemed to guarantee protection from eavesdropping, but as Joe knew to his cost, Butcher had the kind of directional hearing that cost you serious money down Tottenham Court Road.

She sat down in the chair vacated by Eloise. Chip looked at her in amazement then at Joe in anger.

Butcher said, 'It's OK. I'm Joe's lawyer.'

'Yeah?' Now Chip was seriously alarmed and seriously angry. 'Mr Sixsmith, you said this would be confidential . . .'

'It will be,' said Butcher. 'I'm the one who makes sure Joe doesn't go around shooting his mouth off. You're Deb Harvey's nephew, right?'

'You know Aunt Deb?'

'I was able to help her out with a problem she had with a credit company.'

'You're that lawyer, the one from Bullpat Square,' said Chip, sounding impressed.

'The same. Butcher's the name.'

And butcher's the game, thought Joe. Chip was mincemeat in her hands.

'Aunt Deb says you're great,' he said.

'That's nice. So you were saying that all that worries the members about Mr Porphyry is what happens when he passes on?'

'Why should that bother anyone?' demanded Joe, a bit

miffed that Butcher had assumed front-line duty without even a beg-pardon.

'Because the Porphyry family retains a controlling share in the Hoo and the heir apparent is a cousin who lives in a Buddhist monastery in Thailand.'

'That's right,' said Chip. 'I heard Mr Surtees say that if he inherited, we'd all be wearing yellow robes and eating noodles.'

Joe couldn't see how this could have anything to do with anything.

Butcher frowned at the mention of Surtees. She thinks it's lawyers like him who give lawyers a bad name, thought Joe. She ought to get out more!

She gave him a glare as if he'd spoken the thought out loud, then said, 'So it's in everyone's interest to keep Mr Porphyry happy, hope he gets married soon and has a kid he can bring up to take care of the club like he does?'

'That's right,' said Chip. 'Everyone was really chuffed when he got engaged to Miss Emerson. She's really nice.'

'Is she a member?' asked Joe.

Chip looked at him as if he'd said something stupid.

Butcher said, 'It's an all-boys outfit, Sixsmith. Ladies can be guests, but there's no way they can join.'

'Is that legal?' asked Joe. 'Thought there were laws against it nowadays.'

If he thought his indignation would win him house-points from Butcher, he was disappointed.

She said, 'Before you get on your white horse, Sixsmith, ask yourself when was the last time Sir Monty dug into his piggy bank to buy a female player for your beloved Luton.'

'But women don't play in the League,' said Joe.

'Exactly. Chip, when the members got wind of this business about the ball in the swimming pool, what did most of them reckon would happen?'

'Well, nothing, I suppose. I mean, it was something to talk about, but it was so daft really, it being Mr Porphyry and everything, I think they just thought things would settle down and it would go away. You see, you need someone to make a complaint, which in this case would most likely have been Mr Cockernhoe who lost the match concerned. It was in the scratch knock-out competition for the Vardon Cup – that's the club's top award, everyone wants their name on that. But I heard Mr Cockernhoe tell Mr Latimer that he certainly wasn't going to take any action.'

'Why would he tell this Mr Latimer in particular?'

'He's Chair of Rules, that's the committee that deals with disputes and discipline and such.'

'So someone complained. Any idea who?'

'No,' said Chip. He looked so relieved he didn't know that Joe felt guilty at what they were doing to him.

'One more thing, Chip,' said Butcher. 'Mr Porphyry's golf balls have a special identifying mark, right?'

I told you that already, thought Joe.

'Yes. They're stamped with a blue seahorse. Something to do with his family coat of arms.'

'And who does the stamping?'

'Me, usually. We keep the stamp in the pro's workshop. A lot of the members have their own identifying stamps. Initials mostly.'

'Could anyone get at the seahorse stamp?'

'Sure. It wouldn't be hard. The members are in and out of there all the time, getting adjustments made to their clubs, that sort of thing.'

I should have asked that, thought Joe. Which didn't stop him from feeling pissed when Butcher said, 'Thanks, Chip. That's us done here, I think, Joe.'

How come she's acting like she's in charge and I'm one of her volunteers she can boss around? Joe asked himself angrily. What he needed was another line of questioning she hadn't thought of to win back the initiative. He looked around in search of inspiration and saw the crowd between their table and the bar part like the Red Sea to permit the passage of Eloise carrying a tray with a pint of Guinness and two other glasses containing the kind of frothy bluey-green liquid that turned you into something in a fantasy movie.

Eloise flowed towards them in a ripple of bright flesh it was hard to take your eyes off, yet Joe found his gaze refocusing behind her. There, leaning back against the section of the bar momentarily revealed by the parting of the throng, was Stephen Hardman, King Rat's minder.

Even at this distance Joe registered the touch of those chilly eyes. Then the crowd closed back in and he vanished.

'Sorry I've been so long,' said Eloise. 'The lad behind the bar's a bit out of it tonight. Wanted to know if I wanted a frosted kumquat in the Guinness to sweeten it up. Hello. You Joe's secretary?'

This to Butcher so delighted Joe that he forgot about Hardman and could almost have forgiven Eloise if he'd had to fish a kumquat out of his drink.

'His minder, actually,' said Butcher. 'Here, have my seat. We're just going.'

'But you haven't had a drink yet,' said Joe.

'I'll survive.'

'I won't,' said Joe, taking a long pull at the black nectar.

'Please yourself, but I have an appointment with a landlady who believes that the Law permits her to put up to ten asylum seekers in each of her four small rooms and claim a full B-and-B allowance for each.'

The word landlady triggered a memory in Joe. Nothing significant, but at least it suggested a question he could ask to regain control from Butcher.

He said, 'Chip, in the car park we were talking about Steve Waring, remember?'

'Don't recall,' said Chip surlily.

Butcher had stopped looking impatient, Joe noticed. But having got her interest, he couldn't see any way to keep it.

'Yes, we were,' he said. 'So when was he last seen at the club?'

'Don't know,' Chip said. 'Last Tuesday maybe.'

'Same day as Mr Porphyry played Mr Cockernhoe in that cup thing?'

'The Vardon. Yeah, could be.'

Well, that was a sort of connection; the sort that didn't actually lead anywhere, but it would have to do.

Joe finished his Guinness and stood up. It was worth it just to see the relief on Chip's face.

'Thanks, Chip,' he said. 'Enjoy your night out, you two.'

He followed Butcher out of the now very crowded bar. As they headed for the car park, a figure standing by a Chrysler Cruiser caught his eye. He was sure it was the same skinny twitchy guy he'd seen outside Ram Ray's and, if it was, he was still on the phone!

Maybe I should go over there and have a word, thought Joe. But before he could act, he heard his name called and turned to see Eloise coming after him.

'Hi,' he said. 'I forget something?'

'No. It's just that Chip seems really worried about talking with you. Looks to be weighing heavy on him and tonight I don't want anything weighing heavier on him than me. So I just wanted to remind you, Joe, that you promised this would be absolutely confidential.'

She was looking at him with the look she'd fixed on Scrapyard Eddie.

He said, 'On Aunt Mirabelle's grave, I swear.'

Though she wasn't dead, invoking Mirabelle in an oath beat bibles.

'OK,' said Eloise. 'And her?'

She looked towards Butcher, who was watching them with an air of tight-stretched patience.

'She's a lawyer,' said Joe. 'She doesn't talk unless you insert gold sovereigns into her mouth.'

This dreadful slander seemed to convince the young woman.

'OK,' she said. 'Now I'll go and take the weight off Chip's mind. Thanks, Joe.'

She leaned forward. She's going to kiss me again! he thought in amazement. She did, and it was even better than before. This time she leaned right into it and he felt the soft warmth of that scantily dressed body mould itself around him like a wheatgerm poultice as her soft full lips pressed against his. Then she pulled away and vanished back into the depths of the Hole.

'Sixsmith, can we go now?' said Butcher. 'Only watch how you walk or you'll trip over your tongue.'

13

Legal Advice

Butcher sat with Joe in the Morris and listened as he described his audience with King Rat.

He showed her the contents of the green folder. She looked at the photo of Brian Tomlin, his target, and said, 'I know him.'

'And?'

'He's the kind of wheeler-dealer you wear belt and braces with, and you can still end up bare-ass.'

'So this could be a genuine job, not just a way of getting me out of the way?' said Joe.

Butcher sighed.

'I've got a problem with both parts of that question, Sixsmith.'

'Sorry?'

'What I mean is, why would someone like King give you a genuine job? On the other hand, why would he be worried enough about you to want to get you out of the way?'

There was an insult in here somewhere, maybe two, in which case could be they cancelled each other out.

He binned it and said, 'If this guy Tomlin's such a chancer, why would King dream of trusting him anyway?'

She opened her mouth to reply, closed it, opened it again and said, 'Never thought I'd have to say this, but that's a good point. Tomlin's the kind of pond-life King might use to do something dodgy; he's certainly not the kind he's ever going to get close to doing a deal with. All right, let's see how this runs. King wants you out of the way, he knows Tomlin's in Spain, holiday, whatever, so he uses him as an excuse to hire you for a surveillance job.'

'Yeah, but it's only for three days. I'd be back well before the committee meeting,' said Joe, finding himself surprisingly reluctant to admit that the job was just a ruse. 'Also he's sending his PA to help me and he wouldn't do that if he just wanted to get me out of the way, would he?'

As so often in arguments with Butcher, all his get-round-that clincher won him was a long sigh full of intellectual pain.

'She's there to watch you, stupid,' said Butcher. 'He needs to be sure you've really gone.'

Joe shook his head.

'No,' he said, 'she's OK, I don't see her being in on anything dodgy. And she was so lit up at the thought of doing some detective work.'

Butcher laughed.

'What is it with you and nubile young women, Joe? Doesn't matter if she's in on it or not anyway. You do something weird like not turning up at the airport, or heading back home from Spain, and she'll report straight back to King, won't she? She's his PA, after all. But you're right about the time thing. If he wanted you out of the way till after the committee pinned the Scarlet Letter or whatever they do on Porphyry, why not hire you for a fortnight?'

'I'd definitely not have agreed to that much,' said Joe stoutly.

'Not even with all that big money being wafted under your nose?' laughed Butcher. 'Pull the other one. Now, this fellow Waring you mentioned. What's all that about?'

Joe told her.

'So, what's become of Waring?' she said in that amused tone the educated classes use when they're saying something clever they reckon you probably won't understand. 'You say Porphyry seemed particularly interested in him. That why you felt his disappearance might be relevant?'

'Yeah, that's it,' said Joe, reasoning that anything was better than admitting his only reason for bringing the vanishing greensman up was because Butcher had asked all the obvious questions. 'But it looks like a red herring.'

'Don't undersell yourself,' said Butcher. 'You might in your inimitable way have stumbled on something. You see,

I think I mentioned to you earlier I once acted in a case for an ex-employee of the Porphyry estate. Her name was Sally Waring. She had a teenage son.'

'So that could explain Chris's interest. Son of an old employee, give him a hand-up.'

'Your belief in the philanthropic impulses of the ruling classes is touching, Sixsmith. In my experience, the nearest they get to giving anyone a hand-up is their hands up their maids' skirts. Good Lord, I wonder – could this lad Steve be Porphyry's child?'

'Shoot, Butcher, you do get carried away on them socialist principles of yours,' said Joe angrily. 'Chris would only have been a kid himself when this Waring boy was born.'

'Very precocious, the upper classes,' said Butcher. 'OK, how about *his* father? Steve could be his half brother.'

'Talking through your wig, Butcher,' said Joe. 'Anyway, don't matter whose brother this guy Waring is, can't see how him taking off has any connection with my case.'

Butcher might at this point have justly pointed out that it was Joe who'd started the speculation flowing in the first place. Instead she said, 'All right, Joe. But relationship apart, there is one very obvious reason why Porphyry might not want anyone to show too much interest in looking for Waring.'

Joe said, 'What reason?'

Butcher shook her head sorrowfully and said, 'I don't know how it is with detectives, Joe, but a good lawyer never discounts any possibility. It's the only way you can be prepared for whatever the opposition may throw at you.'

'Meaning?'

'Meaning it could be that Waring, going about his business near the sixteenth fairway, observed Mr Porphyry take a ball out of his pocket and set it down in a good lie at the edge of the wood. When Porphyry realized he'd been observed, he suggested to Waring that he might care to take a long, well-paid holiday far, far away. Of course, at that moment he would not realize that even as he spoke his Nemesis, Jimmy Postgate, was fishing his ball out of the pool.'

It took Joe a few seconds to pick the meaning out of this verbiage.

'You mean, Chris really did cheat? No way! No way!'

'Your belief is touching,' said Butcher. 'Reminds me of all the times I've heard devoted mothers stand up in court and assure the jury that there is no way their beloved sons would commit assault or burglary or murder.'

'I'm not his mother,' said Joe. 'Anyway, if he's guilty, why would he hire me? And why would King Rat try to get me out of the way?'

'I'm working on that,' said Butcher. 'I've been trying to find out more about the set-up at the Royal Hoo. If they'd gone public, it would be easy, but as it's a private company, there's a problem with getting hold of the details.'

'Why don't I ask Chris Porphyry?' said Joe.

Butcher looked at him for a moment then said in wonderment, 'There you go again. Just when I'm starting to feel that perhaps I've got it all wrong and that looking at you as an investigator, what we see is in fact what we get, out pops an idea so obvious that a fine-tuned legal intellect like mine has overlooked it. Yes, why don't you ask him. Now, I've got work to do, Sixsmith. Enjoy Spain.'

Joe had put Spain to the back of his mind, which was an area of the Sixsmith intellect so crowded that a Health and Safety inspector would have condemned it out of hand. All kinds of stuff got dumped there and much of it was never reclaimed. But some decision times were not permanently postponable.

'You think I should go, Butcher?' he said through the open door.

'Didn't you tell King you'd take the job?'

'I suppose. But if it's just a trick to get shot of me . . .'

'You got any evidence of that, Sixsmith?'

'No. Was hoping you'd come up with something,' he said sadly.

'You were? I'm touched. But I haven't. And as your legal adviser I have to say that a verbal contract in the presence of a witness is binding. And in Ratcliffe King's case, the binding's done with piano wire. So my advice is, go. Don't pay me now, I'll send you a bill.'

She began to walk away.

'I bet you will, too. Thanks a bunch,' yelled Joe after her.

He started up the Morris. He had a lot to think about, but as he left the car park he didn't forget to check in the mirror to see if there was any sign of the Cruiser and its twitchy owner. There wasn't.

One less thing to worry about, thought Joe.

But it still left plenty.

14

What's Become of Waring?

Back in his flat he shouted hello to Whitey but got no response. It didn't surprise him. During this hot weather the cat spent most of the day sleeping, only rousing himself during the cool of the evening to sally forth and check on his empire. As the flat was on the seventh floor, sentimental visitors sometimes opined it was a long way for a little cat to have to make his way down all those stairs and back up again. Long and dangerous, some of them said.

But if the visitors visited often enough, almost certainly a day would come when, as they got into the lift downstairs, they would find themselves joined by Whitey, who would then ride up to the seventh with them.

'But we never see him going down with us,' a visitor might occasionally say.

'Going down he don't use the lift,' Joe would reply.

He took it in his stride now, but the first time he'd seen Whitey squeeze through the railings of the tiny balcony and vanish from sight, he'd almost died of shock. He'd rushed to the rail and peered over, expecting to see a splatter of fur and flesh on the pavement below. Instead he'd glimpsed a little white rump moving rapidly down the wall from balcony to balcony till it reached the ground. At a pinch, Whitey could make it back up by the same route, but when it came to energy conservation, he was way ahead of the Greens.

Joe checked the time. Eight forty, still early enough to wander round to Beryl's flat and suggest they share a cooling takeaway. Early enough, that is, if you weren't being picked up to go to the airport at five o'clock tomorrow morning.

What should he do? Ring Porphyry and tell him he'd done all he could for him and would be refunding his money? Or ring Mimi and tell her to tell her boss something had come up and he wouldn't be able to take the job after all.

But that would make him sound really unreliable and he guessed King Rat's dissatisfaction could blacklist parts of the Sixsmith Agency other complainants couldn't reach.

In any case, hadn't the fact that this Spanish job was only for three days made even Butcher dilute her doubt of King Rat's motives?

So he'd go. It gave him the excuse he needed to ring Beryl.

She said, 'Hi, Joe. Thought you might have rung earlier to suggest going out tonight to make up for last night.'

As if it had been him who stood her up!

He said, 'Sorry. I was busy on a job.'

'Yeah. Down at the Hole in the Wall, was that?'

Shoot! How the heck did she know that? he asked himself. And guessed the answer almost simultaneously. Aunt Mirabelle. Who had an intelligence system in the Luton area that made the CIA look like amateurs. Correction! The South Beds Bird-watching Society made the CIA look like amateurs. Mirabelle's totalitarian network was KGB or MOSSAD in its scope. One of her minions probably worked at the Hole, and news of Joe's appearance among the ravers would have shot along the line like a sighting of Bin Laden at a bar mitzvah.

And once Mirabelle heard, she'd have been straight on to Beryl to find out if she could throw any light on this latest aberration.

'That's right,' he said. 'Working Chris Porphyry's case.'

He guessed right that this would be a diversion.

'The hunk in the Aston? You actually went to the Royal Hoo and got the job?'

'I surely did,' he said. 'No need to sound so surprised either. Look, what I'm ringing for is, I have to be away for a couple of days, wondered if you and Desmond could keep an eye on Whitey for me. Usual: top up the water and food, don't let the tray get too disgusting.'

Desmond was Beryl's young son, who loved the cat.

'Couple of days?'

'Till the weekend maybe.'

'That's four days.'

'Hey, three, four, no need to get hung up on counting.'

'When I'm doling out your pills in the geriatric ward, you'll want me to get hung up on counting, believe me.'

'I surely will as you'll likely be in the next bed,' said Joe ungallantly.

'I certainly won't be in the same bed.'

This wasn't going too well.

He said, 'Will you do it? Please.'

'Course I will. You don't think I'd let a dumb animal suffer. And I worry about Whitey, too.'

This was better.

'Well, thanks. You've got a key, right?'

'Yeah, if I can recall where I put it. When are you leaving?'

'Five tomorrow morning.'

'Jeez, Joe. What's Mr Porphyry offering you to get you up so early?'

'This ain't that job. This one, I'm working for Mr Ratcliffe King.'

There was a moment's shocked silence then she said, 'Oh Joe, Joe, all these high-up people, don't be getting out of your depth.'

'Hard with high-up people,' he joked.

'Then don't be getting above yourself. Gotta go now. Bye, Joe.'

'Bye,' he said reluctantly.

As he ended the call, the phone rang again.

'Sixsmith,' he said.

'Joe, it's Chris. You said you'd let me know how you were getting on.'

There was no reproach in the voice, just hope. No, worse than hope. Confidence.

'Making progress, Chris,' said Joe.

'Yes?'

He cast around for something reassuring to say and all that came to mind was Butcher's obscurely jokey, *What's become of Waring?*

He said, 'That lad, Waring, the assistant greenkeeper, still no word of him?'

'No. Why do you ask?'

'Just think there might be a connection,' lied Joe. 'You being so concerned about him and all.'

It sounded so feeble that he anticipated the long silence that followed must signal the inevitable onset of doubt about his competence.

Instead . . .

'Oh, Joe, Joe,' said Porphyry. 'What Willie said about you is true. You don't say much, but nothing gets past that razor-sharp mind of yours.'

'Eh?' said Joe, thinking there must be a crossed line or something.

'Yes, I take a special interest in Steve, but I don't see how it can be connected with this business. Thing is, Steve's local. Sally, his mother, used to work for my parents.

Housemaid. I remember her well, pretty little thing . . . I recall telling her I wanted to marry her . . .'

He paused as if in reminiscence.

Joe thought, Oh shoot! He's not going to tell me Butcher was right, is he?

Then Porphyry laughed. It was good to hear him laugh. Young Fair Gods aren't made for sorrow.

'She said, "Thank you kindly, Master Chris, but my George has got first refusal." Then she took me to the kitchen and gave me a huge slice of cook's chocolate fudge cake. Best adhesive known for mending an eight-year-old's broken heart. She got married soon after, handed in her notice when she got pregnant with Steve.'

Joe heaved a silent sigh of relief and said, 'This George . . .'

'George Waring. Worked on the estate. Sort of general dogsbody. Could turn his hand to anything. Might have made something of himself if he hadn't been such a devil for the drink. Killed him in the end, poor blighter.'

'He died of alcoholic poisoning?'

'Not exactly. He was rolling home one summer evening with a few mates, took a shortcut over the fields that involved crossing a stream by a single plank bridge. He lost his balance and fell off. A fall of hardly a couple of feet, next to no water in the brook, but he banged his head on a stone and when his mates went to pick him up, they found he was dead.'

'How? Why?' asked Joe. It was totally irrelevant, but it was better than trying to explain he had no leads on the cheating case and not much hope of developing any.

'Turned out he had an abnormally thin skull. You and me might have had a bump, nothing worse. Poor old George cracked his head wide open and that was that. It was an unfortunate accident, no one's fault, but Sally, his wife, got embroiled with some ambulance-chasing lawyer who said it was the estate's responsibility and wanted her to launch a huge compensation claim.'

'That would be Ms Butcher,' said Joe, relishing the *ambulance-chasing* bit.

'Spot on, Joe. You really are a marvel. There was no case, it was never going to get near court, but this Butcher creature kept nagging away. Then poor Sally was diagnosed with cancer. We made sure she got the best of treatment, but a year and a half later she was dead too. Young Steve was sixteen then. I'd promised Sally I would keep an eye on him. He moved in with her family, who also worked on the estate. I offered to finance him through college, or he could have had a job on the estate, but he wasn't interested. He wanted his independence and he wanted to be a bit nearer town. So rather than see him do something silly and go off the rails, last year I fixed up a job for him at the golf club. He found lodgings in Upleck – do you know it? Handy for town and on the right side for work. I bought him a little motor scooter so he could get to the Hoo nice and easy. He seemed really happy, which is why I can't understand what made him take off.'

So much for Porphyry's special interest. Guilt money, Butcher would probably call it, or at best feudal patronage, but to Joe it seemed like the decent concern of a decent guy. Whatever, it also smelt like a pongy red herring.

Still, when there's nothing else in the fridge, red herring is what you dine on.

'You got the address of his digs?' he asked.

'Yes. Hang on.' A pause then Porphyry dictated, 'Mrs Tremayne, 15 Lock-keeper's Lane, Upleck. Anything else, Joe?'

No curiosity as to why he wanted the address, which was just as well. I'm the basket he's put all his eggs in, thought Joe. And basket just about sums me up!

Something else from his talk with Butcher popped up.

'There's some kind of agreement you've got about how things work at the Hoo, right? Like when the place was set up as a club, there must have been something legal about who got shares and so on.'

'Oh, you mean the deed of foundation.'

'Do I? Yes, I suppose I do.'

'Yes, it was my grandfather who set up the club, of course. A private arrangement between himself and a few friends initially. But he once told me when I was only a nipper, a necessary qualification for being a gent used to be that you could read and write. That was so that you could make sure you kept a clear and detailed record of all the gentlemen's agreements you entered into. I've got a copy somewhere.'

He chuckled. Was that a joke then? wondered Joe.

'Don't suppose you've got a copy handy?' he said without much hope.

'As a matter of fact, I think I have,' said the YFG. 'I dug it out for the club's AGM in the spring. Something had come up, I forget what it was, but Arthur Surtees thought it as well to cast his lawyer's eye over the original foundation document. Now where did I put it? Oh yes. Tucked behind the sherry decanter so I'd be reminded to put it somewhere safe every time I had a drink.'

Didn't work, did it? thought Joe.

'All right if I take a look at it?' he said.

'You think there might be a connection?'

'Can't say. Just covering all angles.'

'Joe, you're a marvel. I'd never have thought of such a thing. Shall I bring it round to your place now?'

'No!' said Joe. Fobbing the poor devil off with red herrings over the phone was one thing, but he couldn't face the prospect of looking into those trusting eyes. Besides, he needed his sleep.

'You got a fax machine?'

'Yes.'

'Good. Just fax it will you. Hang on.'

He opened the address book by the phone and dictated Butcher's fax number. She was the one who wanted to see it.

'One thing more, Chris,' he said.

Typically, he'd almost forgotten the one thing he'd picked up at the Hole that might give a real pointer to who could be behind the frame-up, assuming that's what it was.

'Someone had to put a formal complaint to this Rules Committee before it could consider the case. I gather it wasn't Syd Cockernhoe, the guy you beat. Any idea who it was?'

To Joe's delight, Porphyry said, 'Oh yes,' instantly.

Then the delight faded as the YFG continued, 'That would be me.'

'You?'

'Yes. Couldn't have all those foul rumours flying around. This needed to be brought in the open and sorted out publicly. So I had a word with Tom Latimer and asked him to put the facts before the Four Just Men. You'd have done the same, I think, Joe.'

'Maybe,' said Joe. 'Pity though. If you'd left it to someone else, we might have got a pointer to who it is that's after you.'

'Golly. Never thought of that. That's why I need someone like you, Joe. Shall we meet up some time tomorrow for another chat?'

Joe took a deep breath.

'Not tomorrow. I've got to be away a couple of days. On enquiries.'

'OK, Joe. Understood. Ring me when you can.'

'Yeah, I'll do that.'

Joe sat by the phone and told himself he hadn't lied. If Porphyry interpreted what he'd said as meaning enquiries on his behalf, that was his problem.

But he didn't feel good.

His phone rang again.

'Joe, Chris here. Listen, talking about young Steve got me thinking. I got a call from him that night . . .'

'Which night?'

'You know, the night all this bother started. I didn't hang around the club too long after Jimmy showed up saying he'd picked my ball out of his pool. Bit of an atmosphere and I needed to think. So I went home, and a bit later my mobile rang. It was Steve.'

'Yeah? So what did he say?'

'Nothing really. We got cut off. I tried ringing back but just got his answer service.'

'But it was definitely Waring.'

'Oh yes. I recognized his voice. He said, "Hi, Mr Porphyry –" then we got cut off.'

'So what time did this call come through?'

'About nine thirty, I think. This help at all, Joe?'

No, probably not the slightest bit, thought Joe.

He said gently, 'We'll have to see, Chris. Good night now.'

Why is it I never talk to this guy without feeling lousy? he asked himself as he switched off.

Maybe it was because he'd got so used to being with people who at best regarded him as a lucky PI and at worst thought of him as a joke that it was hard to deal with someone who managed to find more evidence of his skill and insight every time they talked!

He needed someone down to earth and sensible to talk

to, but when he looked around the flat, there was still no sign of Whitey.

He put his front door on the security chain and left it slightly ajar so that if the cat returned via the lift he could get in. The balcony door was wide open anyway to admit what little breeze there was. He recalled the scented air conditioning at ProtoVision House. Nice work if you could get it. But lower down the food chain all you could do was take off all your clothes and lie naked on top of your bed by an open window.

It had been a long day full of incident and information, a day made for lying idly in the sun but which had seen him moving sweatily between the Royal Hoo and Ram Ray's garage and the Law Centre and King Rat's palace and the Hole in the Wall, a day that might have had a lesser man lying awake pondering its significances and implications.

Joe did ponder, for all of five seconds, before bundling up the day and all its events and dumping them out of sight at the back of his mind. And in another five seconds he had plunged effortlessly into his customary deep sleep which Beryl claimed was indistinguishable from catalepsy.

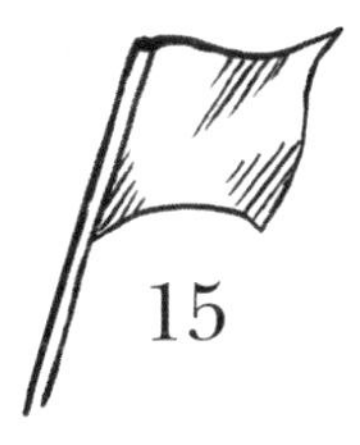

15

Twitch

Except with regard to Luton winning the Premiership title, the FA Cup and the European Championship all in the same season, Joe was not a dreamer.

Tonight, however, he can't have plunged to his usual depths of sleep because he found himself dreaming.

It was a really weird dream in which a pair of mighty hands seized him by the ankles, bore him through the air and hung him upside down over the railing of his balcony. The early July dawn was already painting the dreaming spires of Luton and its surrounding landscape in a beauteous light. He was facing outwards, and even upside down, the view looked really good. Blasphemously he thought, Maybe I'm being tempted like Jesus. A voice was calling his name in the kind of smoky rasp you would expect from the devil's throat and it wouldn't have surprised Joe to hear his assailant proclaiming, 'All these things I will give thee, if thou wilt fall down and worship me.'

Instead the voice cried, 'Sixsmith, what you playing at? You are dead meat, man! Dead meat!' And at the same time his body was pendulumed so violently that his head struck the underside of the balcony.

The first collision roused both pain and suspicion. A lesser detective might have leapt at once to the conclusion that he wasn't dreaming, but Joe had learned a long time ago that it was better never to leap to conclusions but let them come to you in their own sweet time.

The second collision brought the conclusion a lot closer and the third confirmed its arrival.

This was no dream. He really was being dangled over his seventh-floor balcony by a homicidal maniac.

As if to reward this admission of reality, the swinging began to slow down. Which was nice, until it occurred to him this could mean either the swinger was tiring or maybe was thinking of letting go.

One result of the deceleration was that Joe was once more able to take in the view, but like one of his favourite songs almost said, What a difference a couple of seconds makes!

Now the soft beauty of the morning had completely evaporated and the gentle sun was a spotlight, picking out the little square of pavement far below against which his head was about to splatter.

He bent his neck so he could look up. Even if he hadn't been able to recognize the rage-twisted features peering down at him, he would have made a good guess at the huge hands bolted tight around his ankles. Last time he'd seen those fists they'd been remodelling the face of Ernie Jagger, the Battersea Bruiser.

He was literally in the hands of Eloise's ex, Jurassic George.

Knowing how to say the right thing at the right time is truly a gift from heaven, which was why on the whole Joe usually opted for silence or a neutral 'U-huh.' But neither of these options seemed suited to his present circumstances. So Joe let his mind go blank and said the first thing that came into it.

Which was, 'Hey, George, man, how're you doing? That was a great job you did on Jagger. Those left hooks! Just beautiful.'

It was an inspired social gambit. Boxers are simple men, a condition refined by frequent blows about the head, and though they are generally indifferent to appeals to their better nature or the higher aesthetic, the one way of catching their interest is to make complimentary remarks about their ring technique.

Above him there was a change of atmosphere, or not so much a change as the kind of hiatus you sometimes get when a big black thundercloud seems uncertain whether to launch its floods and lightnings *here* and *now* or post-pone them a bit till *there* and *then*. The swinging from side to side stopped altogether and the voice modulated from threatening rasp to modest roar.

'Yeah, well, I just saw a gap, know what I mean, and I threw that first left and the gap got bigger, yeah, so I chucked in another couple and set him up to finish the job.'

Joe would have preferred it if George hadn't felt the need to relax his grip with his left hand in order to illustrate the hooks. True, the man's right hand seemed to have strength enough to hold his weight indefinitely, but if George should feel moved to demonstrate the combination with which he dispatched the unfortunate Bruiser, this diversionary tactic could prove counterproductive.

Time to change the focal point of the flattery.

'Nearly took his head off!' said Joe. 'But it wasn't just strength, though, no way, George. Your footwork, man, you've really been working on your footwork. Float like a butterfly, sting like a Centurion tank, eh?'

To his disappointment, all the fulsome compliment earned Joe was a mandatory shake of the ankles.

'Sting like a bee, I think it is,' growled George. 'Ain't that right, Twitch? Sting like a bee.'

Keep it simple, Joe admonished himself. Real simple!

Another head appeared over the balcony rail. This was a smaller head and it only came up to George's shoulder. The features were indistinguishable, but the way it jerked to the side from time to time as if dislodging a troublesome insect was a giveaway.

This was the watcher outside Ram Ray's and the Hole. Twitch. What else would he be called?

'Yeah, like a bee, George,' agreed Twitch. 'Listen, George, mebbe you should pull him up. He slips, we're all in shit, you dig?'

Joe fell in love with Twitch. Here was a real gem, a man of sense and sensibility who appreciated that while the odd body plummeting from the seventh floor might be regarded as a natural hazard in neighbouring Hermsprong, here in well-regulated Rasselas it could provoke complaint and investigation.

George seemed unconcerned.

'He ain't gonna slip,' he declared reassuringly. Then spoilt it by adding, 'He hits that pavement, it's 'cos I let the motherfucker drop.'

By now Joe had woken enough to be getting his head around what was happening here.

It was Eloise. Distracted by their break-up, George had set his minion Twitch on to watch Eloise. And what had he seen?

Oh shoot! thought Joe.

He'd seen Eloise, the girl of George's dreams, with her scantily clad body pressed close against Joe Sixsmith's, her mouth feasting on his, and he'd seen it twice in one day. Not only that, Twitch had probably been using that phone he was playing with to take photos.

He felt he could put things right if only he could talk to George face to face instead of face to foot.

The one good thing about being upside down was that all that blood draining into his brain seemed to be speeding up his intellectual processes. For instance it was clear to him now that the young woman must also have spotted Twitch lurking, and far from being overcome by a desire to explore his manly body, the two close embraces had just been her way of winding up George in absentia.

All he had to do was share this insight.

He called, 'George, I can explain about Eloise . . .'

It was a mistake. The sound of the girl's name from the unhallowed lips of her molester clearly brought the Jurassic mists rising once more and Joe felt himself swung so violently that if he'd been released at either extremity of the arc, he would have landed twenty or thirty feet from the target point he'd focused on before.

Eventually, perhaps because of the increasingly twitchy Twitch's protests, the swinging ceased once more and Joe's enhanced but jangling brain could get to grips with the pressing problem of how to deny there was anything going on between him and the girl without actually mentioning her name.

He let himself go limp, which wasn't difficult, and called up in a broken voice, 'George, after I die, man, do me one promise. You owe me that, man. Promise you'll go and see Beryl and tell her I love her.'

That hiatus again. For a moment he feared that George's cauliflowered ears might have misheard Beryl for Eloise and he closed his eyes in anticipation of being let go.

Then the voice rasped, 'Beryl? Who's this Beryl?'

'Beryl Boddington. My fiancée,' croaked Joe.

'Your fiancée? You two-timing my Eloise?'

This sideways bound of logic impressed Joe, himself no mean leaper on the dance-floor of debate, but this was no time for abstract analysis.

Keep it simple.

'No . . . Beryl my one and only love . . . She's a scary woman, George . . . no way I'd dare two-time her . . . You tell her I was always true . . .'

There was a moment of complete stillness which, thought Joe, was perhaps really death. Then he felt himself swung high once more, this time the grip on his ankles was released, and now he was flying through the air.

He had time to think, 'I'm going to die,' before he hit the ground a bit earlier than he'd expected.

There was surprisingly little pain, which meant he must have been killed instantly. If Aunt Mirabelle had got it right the next voice he'd hear would be the voice of St Peter.

But oddly St Peter sounded a lot like George.

'You saying you're not screwing my girl, Eloise?'

Joe opened his eyes. He was lying on the floor of the balcony. Way above him loomed Jurassic, who now prodded him with a booted foot and repeated the question.

'You saying you're not screwing my girl, Eloise?'

Joe tried to think of someone who in a similar situation might have replied, 'Well yes, I am, actually. Screwing her, I mean. As often as I can.'

James Bond maybe? Had to be someone in a movie. No one in real life would even dream of it!

'Yeah, that's what I'm saying, George. I love my fiancée, Beryl.'

'What about them photos? You telling me you're not feeling her up on them photos?'

I was right, thought Joe. That bastard Twitch (he'd fallen out of love with Twitch) had been taking pictures and sending them back to George.

'No!' he declared. 'She was just pretending to mess with me to make you jealous.'

'Why'd she do that?'

''Cos she's still got feelings for you, man! She knew your boy was there, spying. Hard to miss him, all that twitching.'

George glowered at the now spasmodic Twitch, who said defensively, 'Looked like he was really feeling her up to me, George,' confirming Joe's disenchantment.

It was decision time. Joe could actually see the thoughts making their slow progress across the boxer's face. If he fought like this, how did he ever manage to win? Then his gaze fell to those huge fists which looked like they'd been carved by that Greek guy Mickey Angel out of solid granite for some gigantic statue.

He urged, 'She loves you true, George. You gotta see that. How could she settle for a guy like me when she could have a hunk like you?'

He could see how this logic made its mark, but in

George's primitive mind a photo was still worth a thousand words. He needed supportive evidence.

'This fiancée, Beryl, where does she live?' he demanded.

'Next block, number 23,' gabbled Joe, thinking, I've got him!

'I need to talk to her.'

'Yeah, sure. Er, why is that?'

'She tells me she's your fiancée, then maybe I don't smash you to a pulp,' said George.

Joe's mind was racing. Beryl was sharp. A couple of quick winks as he explained the situation and she'd be well up to confirming their engagement and convincing George there was no way her man would have strayed. Beryl could be really scary when she chose. OK, he would have to pay for it later, but it would be worth it whatever the price.

'Let me get some clothes on and I'll take you round there,' he said, scrambling to his feet, which George immediately swept from beneath him, sending him crashing back to the ground.

'No, you stay there. I'll talk with this woman without you winking and nodding and fast signing in the corner.'

Shoot! The monster wasn't so simple after all.

But there was always the phone . . .

Not if you're locked naked on your balcony seven floors up, there wasn't, he thought disconsolately as the boxer slammed the balcony door shut and turned the key in the lock.

Through the locked door he watched his unwelcome visitors make their exit from the flat. He could see the so-called security chain dangling loose. Presumably a single push from George's bull-like shoulder had ripped it from its staple on the wall. He thought of trying to smash the glass panel in the balcony door, but it wasn't worth the bother. After some early fraternal visits from a few of the brothers in Hermsprong, the Rasselas inhabitants had demanded and got shatterproof glass put in all their windows. Height was no disincentive to agile thieves who had a Whitey-like ability to scale the sheer side of the tower block from one balcony to the next. Joe peered down and shuddered at the thought of even making the attempt to descend. He might at a pinch be able to drop down on to the balcony below, but by the time he had persuaded the flat-owners that they shouldn't take the dramatic entry of a stark-naked man into their premises personally, George would almost certainly have arrived at Beryl's.

No, all he could do was wait and hope that her natural intelligence and quick wit would get him off the hook.

Of course there was a strong likelihood that being rousted out of bed by a belligerent boxer at this ungodly hour would make her react to the suggestion that Joe was her fiancé with a derisive laugh and unambiguous denial.

In which case George would return . . .

In which case, dropping on to the balcony below didn't seem quite such a desperate act . . .

He sat with his back against the railings so that he could watch the main entrance across the living room.

At least he wasn't cold.

Even at this hour the newly risen sun had enough warmth to warn him of another red-hot day in prospect. Which he might or might not live to see.

Oh well. No point worrying.

His mouth opened in a huge yawn. He had after all had a very disturbed night. A few seconds later the old Sixsmith philosophy that, however bad things were, losing sleep over them only made them worse, kicked in and the yawn turned into a gentle snore.

Joe was asleep again.

16

Wondrous Regiment

Joe's second awakening was a lot less violent than the first but still fell well short of the ideal which included the warm memory of a good woman and the smell of frying bacon which said good woman had just got up to prepare.

A foot prodded at his ribs. He half opened one eye and looked at it. The foot prodded harder. He didn't mind too much because his first assessment had told him it wasn't a size-thirteen foot, therefore it did not belong to Jurassic George. This foot was shod in a size five or six sensible flat-heeled shoe, and it was attached to the end of a shapely leg wrapped in a black silk stocking. This was interesting. He followed the stocking up with his eyes till it reached the hem of a skirt which in turn led him to some kind of uniform blouse. A nurse. It was a nurse. Meaning the stocking wasn't silk but probably lisle or some such stuff. He must be in hospital. Well, that wasn't bad either. Except what sort of hospital even in the cash-strapped National Health expected its patients to sleep on the floor?

'You going to lie there all day, Joe Sixsmith?' said a voice. A familiar voice.

He opened both eyes fully and took in the face peering down at him.

'Beryl, that you?'

'Yes, it's me and I wish it wasn't. What the hell you playing at, Joe Sixsmith? I just had some gorilla beating on my door and waking all the neighbours, asking if I was your effing fiancée!'

'That would be Jurassic George.'

'I know who it was. I read the sports pages too.'

'So what did you say to him?' asked Joe, struggling to his feet.

'I said if he didn't turn the volume down and the language off I'd punch his lights out,' said Beryl.

Joe looked at her with mingled admiration and sorrow, the first because she was clearly Wonder Woman, the second because he could see no way he could ever deserve her.

'So what did he say?' he asked.

'After he calmed down, he gave me some garbled story about him going to tear your head off because he'd heard you were balling his young and gorgeous girlfriend, and you saying he'd got it wrong 'cos I was your ever-loving fiancée and there was no way you could even look at another woman.'

'And what did you say?'

'I said there was no way any young and gorgeous girl would let you ball her, but in any case you'd be too scared to even think about it 'cos, if you did, I'd be the one to tear your head off. After that he went away and I got dressed. I'm on early shift and I thought I'd better look in here first to find out just what the hell's been going on.'

'Beryl, you are a real star!' said Joe.

He reached forward to give her a grateful hug. She started back, crying, 'Don't even dream about it, not in that state!'

Only now did it occur to Joe that he was stark naked. It was funny, he'd been stark naked with Beryl before and she'd been in a similar condition and they'd both really enjoyed it. But now it was just plain embarrassing.

He moved past her into the living room in search of clothing. At least that was his intention, but Beryl mistook it and retreated before him. The back of the low settee caught her just behind the knees and she fell over it backwards, her legs kicking in the air. Joe rushed forward to help her.

At the same moment, King Rat's PA, the gorgeous Mimi, dressed as if she planned to step right from the plane into the wine-dark Med, rushed through the open door saying, 'Joe, I'm sorry I'm a bit late, we'll need to rush . . . Oh my God!'

In such circumstances in a French farce or a British sitcom, the character in Joe's situation would probably have said, 'It's not what it seems . . .' but Joe knew from his gumshoe guru, Endo Venera, that unless you were watching one of those Ag Christie shows on the telly, it was wise to assume a guy with a smoking gun standing over a bleeding corpse was guilty as hell. OK, maybe his gun wasn't smoking, but a naked man standing over a woman in a nurse's uniform with her legs kicking in the air was a situation it would take even that Aircool Parrot a couple of hours in the library to explain away.

He said, 'Don't think I'm going to make it, Mimi.'

She managed a grin and said, 'Looks to me like you're halfway there, Joe,' and left.

Beryl pulled herself upright.

'And who the hell was that?' she demanded. 'Maybe I should have let Jurassic George tear your head off, after all!'

'No, no,' protested Joe. 'That wasn't Eloise. That was Mimi. We were flying off to Spain together . . . Hang about till I get dressed . . .'

He should have stuck to silence. Even that small beginning of explanation was a mistake. When he returned from his bedroom, fastening up his trousers, the living room was empty.

But not for long. Through the open door stepped Whitey. He looked around as if to say, *I leave the place for a few hours and it's a tip!* Then he moved purposefully into the kitchen.

He was right, thought Joe. Nothing so bad that a spot of breakfast wouldn't help.

From the kitchen came an imperious howl.

'I'm coming, I'm coming,' said Joe.

An hour later, his belly distended by a Full English Breakfast (minus of course that percentage which Whitey felt was his due), Joe felt able to bring the full beam of his mental searchlight to bear on recent events and his best response to them.

Going back to bed was a distinct possibility till it occurred to him that at some point Jurassic George was going to approach Eloise with a view to telling her all was forgiven and folding her to his bosom.

Now Eloise he knew to be a girl of spirit, and while she might react by returning the embrace with an equal passion, she might also knee him in the crutch and tell him to get his big bear paws off her lily-white body which belonged to another, and take a hike. In which case the likely direction of the hike could be back to Rasselas.

He'd already taken the precaution of shutting, locking and bolting his front door, but when he looked at the devastated security chain, even this didn't make him feel secure. Best, he decided, to be out of here and on the move.

First, though, he stripped off again and got under a nice hot shower. The Full English had fortified the inner man, but the outer man was indicating by a network of twinges and bruises exactly where Jurassic's assault had left its mark. In the shower he sang, not to keep up his spirits, which were self-raising anyway, but because a singer needs to exercise his vocal cords and the shower was the only place he could do it in the flat at this hour of day without the neighbours banging on the walls. He did Vaughan Williams' *Songs of Travel,* which had won him plaudits at the last Luton *Singfest,* then he tried Bach's '*Ich habe genug*' with which he was hoping to impress Rev. Pot sufficiently to put him forward for the baritone solo in the Luton Combined Choirs' performance of the *Christmas Oratorio* at the end of the year. It still needed a bit of work, he judged, so for his finale he moved on to a selection more in favour on Entertainment Night at the Supporters' Club, building up to his show-stopping 'Ol' Man River'.

This usually left him as uplifted as his audience but as he stepped out of the shower, his thoughts moved naturally from the Supporters' Club to Sir Monty Wright and thence to Monty's cohort, Ratcliffe King, who had paid him good money to be on a plane to Spain at this very moment.

While King Rat wasn't a real and present danger – unlike Jurassic, whose battering ram of a shoulder might at any moment be applied to the door – he was in the long run a far more potent enemy.

Probably Mimi had already put him in the picture so it might be a wise move to try and take the sting out of his anger by ringing up to explain and apologize and offer atonement.

He went to the phone and saw the *message* light on the answer machine had come on while he was showering. He pressed *play.*

'Joe, hi! It's Mimi. Listen, I'm just boarding our flight. Now don't get your boxers in a twist worrying about missing it. We've all been there and I know how easy it is to lose track. Anyway, things are busy here and the next flight I could get you transferred to leaves at two p.m., OK? So I'll take care of things till you show; quite looking forward to doing a bit of the real PI stuff instead of just being your gofer! But, Joe, Mr King wants me to report in soon as we get ourselves settled at the hotel and make contact with Tomlin. I can hold back till this evening, no problem, but if you haven't shown by then, he'll have to know. So don't let me down. Give me a ring to say you've got the message, OK? Cheers.'

I am surrounded by wonderful women, thought Joe. Whoever said that stuff about *a monstrous regiment* got it wrong. Must have meant *wondrous!*

That dealt with the King Rat problem, and flying to Spain seemed a very good way of dealing with the Jurassic George problem.

He picked up the phone and rang Mimi's mobile number. He got the message service. Of course, she'd be switched off on the plane.

He said, 'Hi, Mimi, got your message, I'll be on the two o'clock. And thanks a bunch. I owe you.'

As he spoke he found himself thinking, What was it she'd said? *We've all been there.* Might be worth asking her about that when I get to Spain!

He shoved the unworthy thought out of his mind and rang Beryl's mobile. Her phone was off too, for which he was somewhat relieved.

'Hi,' he said. 'It's Joe. Listen, sorry about all that stuff this morning, but when you hear everything that's been happening, you'll understand. Main thing is, I'm still going to be away for a couple of days, well, four actually. So if you could do what you said about keeping an eye out for Whitey I'd be truly grateful. I expect you're up to your elbows in new-born babies or something now, so I'll ring you later, OK? Thanks a lot and I'm really sorry that moron George got you involved. Bye.'

There. Nothing there to get her heating up again. You are the master of diplomacy, Sixsmith. Now show you are also the master of self-preservation and get the hell out of here!

He grabbed the bag he'd packed the previous night and headed down to his car.

17

A Message from Frank

First stop was his office to check his mail, except that when he got there the postman hadn't been yet. He doubted it would hold anything but requests for money, whether official, commercial or charitable. It was far too early to go to the airport, but maybe hanging around here wasn't such a good idea. George, though no Nobel Prize-winner, was quite capable of checking the Yellow Pages.

In any case, his conscience told him, after his deception of the Young Fair God last night, he really owed it to him to put these hard-won hours at his disposal. But how?

All he could think of was Steve Waring. Porphyry had supplied the address of the lad's digs. Joe didn't have a great memory except for song lyrics, but he'd found he could extend this specialized skill to other areas such as addresses by fitting their rhythms to a melody in his repertoire.

Mrs Tremayne, 15 Lock-keeper's Lane marched very nicely with 'Give me some men who are stout-hearted men' from *The New Moon.* As for *Upleck,* this was a suburb of Luton whose name was engraved on Joe's heart as the site of the bus shelter in which he'd had his first experience of *coitus* which, perhaps fortunately, had been *interruptus* by the approach of the last No 27 bus. Later he sometimes mused that a five-mile walk home might have been a small price to pay for letting this supremely important encounter run its full and natural course.

He couldn't really see how a visit to Waring's might be helpful in the case, but as he couldn't see how anything other than a small miracle was going to help, he might as well drive out there. At least it was unlikely he'd run into George in Upleck.

A quarter of an hour later he was driving past the famous bus shelter. He slowed down to take a closer look. It looked as drab and draughty and uninviting as these things usually did.

What're you expecting, Sixsmith? he asked himself. English Heritage sticking a blue plaque on it?

Lock-keeper's Lane had indeed once been a lane, and a busy one too, carrying traffic down from the main highway to the Luton–Bedford Canal created to form a link with the Ouse to the north. Twentieth-century improvements in road and rail services had long since put paid to the canal's commercial claims to survival. From time to time proposals were made to revive it recreationally, but they always collapsed under the sheer weight of investment necessary to reconstitute the canal from the sorry string of silted-up, overgrown and usually stagnant pools it had degenerated into. At its urban end, Lock-keeper's Lane had become just another dusty suburban street with few of its inmates sufficiently curious even to wonder where the name came from.

It was still early enough in the morning for both kerbs to be lined with parked cars. Joe drove slowly, looking for a space. His luck was in. As he approached the estimated location of No 15, a silver Audi A8 4.2 Quattro pulled out and he gratefully slipped the Morris into the space.

The house had a sign in the window saying *Rooms to let – vacancies.* Joe rang the bell and a couple of moments later the door was opened by a woman who looked like Princess Anne in a bad temper after falling off a horse which had then kicked her.

'Yes?' she exclaimed.

'Mrs Tremayne, is it?'

Joe took the yellow-toothed snarl as an affirmative and pressed on.

'Sorry to bother you, but it's about one of your lodgers, Mr Waring –'

'Him? Why's everybody so interested in him all of a sudden? And why can't they be interested at a decent time of day?'

'Mam!' yelled a voice from within. 'Something's burning!'

'Well, turn it off then! Jesus, what do they teach them nowadays?'

She turned on her heel and vanished inside. After a while Joe took the still-open door as an invite and followed. A spoor of charred bacon led him into the kitchen where a teenage boy sat at a table eating bran flakes while his mother scraped the blackening contents of a frying pan on to a plate.

'Here,' she said. 'Take that in to Mr Logan. Hurry up, before it gets cold.'

'You mean that would make it worse?' said the boy, looking at the plate with exaggerated revulsion.

'Just for once in your life, Liam, do something without being smart, all right?'

Joe caught the boy's eye and gave a sympathetic smile. He got blanked for his pains. He's a teen, thought Joe, probably sensitized to trouble and something about me says I could be trouble.

The boy seized the plate, kicked the door open and went out of the kitchen.

'Right,' said Mrs Tremayne, turning her attention to Joe. 'So what the hell do you want?'

The interval since their first brief exchange had given Joe time to ponder.

He said, 'Who else has been interested in Mr Waring, then?'

'His brother,' replied the woman, surprised by the directness of the question.

'His brother?' Joe recalled the YFG talking about Steve being an only child. 'Which brother would that be?'

'His brother, Stephen.'

'So Steve's got a brother called . . . *Stephen*?'

'Yeah, why not? I've got a sister called Elspeth. Anyway, that's what his friend called him.'

'Whose friend?'

'Mr Waring's brother Stephen's friend who helped him clear out his things.'

At this point Mrs Tremayne registered that somehow she'd been bounced into co-operation and exclaimed, 'Who the hell are you anyway and what am I doing standing here in my own kitchen answering your sodding stupid questions?'

'I'm a friend of Mr Waring and I'm here to clear out his things,' said Joe who, not being a very good liar, was happy to pick up his lies ready-made, off the peg. 'Looks like I got my wires crossed.'

'That's right, so why don't you sod off before I cross your wires some more?'

She didn't look like the kind of woman who made threats lightly, but even though Joe didn't really know what it was he was looking for, he knew he needed more time to look for it and cast around for something to gain a stay of execution.

Money. He'd never met a landlady yet who wasn't interested in money.

He said, 'Mr Waring all paid up when he left, was he?'

'No, he was not! Why're you asking?'

'Just thought if you could work out what he owed, I might be able to sort things out when I see him.'

She regarded him speculatively.

The door opened and out of the corner of his eye he saw the boy come back into the kitchen.

'And maybe I could pay a little on account,' added Joe, recalling the saying of that great student of female psychology Merv Golightly that most women were suckers for promises except landladies, who were softened by nothing but hard cash.

Mrs Tremayne was nodding as if at last she was hearing something that made sense.

Liam said warningly, 'Mum . . .'

'Don't interrupt,' she snapped.

'Mr Logan says he doesn't want it. He says he'll buy a Mac on his way to work and knock it off his bill.'

Now he had his mother's full attention.

'He says *what*? We'll see about that!'

She snatched the plate from the boy's hand. Young Liam was a lad of some discernment, thought Joe. Cold, the breakfast looked even worse.

With her Habsburg lip thrust out like a locomotive's cow-catcher, Mrs Tremayne stormed out of the kitchen.

Joe caught the boy's eye and tried to share a poor-sod smile, but Liam wasn't having any.

On the whole, Joe got on well with kids. Just because most of today's teenagers chose to shuffle around with their pants at half-mast, talking in grunts and looking like they hated the universe didn't mean they were flesh-eating zombies on their way to an eat-in. Except on Hermsprong, where it might.

This boy seemed to have his wits about him. And there was that warning note in his voice when he'd come back into the kitchen and heard what Joe said to his mother . . .

He said, 'You get on all right with Mr Waring?'

'Steve? Yeah, he was cool.'

'Didn't say anything to you about going away, did he?'

'Nah.'

'This brother who collected his stuff this morning, did he look much like Steve?'

'Nah.'

'Didn't show any ID or anything, just to prove he was Steve's brother, did he?'

'Nah. You a cop, yeah?'

There it was. He'd been right. The kid had sussed he was nosing around soon as he'd seen him, but he'd jumped to the wrong conclusion.

Joe said, 'Sort of. PI.'

This finally got the boy's interest.

'You mean like private?'

'That's what the P means, I think.'

The boy looked like he might have some other suggestions, but he kept them to himself.

'You think something's happened to Steve?'

'Would it surprise you?'

Liam thought about this. Involvement was humanizing him. Also, Joe guessed he really did like Waring.

'Don't know. Thought it was odd he went off without his Frank Lampard picture.'

'What's that then?'

'He was a big Chelsea fan. Couple of years back he'd gone down to watch them and that night when he was wandering round the West End, he saw Frank getting out of a cab to go into a posh restaurant and he went up to him to ask for his autograph. Some of the guys with Frank told him to bog off, but Frank said no, it was fine, and he asked what Steve's name was and he signed this photo of him that was in a fan mag that Steve had.'

'And that was one of Steve's treasured possessions, was it?'

'Oh yeah. He'd got it in this gold frame and he had it on the wall at the bottom of his bed where he could look at it.'

'And you were surprised it hadn't gone.'

'Yeah, but I expect his brother took it this morning.'

'Couldn't check, could you, Liam?'

The boy went out. From what must be the dining room came the sound of Mrs Tremayne in full flow, counter-pointed by a desperately querulous male voice.

Joe moved across the kitchen. On a shelf between two wall units he'd noticed a jar full of ballpoints alongside a blue duplicate receipt book. He opened it and looked at the last carbon. It had today's date on and was headed *Re Mr S. Waring*. Beneath this he read *Back rent received up to and including breakfast Wed July 12th £135 payment.* Then on another line *To cover period July 12th to present July 19th £40.* And finally *Total received £175 cash,* followed by Mrs Tremayne's signature.

This confirmed what Joe had guessed. No landlady let anyone remove an errant lodger's belongings without she got payment first. It also explained Liam's admonitory tone. The boy hadn't wanted his mother to get involved in ripping off a cop.

He heard footsteps outside and quickly replaced the receipt book.

A moment later Liam returned clutching a photo in a cheap gilt frame. Across it was scrawled, *To Steve, good luck, mate! Frank.*

'He didn't take it,' said Liam. 'Steve will be gutted. He really liked that picture.'

'Yeah,' said Joe. 'Nice message.'

He was thinking, you send someone to pick up your stuff, you mention what you value most. But you come to clear all traces of a guy out of his lodgings, you don't look at what's hanging on the wall.

He said, 'This brother who came, you see what he was driving?'

'His mate was driving, but it was a silver Audi,' said Liam, confirming what Joe had guessed. But the boy hadn't finished, 'That's how I knew it was all right.'

'Sorry?'

'Yeah, I saw Steve in the car before.'

'You did?' said Joe, feeling the not unfamiliar feeling that another promising theory might be on the point of crumbling. 'When was that?'

'I don't know, week back maybe.'

'Morning, night? Weekend, weekday? Before the heat-wave started, after the heatwave started?'

'Don't remember,' said the boy with that indifference to temporal matters which is one of the blessings of child-hood and one of the penalties of age.

'So where was this?' said Joe, moving from time to place.

It was a clever move. Suddenly he got precision.

'Coming down Plunkett Avenue from the bypass about half a mile away,' said Liam. 'I'd been round at my mate Trent's . . .'

'So this was evening?' interrupted Joe.

'That's right, late on, still light but fading . . .'

'So nine-ish?' said Joe.

'Bit later. Mum got real ratty, says I should be in by nine on a school day. Anyway, this silver Audi goes by and there's Steve in the passenger seat. I gave him a wave, thought I might get a lift, but he didn't see me.'

'So did you mention this next time you saw him?'

Liam's face went slack, which in another age might have been taken as evidence of incipient idiocy, but which Joe recognized as signifying the modern teenager's entry into deep-thought mode.

'No,' said the boy finally. 'Didn't mention it 'cos I didn't see him again.'

'You mean . . . ?'

'Yeah. He was up in his room when I got back, and next morning must have been the day he took off. What do you think I should do about the picture?'

'Best keep it safe,' advised Joe. 'You a Chelsea fan?'

'No,' said the boy indignantly. 'Luton!'

'Good lad!' said Joe. 'Could be a cracking season ahead, specially with Sir Monty coming up with the cash to sign the Croat kid.'

'Mebbe,' said the boy with that natural scepticism which marks the true Luton supporter. 'Tell you next April.'

Joe's musically attuned ear told him the dining-room duet was reaching its climax. It didn't sound as if Mrs Tremayne was going to return in a better temper than when she left, which was an excellent reason to be on his way. He'd got all he was going to get here, though as usual he'd no idea whether it was worth the effort.

'Mebbe see you at the ground some time, Liam,' he said. 'Say goodbye to your mum for me.'

He made his way out, glancing at his watch. Still a couple of hours before he needed to think about getting to the airport. His visit to Lock-keeper's Lane had proved more productive than he'd anticipated, but he refused to let himself get carried away, mainly because his limited imaginative powers couldn't picture any destination he might be carried away to.

But he did know where it was worth looking for a silver Audi 8 Quattro.

He paused at the mini-roundabout at the top end of Lock-keeper's Lane to work out the best route to the Royal Hoo.

Straight across was going to be quickest, he decided.

And it was little surprise to discover after he'd negotiated the roundabout that he was driving along Plunkett Avenue.

18

A Patch of Oil

It occurred to Joe as he was parking his car that on this occasion he didn't have the protective cover of an invitation from the YFG.

On the other hand, no one here was going to know that, he told himself, and in any case he wanted to keep a low profile.

He checked his gear. He was dressed for his Spanish trip. If it had been a holiday he would definitely have travelled in the parrot shorts, but as it was business he'd opted for canary yellow chinos, green T-shirt and blue deck shoes. Nothing there to cause offence in a place where plus-fours and tartan trews were regarded as sharp gear.

It was still early, but golfers must like an early start for there was already an impressive array of high-price metal on display in the car park, including two silver Audi 8's.

The first he looked at was the 3-litre diesel model.

'Some poor sod on the bread-line,' mused Joe, making for the other.

This was the big boy, the Quattro 6. He strolled round as if admiring the lines. No sign of Waring's belongings inside. Must be still in the boot. He noticed that the tyre had picked up some mud which was quite a feat round Luton during the heatwave. Except of course he was in Royal Hoo mini-climate land where you could probably summon the steward and order mud.

'Mr Sixsmith.'

He looked up to see Chip Harvey approaching carrying what looked like a portable mummy case.

The young man didn't look happy to see him. It was understandable. Last time they'd met here, he'd been the YFG's guest and a well-heeled prospective member. After last night he was just old Joe, the snoop.

He said, 'Hi, Chip. How're you doing? Have a good time last night?'

'OK,' grunted Chip, which didn't come across as the modest disclaimer of a guy who had raved it up round the clubs before being taken to the bosom and wherever else he fancied of the gorgeous Eloise. Maybe things hadn't panned out.

He said, 'Just admiring the Audi. Nice wheels.'

'OK if you like that sort of thing,' said Chip with the

disdain of youth to whom *Vorsprung durch Technik* means dull in any language.

Then to Joe's surprise he reached down and started to unlock the boot.

'Hey, this isn't your machine, is it?'

'Don't be silly,' said Chip as the lid slowly rose allowing Joe to see that he'd got another guess completely wrong. The boot was empty except for a piece of dark blue carpeting of a quality Joe couldn't afford for his living room.

Chip's sharp young eyes spotted an imperfection that Joe had missed.

He reached in and touched the carpet with his index finger. He raised it to reveal the tip was oily. Frowning, he took a handkerchief from his pocket, wiped his finger and then rubbed the linen square vigorously over the offending piece of carpet. It took a lot of rubbing till he was satisfied, by which time his handkerchief was ruined.

'You do car-valeting too?' enquired Joe.

'These things cost too much to get them dirty,' said Chip, laying the mummy case gently inside. It was made of a rich black leather with a zipper and some strap buckles that looked like they could be real old gold.

'Just what is that thing?' asked Joe.

'It's a travel case,' said Chip. 'You put your golf bag and clubs in it so they don't get knocked around when you're flying abroad.'

'Shoot! You mean it's going to go in the plane's hold and you're worried about a bit of oil?'

'I'm not worried, but Mr Rowe might be.'

'That would be Colin Rowe?'

'That's right. It's just been delivered and he asked me to put it in his car. He plays abroad a lot so he needs his clubs well protected.'

'What happened to his last one?'

'Got ripped up coming back from Portugal the other week.'

'There you go! Way those handlers throw things around, he'd be better off using a couple of bin-liners. I mean, this thing looks more pricey than most of what I take on holiday!'

'You'd be amazed. Special order, we don't keep these babies in stock. But Mr Rowe wanted an exact replacement. Insurance paying, why not?'

'Suppose. Mr Rowe, is he one of the good guys or one of those who talk like you're not there?'

He'd moved off the acceptable ground of talking about how rich and important the Hoo members were.

Chip slammed the lid down, and turned to face Joe.

'Mr Sixsmith . . .'

'Joe . . .'

'*Mr Sixsmith.* I really don't want to talk to you about what goes on at the club.'

'No? What's happened since last night?'

'I didn't want to talk to you last night either, but at least we were in a pub. Here, well, this is where I work . . .'

'And this is where you're going to get the money to put you on this tour thing, right?'

'That's right. The members are being very generous, giving me this chance to show what I can do . . .'

'With Chris Porphyry leading the way, wasn't that what you said?'

'Yes, maybe. But there are plenty of others and I need to think about them too. If you're going to make it to the top in this business, you've really got to put your game first.'

Joe's areas of expertise were not all that extensive, ranging from the workings of the internal combustion engine to the history of Luton FC with not a great deal in between, but one thing he had learnt by bitter experience was you had to be very careful what you said to a woman, 'specially one who was willing to give Jurassic George his marching orders when his training schedule got in the way of her raving schedule. He'd guessed earlier things hadn't gone too well for Chip last night. Now he thought he knew why.

'Didn't say this to Eloise, did you?' he asked.

'You been talking to her?' said Chip suspiciously.

'No need. But I'd guess you went on about how pissed you were at her inviting me along to the Hole. And she said she didn't take kindly to being told what she could and couldn't do, and what was your beef? And then you told her about the support package and you probably rattled on about your career in golf being the most important thing in your life, and you didn't want it messed up. And she said in that case better you headed off home and got your head down before nine o'clock so you could be sure of waking at the crack to get out and practise.'

'You have been talking to her!' declared Chip indignantly. 'I don't suppose she said she was sorry?'

'As in, sorry I was wrong?' said Joe. 'Chip, I don't know much about handling women, but two things I do know. One is, never tell them anything is more important than the way you feel about them. The other is, don't matter they're so much in the wrong they could go to jail for it, there's always part of them that knows they're absolutely in the right.'

'Well, thanks for that good advice,' said Chip, moving away. 'But me and Eloise are history now, so it doesn't make much difference.'

'Believe me, you're well out of it, Chip,' said Joe, recalling with a shudder Jurassic's subtle way with a rival.

He'd fallen into step with Chip, if taking one and a half steps to the youngster's one could so be termed. He got a distinct impression the boy was trying to shake him off.

Breathing hard, he said, 'When you were talking to Mr Rowe just now, he say anything about your career?'

'Well, yes, he did,' admitted Chip. 'He said there'd been a lot of interest in the support package and, all being well, as long as I didn't blot my copy-book and knew who my real friends were, I had a bright future.'

Yes, thought Joe. And then he tossed you the key to his super-luxe wheels and told you to run along and put his new highly expensive travel case in the boot. It's called putting you in your place.

Joe had experienced plenty of being put in his place, which he paid little heed to on the grounds that he found his place so very much to his liking that he had no notion of trying to get out of it. Also it was often very helpful to a PI for folk to be so certain you were in your place they didn't watch you as close as they should have done.

But to a young man with ambitions, being sent off to put the bag in the Audi was like saying, this is where you are and that's where you'd like to be, so keep your nose clean else you'll never take even the first step.

Talking of steps, the boy's had now lengthened so much he was several yards ahead. The distance didn't stop Colin Rowe glowering at him as he came out of the pro's shop and spotted the approaching procession.

Chip reached him and said in a loud voice, 'Case is in your car, Mr Rowe. Here are your keys.'

'Thanks, Chip,' said Rowe.

The youngster went into the shop. Joe approached, trying to give the impression of a man who just happened to be walking in that direction .

Rowe, now smiling broadly, said, 'Joe, nice to see you again. Taking another look at us, are you? Wise man. Second impressions are always best, that's what we say in the estate business.'

'Meeting Chris for coffee,' said Joe, following his practice of sticking to a simple lie. 'Thought I'd get here early and take a stroll around, if that's OK?'

'Of course it is. Take a good look. You've certainly given yourself plenty of time. I like a man who's thorough. Did Chris show you our changing rooms? Just over here.'

He led the way to the main building through a door marked *Members Only.*

Joe's experience of changing rooms was limited to what was on offer in the world of Sunday-morning football, which at the luxury end amounted to little more than a hut with wooden benches, four-inch nails driven into the wall to act as coat-pegs, and a couple of luke-warm showers whose thin trickle somehow managed to spread more water over the muddy floor than over your muddy body.

This was something else. The benches were upholstered in dark green leather, the walls were lined with richly glowing mahogany lockers each bearing a gilded name in cursive script, while the floor was covered with a carpet even more expensive than the one in the Audi's boot, and the only mud in sight was that carried in on Rowe's hand-made shoes.

'Showers through there,' said Rowe, pointing.

Joe advanced through a small antechamber lined with shelves bearing bars of soap, bottles of shower gel and hair shampoo, and gleaming alps of snow-white bath sheets. Beyond this there must have been a dozen or more cubicles, each as spacious as his own bathroom back on Rasselas.

He said, 'Hey, how do I get the tile concession?'

Rowe laughed and said, 'That your line of business then, Joe, construction?'

'Sometimes,' said Joe. 'More facilitating, know what I mean?'

'Yes, I see,' said Rowe, nodding vigorously, presumably to indicate he did know what Joe meant, which was good as Joe himself didn't have the faintest idea, but he'd really liked the word when he came across it in his crossword.

Rowe had got most of his kit off by now. A thing Joe had noticed in his admittedly limited dealings with the upper classes was the higher you got, the less it bothered them flashing their flesh. Himself, he'd been brought up so proper by Aunt Mirabelle that he could have changed out of overalls into evening suit under a tea towel without bringing a blush to a maiden cheek.

Feeling rather uncomfortable as Rowe dropped his boxers and started to cram his pretty hefty parts into an athletic support, Joe said, 'Leave you to it, then.'

'Sure. Hope to catch you later. And hey! We haven't forgotten you promised to join us for a round some time.'

In your dreams, thought Joe as he made his escape.

And in my nightmares!

19

Go with the Garbage

To Joe Sixsmith, the detective process was more like an act of creative imagination than a rational process, though of course if you'd suggested this to him in a pub, he'd have advised you went home and drank a couple of litres of water and hoped you'd wake up feeling better in the morning.

Someone, probably Butcher, had once told him he had something called *negative capability*, which meant he didn't let being surrounded by stuff in a case that made no sense bother him.

Joe had laughed at her joke. Why should he let anything bother him when, like a good pilgrim, he had his own Good Book, Endo Venera's *Not So Private Eye*? Often when the way forward seemed a bit uncertain, one of Endo's elegantly phrased maxims would float into his mind.

It would be nice, opined Endo, *if investigation was all high life and high-balls, but sometimes you gotta go with the garbage.*

At the moment, iced coffee on the terrace (the Hoo equivalent of high life and high-balls) seemed very attractive, but that would mean maybe running up against the other two corners of the Bermuda Triangle. Just because he was beginning to feel some uneasiness about Colin Rowe didn't mean they were necessarily tarred with the same brush, but at the very least they might start pressing him again to play a few holes with them. Also Butcher had implied Arthur Surtees was a guy to be scared of, and when a lawyer as scary as Butcher told you that about another lawyer, only a fool didn't pay heed.

So when Joe came out of the locker room, instead of heading left round the front of the clubhouse he made his way right round the rear, towards the service area behind the kitchen where the garbage was.

Though Endo Venera gave many graphic and often unsavoury examples of significant finds he'd made among garbage, Joe didn't really have it in mind to start rifling through the rubbish. Not that it would have been all that easy anyway. Normally even behind the most elegant of restaurants, the waste area is unhygienic and squalid. Not at the Royal Hoo. Here there were no loosely tied black plastic bags, easy for PI's and vermin to penetrate, but a neat line of elegant green bins with hinged lids sufficiently tight fitting to contain all but the slightest whiff of decay, even in this hot weather.

Also there was a witness, a figure lounging against the wall alongside the kitchen doorway, a cigarette between his lips.

Joe recognized him as the club steward.

'Morning, Bert,' he called as he drew near.

The man straightened up like a sentry caught lolling against his box and the cigarette vanished as if by magic. But when realized who it was addressing him, he relaxed once more and the half-smoked fag emerged from behind his back.

This told Joe something he was quite glad of. Whoever else he might be fooling at the Hoo, the steward had got him sussed.

'Morning Mr Sixsmith,' said the man politely, which told Joe a little more. Bert might know he was just an employee like himself, but being the YFG's employee still got you a bit of respect.

'Name's Joe,' he said, offering his hand. 'I'm a private investigator.'

'Yeah, I know. Bert Symonds.'

They shook hands.

'You knew all the time?' said Joe, curious.

'Wondered when I first saw you. I thought, hasn't Mr Porphyry got enough bother on his hands without . . .'

He hesitated and Joe helped him out by saying, 'Without putting up someone like me for membership.'

'That's it. Don't take it personal. I mean, they're so bloody choosy here, you wouldn't believe. Even Sir Monty Wright got blackballed.'

'Well, I was way ahead of the field there,' said Joe, who had quickly worked out this was probably a good guy to have on your side. Also he'd learnt early to differentiate between the casual thoughtless racism you met at all levels of English society and the bred-in-the-bone KKK variety. A quiet word often sorted out the former while the latter was usually beyond the reach of anything this side of divine revelation.

Bert said, 'Anyway, the name rang a bell. You played footie in the same works team as my cousin, Alf, right? I remembered him talking about this mate who set up as a gumshoe when they all got made redundant.'

'Alfie Symonds? Hey, man, how's he doing?'

'Moved down to Romford, got a new job there. I gave him a call to check you out. Description fitted and Alfie says you're all right. He sends his regards.'

'Give him mine. So, Bert, you enjoy working here?'

He saw the man's expression shadow into caution and he didn't wait for an answer but plunged straight on, 'Look, what I'm doing here is this. Mr Porphyry's in a spot of trouble – well, I don't expect I need to tell you anything about that.'

The man nodded.

'OK. So it looks like he's been cheating, only he says he wasn't, so he asked me to help him find out what's really going on. That's it. I'm working for Mr Porphyry and you work for the club, and I don't want to get anyone into bother. So if you'd rather I didn't ask you any questions, just say so, and I'll be on my way.'

Bert took a long drag at his cigarette then said, 'You ask, and if I don't want to answer, I won't.'

'Fair enough,' said Joe, wondering, What the hell is there I can ask this guy? It felt like a golden opportunity, but the trouble with golden opportunities was that, unless you got decent notice, they were often easier to let slip than to grasp.

He said, 'You think he cheated?'

Bert said, 'They all want to win so badly, I'd not trust any of them not to bend the rules a bit.'

This was a bad start. Joe had expected some version of the unequivocal denial of the possibility he'd got from everyone else he'd asked.

He said, 'This sounds a bit more than just bending the rules.'

'It does,' agreed the steward. 'And yes, that would surprise me in Mr Porphyry's case.'

'But not in some of the others'?'

'There's one or two who'd forge their own wills,' said Bert.

This was an interesting concept but Joe decided not to pursue it.

'Such as?' he said.

Bert shook his head and said, 'Next question.'

'Would anyone have any reason you know of for wanting to set Mr Porphyry up?'

'Frame him for cheating, you mean? Well, he's very popular.'

'You mean you can't think of a reason?'

'I mean him being very popular might be a reason to some folk.'

This was the kind of psychological subtlety that made Joe blink.

'You mean, people might not like him 'cos everyone liked him?'

'Something like that.'

'Nothing more definite? I mean like he's been cosying up to someone's wife or something like that.'

'No,' said Bert very firmly. 'Not that there aren't plenty would like to cosy up to him, but he treats 'em all the same.'

'Maybe one of them's been lying about it just to show the others she's ahead of the game, and one of her mates dropped a hint to the husband,' said Joe, who did have some basic grasp of the subtleties of female psychology.

Bert shrugged and lit another cigarette from the butt of the old one.

'And he persuaded Jimmy Postgate to lie about the ball dropping into his pool? No way! That old boy loves Mr Porphyry. Wanted to change his story when he realized the trouble it was causing. Anyone else would have said yes, let's brush it under the carpet, but not Mr Porphyry. Look, I really ought to be getting back in. Things will be livening up on the terrace. The members who set out at the crack will be finishing their round and wanting a drink and there's a lot who just drop in for a coffee mid morning. All right for some, eh? So if there aren't any more questions . . .'

Joe raked over the dead leaves in his mind desperately.

'You know Steve Waring?' he said. 'Worked on the greenkeeper's staff.'

'Yeah, I know Steve. Nice lad. Not been around lately. They reckon he's gone on the wander. Ran up a few debts then decided to take a little holiday before the duns came round. That would be Steve!'

He spoke with the baffled admiration of the labourer inextricably tangled in the chains of employment for the layabout who with one not so mighty leap is free.

'So when did you last see him?'

'When? Not sure. But I can tell you where 'cos it was right here. It was late on one night, and I'd slipped out for a quick fag when I saw Steve heading off home . . .'

'He worked late evenings then?' interrupted Joe.

Bert laughed.

'This time of year, oh yes. Everything's got to be immaculate at the Hoo. That mad Scots bugger's got his lads tidying up behind the last players out on the course and they're still coming in after nine in the summer.'

'Did you talk to him?'

'Yes. He came over and bummed a ciggy off me. I always told him it was an unhealthy habit for a young man, but he said he'd give it up when I dropped dead.'

'You talk about anything interesting?'

Bert sucked in the remaining inch of his cigarette as though inhaling memory.

'That's right,' he exclaimed. 'Now I think about it, it

was that very same night! The one when Mr Postgate came into the bar with the ball just as Syd Cockernhoe was telling the story of how Mr Porphyry had nicked the match from him. Of course the whole place was buzzing with speculation after that, so naturally I filled young Steve in.'

'How did he take it?'

'He said it had to be a mistake 'cos any story about Mr Porphyry cheating was a load of old cobblers. He really rates Mr Porphyry, does Steve.'

'And then?'

'Then I had to get back inside.'

'And Steve?'

'He went off, I suppose . . . no, hang about. He asked me something . . . what was it? He asked me if Mr Rowe was still in the bar. I said yes, he was, drinking with Mr Surtees. And *then* I went in.'

'How did Steve usually get home?'

'He had this scooter thing, one of those that folds up next to nothing. We used to joke you could get close to twenty mph on it, downhill with a following wind, and Steve would say that one day when he'd made it rich, he'd turn up in the car park here with a machine that would make the rest of them there look like old rust-buckets.'

'Did he used to leave it in the car park?'

'Don't be silly! No, he used to stick it round the back of the greenkeeper's shed.'

'Where's that?'

'Carry on down the service road there. It's on the left. That it?'

'Just one thing more. This Rules Committee – the Four Just Men, isn't that what they call it? I know Tom Latimer's on it. Who're the other three?'

Bert considered, saw no harm in answering this and said, 'Mr Surtees, Mr Lillihall, and Mr Plimpton.'

'Arthur Surtees, the lawyer, that would be?'

'Right,' said Bert. 'Him and Mr Latimer call the shots, the other two are just there to make up the numbers. At least, that's what I hear. But I've not said anything to you, right?'

'Of course you haven't, Bert. Cheers, mate.'

'You take care now, Joe. One of the things I haven't said to you is, there's some mean bastards in this club. Cheers.'

Joe would have liked a list of names, but Bert had vanished into the building and in any case Joe guessed that the only response he would have got would have been, 'Next question.'

He set off down the service road in search of the greenkeeper's shed.

It took some finding, not because it was obscure but because it turned out to be a shed in the same way that Balmoral is a holiday cottage. Originally an old barn in the same creamy stone as the clubhouse, it stood foursquare and solid in a small copse of beech trees. Converted into a country dwelling, it would have made a developer a small fortune. There was no one in sight, so Joe wandered down the side of the building and round the back. No scooter here, but there was a large patch of oily grass against the rear wall.

Before he could examine it closer, a voice grated, 'Help you?'

Joe turned to find himself the object of a suspicious gaze. As the gaze was emanating from the sun-ravaged features of Davie Davie, and as Joe was poking around behind the building in which presumably the head greenkeeper kept all that was most precious to him, he couldn't blame the guy for being suspicious.

Joe had to make a decision. Did Davie, like Bert, know he was a PI? Or was he still under the impression he was a chum of the YFG's?

He made his choice and said, 'Oh hello, Davie. Just having a look around while I'm waiting for Mr Porphyry and I seem to have got a bit lost.'

It sounded pretty stilted to Joe, but most of what Davie heard at the Hoo must sound pretty stilted to his Caledonian ears.

He said, 'If it's the clubhouse ye're wanting, ye'll need to walk back along the track a ways.'

'Thanks. Some places I've been, this would have done for the clubhouse, yeah?'

'Aye, well, it does the job, sir,' said Davie with the modest pride of a man who knew his worth.

The *sir* confirmed to Joe that his cover remained in place here at least.

As the Scot turned away, Joe took a pound coin out of

his pocket, palmed it, then stooped and said, 'Hey, it's my lucky day. Oh shoot, it's a bit oily.'

He held the coin up and ostentatiously began to wipe it with his handkerchief. Davie again was regarding him suspiciously, but this time it was the suspicion of a Scot who knew it was written somewhere in the Old Testament that he would be able to spot lost money in his back yard long before any poncy Anglo of no matter what shade.

Joe quickly moved from the coin to the oil which he was sure the greenkeeper would have spotted.

'Seems to be a patch of the stuff down there,' he said indicating the area he'd been examining when interrupted. 'One of your mowers must be leaking or something.'

'No way!' Davie snorted indignantly. 'One of my lads parks his bike there and that's what's got the leak. When I was his age I'd have had it sorted in two jinks of a cat's tale, but nowadays they've nae pride in what they possess. It all comes too easy, that's my way of thinking.'

'But I bet you don't let him get away with anything when he's working on the course,' said Joe. 'From what I've seen, it's immaculate.'

'Aye, they leave their standards behind and work to mine once they're out there,' said Davie. 'To give him his due, this laddie did a fair day's work when I made him put his mind to it.'

'Did? He's gone, has he? I only ask 'cos the oil seems quite fresh.'

This was pushing it a bit, but golf club greenkeepers have to get used to vacuous waffle from their members and Davie replied, 'Aye, he took off a few days back, but his machine was around till yesterday, I'm sure. He must have snuck in to collect it, scairt of running into me likely, the way he let me down. I'll be hard put to get a decent replacement this time of year.'

'Plenty of lads out of work would surely jump at the chance,' said Joe.

'You'd think so, but most of them are likely sunning themselves on a holiday beach, and those that aren't don't like to get their hands dirty,' said Davie sourly. 'Good day to ye.'

Joe walked away, his mind buzzing like the mysterious scooter and probably making as much smoke.

Exactly a week ago, the morning after Porphyry's disputed victory in his Vardon Cup match, Waring had risen, eaten a hearty breakfast, walked out of No 15 Lockkeeper's Lane and vanished off the face of the earth.

The night before, he had been given a lift home by

someone driving a silver Audi 8, almost certainly Colin Rowe.

His motor scooter had remained here behind the green-keeper's shed till yesterday or maybe early this morning when someone had removed it. Also this morning someone had turned up at Lock-keeper's Lane to collect Waring's belongings from his lodgings, and pay his rent up to date. That person, or rather those persons, had also been in a silver Audi 8 identified by young Liam Tremayne as the same in which he'd seen Waring travelling the evening before his disappearance.

And Colin Rowe's Audi was presently standing in the Hoo car park with mud on its tyres and an oil stain on its boot carpet.

This needed a bit of thinking about.

He glanced at his watch, and realized that he'd need to do his thinking on the way to the airport.

His phone rang. The display read *Butcher.* He looked around guiltily, wondering if the Hoo embargo on mobiles extended here. But no one came running out of the trees shaking their fists and brandishing their niblicks, so he put it to his ear and said, 'Hi, Butcher.'

'Sixsmith, what are you doing? Basking by the hotel pool, charging your pint glasses of sangria to King Rat's account?'

'No. I'm still here.'

'Still in Luton? Oh, Joe, Joe, you do like living dangerously. His Majesty won't like you changing his plans.'

'It's just the timetable I've changed. I'm catching a later plane. Just setting out for the airport.'

'Oh good. Then call in here as you're passing. Something I want to show you.'

'What is it? I'm a bit pushed. Couldn't you just . . .'

'Got to go now, Sixsmith. See you soon.'

She switched off.

'Oh shoot,' said Joe.

There had to be a trick to ignoring bossy women, but Aunt Mirabelle hadn't taught him it. He hurried back to the car park.

20

Lightning Strikes Twice

At the Law Centre, Butcher saw him straightaway, which had to mean something.

She said, 'When I got in this morning my fax had spewed out a lot of stuff about the Royal Hoo.'

'Yeah, I gave Porphyry your number.'

'You not got a fax of your own, Sixsmith?'

'Course I have. Only it doesn't work too good.'

Merv Golightly, who'd been present in Joe's office when the machine churned out fifty pages of midnight blackness, had said, 'Joe, whoever sold you that fax got the vowel wrong. Why didn't you come to me? I know this guy who's going bankrupt . . .'

'In any case,' Joe went on to Butcher, 'this was stuff you wanted to look at.'

'Which I've done. Have to say that when old Porphyry set up the club, he really tied up the loose ends so the family kept control.'

'You're not going to start talking all that legal mumbo-jumbo to me, Butcher?' said Joe fearfully.

'No, Joe. I'll give you the idiot child's version,' she said. 'Grandpapa Porphyry got his lawyers to tie up the business side of things. Members are shareholders, with the current head of the Porphyry family the majority shareholder. Any shares owned by ordinary members – that is, members other than said Porphyry – are non-transferable. They cannot be sold outside the club or inherited. On the death of a member, his share reverts to the club, where it remains in a share-pool till such time as a new member is elected who must purchase his qualifying share at its current market value, which, as there is no market, is decided by a small committee known as the Prop, which is short for Proportionality. You still with me?'

'I was till this last bit,' said Joe.

'Do pay attention. The intention is that new members should be chosen for their clubbability not their wealth, and charged not on a fixed scale but according to what they can afford to pay.'

'Got you!' said Joe. 'You mean like if I got elected, they'd say, Welcome aboard, Joe, you're such a nice guy we really want you here at the Hoo. Here's your membership share, that will be a fiver please. Whereas if Sir Monty Wright had got elected it would have cost him half a mill maybe.'

'You're doing well,' said Butcher approvingly. 'But don't get your hopes up; there's an annual fee which you could probably afford, only you wouldn't be able to eat, drink, pay your rent, or buy new clothes, which in your case might not be such a bad thing.'

'You ain't no fashion plate yourself,' retorted Joe. 'So OK, everything's neat and tidy, that what you got me here to tell?'

'More or less. But what one lawyer puts away neat and tidy another lawyer can usually find a way to muss up, if he or she puts her mind to it. If at any time there should be more than four membership shares floating around this pool – because, say, the Almighty decided He'd had enough of these privileged prats sunning themselves on their exclusive terrace and took a lot of them out with one of His thunderbolts – in that case members are allowed to buy extra shares which they can hold in trust for any future member they themselves may care to propose, the advantage of this being that in such a case such a proposition would be decided by simple majority without option of blackball.'

'Now I'm starting to hurt,' said Joe. 'Why?'

'To keep numbers up, I suspect. And also because grandpapa Porphyry didn't trust his friends not to become such a complacent, snobbish, coterie-forming bunch of twats that they'd end up blackballing the club out of existence.'

'Butcher, I got a plane to catch,' said Joe looking at his watch. 'And if I don't catch it, I'm going to have to explain myself to King Rat. I'm already running late, so can we cut to the chase here?'

'OK. Termination of membership. Possible reasons: death, resignation, expulsion. In each and all of these cases, the membership shares go into the pool. Possible reasons for expulsion: anything which in the judgement of the Committee is deemed to have brought the club into disrepute. So, a judgement call, except in one particular instance. There is one crime regarded as heinous beyond all mitigation of circumstance or misfortune. If a man is found to have cheated at golf, the penalty is instant expulsion, without debate or appeal.'

Finally Joe was starting to see where Butcher was going.

'So if Mr Porphyry was found guilty, he'd be chucked out and his shares would go into this pool thing? But I mean, it's his club, or at least it's his family's club . . .'

'Wrong,' said Butcher. 'The club belongs to the shareholders who are the members. The fact that there is a majority shareholder who calls the shots is immaterial. This is where Grandpapa Porphyry's neat and tidy arrangements fall down. I'm sure he was sufficiently a realist to know that nothing lasts for ever. Everything changes. It might even be that eventually he would have a descendant who didn't care for golf and wanted to realize this particular asset. That would be fine, a matter of commercial choice. What he didn't envisage was that one of his descendants could be caught cheating at the game and expelled from the Hoo.'

'And this means all of Mr Porphyry's shares go into this pool? And the other members can buy them up? Shoot, Butcher, would someone really do this to a nice guy like Christian just so they can get one of their chums into the Hoo without risk of blackball?'

The lawyer looked at him in amazement then began to laugh.

'Joe, Joe,' she said. 'This isn't about membership of a stupid golf club, it's not about blackballing – though I've a strong suspicion that a blackball is where it all started. The point is that if one guy or a group of like-minded guys get their hands on Porphyry's shares, then they'll have a majority holding and they can do with the club whatever they damn well like.'

'Such as?'

'Such as apply for development permission, which with the right connections isn't too hard to obtain. God, the properties already scattered around the Hoo site must be worth millions on the open market. As for development, think what an expanding supermarket chain might be willing to pay for a chunk of that land!'

'You mean, Wright-Price? Sir Monty?' said Joe aghast. 'You saying Sir Monty's set this thing up just to get his own back 'cos he thinks Christian blackballed him?'

'I think that getting Porphyry disgraced at the same time as adding a lot more dosh to his already obscene bank balance would be an irresistible combination to that nasty bastard,' snapped Butcher. 'And don't give me any sentimental crap about his charitable works and all the good he's done that sad football club of yours. When you see a smile on the face of the tiger, you need to ask yourself what it's been eating!'

Joe didn't argue – with Butcher in full spate, argument was futile – but he couldn't agree. OK, Sir Monty was sharp. You didn't get to be a multi-millionaire without cutting corners. But when it came to sporting morality, the Luton chairman made Aunt Mirabelle look like an estate agent. He thought one of City's players was diving, that got a last-chance warning. One more dive and it didn't matter if you were a full international and player of the year, you were out! How could a guy like that be mixed up in framing a fellow golfer for cheating?

Joe's head was in a whirl. From an objective, professional point of view, his investigation had made great strides forward, but he wished with all his heart he'd somehow managed to catch that early flight to Spain with Mimi.

Which reminded him. He glanced at his watch and began to rise.

'Where are you going?' demanded Butcher.

'The airport, I told you . . .'

'Sixsmith, you are unbelievable! Haven't you been listening to me? I've laid it out for you why I think your client's been set up! And if I'm right and this all leads back to Sir Monty bloody Wright, ask yourself who helped him get where he is today. Ratcliffe King, that's who, the man who's fixed it to get you out of the country. And all you can do on hearing this is rush off to the airport to make sure he's not disappointed!'

Joe said, 'Sounds a pretty healthy option to me. In fact, only last night you were telling me that I'd be mad to cross King Rat once I'd made a deal with him.'

'So when have I expressed belief in your sanity? You've got responsibilities to your client here, Joe.'

'Yeah? Well, Mr King's a client too. His job's urgent. The golf-club thing ain't. I mean, this committee won't be considering Porphyry's case for another couple of weeks, and I'll be back long before then.'

'I'd bet Christian Porphyry's thinking it's a bit more urgent today,' said Butcher. 'You've not seen the *Crier*?'

She produced a copy of the tabloid which appealed to those local readers who found the *Bugle* too intellectual. Under the headline **STORM IN A TEE CUP?** was a brief account of the cheating accusations levelled at Porphyry. Joe could almost hear the glee in the last sentences: *Only a week ago the engagement was announced (though not in the* Crier*'s classifieds!) of Mr Porphyry to Tiff, only daughter of Bruce Emerson, proprietor of the* South Bedfordshire Bugle. *We look forward to following the affair in the* Bugle*'s pages.*

'Shoot,' said Joe defiantly. 'That's rough, but it doesn't change things. Anyway, looks like you're making a lot more progress than I've managed. You take over, why don't you? Speed you work, you could have it all sorted by the time I get back.'

Butcher banged her tiny fist on her desk, toppling several piles of paper.

'Bullshit!' she cried. 'You're running away, that's what you're doing! Never thought I'd hear myself say this, but there are things you can do far better than me. I'm good at this stuff –' she gave the confusion of papers on her desk a further violent shuffle – 'but it's not this stuff that's going to get things sorted, not without a lot more evidence. That's your job, Joe. The dirty nails, hands-on work. You're doing well, you're doing things right, otherwise they wouldn't want to be rid of you. So sit that well-upholstered backside of yours down and tell me what you've got, all of it, and let's try to work out how we can stymie these bastards!'

Joe, shaken more than he cared to admit by the onslaught, shook his head, as much to clear it as in denial. For once what Butcher was saying seemed to accord with Endo Venera's advice, *go with the garbage*, meaning in the lawyer's case that this was all he was good for.

He said. 'I gotta get out of here.'

'You're going to Spain then?' she said disbelievingly.

'Didn't say that. What I mean is, I got to get away from here. From you. Need a bit of time to think. My brain don't work like yours, Butcher. You see things in a tangle, then you see them clear. Me, I need to be picking and unpicking till I work out what I've got.'

He expected another outburst. Instead the little lawyer came round the desk and gave him a hug and her soft-spoken words sounded remarkably like an apology.

'You're right, Joe. That's your way and it's a good way. For you it's the only way, which means it's the best way. You get it sorted in your mind then give me a ring, OK? I'm sorry I yelled at you.'

This was like Aunt Mirabelle jumping on the bar at the Supporters' Club and leading a chorus of 'I'm a-rootin' for Luton', the club song. It was time to get out before she asked him to marry her.

He said, 'That's fine. Didn't notice. Really. I'll be in touch, yeah?'

He hurried out to the Morris and drove away. His mind was in a turmoil. He knew he had decisions to make and he'd no idea how to set about making them.

It wasn't till a couple of minutes later he realized he was heading for Rasselas.

He relaxed behind the wheel and felt his mind clearing like a freshly poured bottle of pils. This was the way it often happened. Somewhere deep inside there was something that made important decisions affecting his wellbeing, then let him know at its own sweet leisure. Bit like the NHS. King Rat wasn't going to be happy when he found out. Well, that was tough. But lovely little Mimi deserved an explanation.

After he parked at the tower block he dug her number out of the green folder and punched it in as he went up into the building. The lift was on the seventh floor. He summoned it down as Mimi's voice said, Hi!' in his ear.

'Mimi, it's me, Joe,' he said. 'Look, I'm really sorry, but I'm not going to make it.'

'Surprise!' she said with that gurgling laugh that made a guy feel real good. 'Shame. It's lovely here.'

'Listen, I don't want you to get into trouble. I'll ring Mr King and explain . . .'

'No need. I've just had Ratcliffe on the line. Wanted to know why I hadn't told him you were still in Luton.'

'Shoot! I'm sorry. Is there anything I can do . . . ?'

'Nothing, thanks all the same. He fired me.'

'What? That's terrible! Mimi, I'm . . .'

'Hold it there, Joe. It's OK. I've been looking for an easy escape route for a while now and they don't come any easier than getting sacked.'

'But what will you do?' said Joe, still guilt ridden. 'I mean, without a job . . . and what about money . . . ?'

'Well, first I'll finish my margarita, then I'll do some serious work on my tan. That should take three or four days. Meanwhile I'll get back to the three or four guys who've been dangling tempting job offers in front of me for the past six months and decide if there's anything there I fancy. As for money, well, when I saw you this morning I said to myself, I don't think this guy is serious about coming to Spain. So I took the precaution of paying for my hotel room in advance with the company credit card before the Rat put a stop on it. Oh, and I hit a couple of money machines and got myself a whole hatful of euros too. So I'm fine. Hope you will be too, Joe.'

'Any reason I shouldn't be?'

'I don't know why Ratcliffe wanted you in Spain, Joe,

but I do know he doesn't much care for not getting what he wants. You see Stephen Hardman coming towards you, better turn and run! In fact, maybe a little holiday abroad wouldn't be such a bad idea.'

'I'll think about it. Mimi, something you can maybe help me with. Mr King used to be in close cahoots with Sir Monty Wright. They got anything going lately?'

There was a silence long enough to get Joe apologizing again.

'Look, sorry, shouldn't have asked. Even though he's your ex-employer, I know you can't go mouthing off about your work there . . .'

'No, I was just thinking. In fact, I never had any dealings with Wright-Price. No reason to, Ratcliffe was just a non-exec director, nothing hands on. But he has spent a lot of phone time talking to Sir Monty lately, don't know what about. Could be just exchanging recipes. That it, Joe? The ice is melting in my margarita.'

'Yeah. And thanks for being such a sport.'

'No sweat. Like I say, I was ready for fresh fields and pastures new. Take care, Joe.'

'No, hold on,' said Joe. He rarely got flashes of inspiration but sometimes a trigger could produce a flash. 'Pastures new, I mean New Pastures – you ever hear of an outfit with that name?'

'Yes. How do you know about them, Joe? It's a land-holding company that Ratcliffe set up a couple of months back.'

'Thanks, Mimi. See you around, maybe.'

'Hope so, Joe. Bye.'

The lift had arrived and Joe had stuck his foot in the door to hold it there. He now stepped inside. As the door closed he saw the swing doors of the main entrance begin to open. His first instinct was to hold the lift for the newcomer. Then he saw who it was.

Jurassic George.

'Oh shoot!' cried Joe and hit the 7 button. Fortunately though a long way from the smooth swift sweet-smelling elevator in ProtoVision House, the lifts on Rasselas were just as far removed from the mechanically and physically dangerous mobile urinals you found on Hermsprong.

The door closed. The ascent began. Not even a super athlete could make it up seven flights of stairs as fast as the lift, but Joe still sprinted down the corridor. Once in his flat he locked and bolted the door. The security chain dangled uselessly from the woodwork. Joe grabbed a stout dining chair and wedged it under the handle.

'There,' said Joe. 'Let's see you get through that!'

Breathing deeply he opened the balcony window to get some air. Below him Luton slumbered in the heat. It was good slumbering weather, specially if you were lying beside a pool with some like Mimi . . .

Beryl . . . he corrected guiltily. He meant someone like Beryl . . .

In Aunt Mirabelle's strict theology, even a fantasized infidelity deserves punishment, so she might have been unsurprised by what happened next, but Joe was figuratively as well as literally bowled over when he felt himself hit from behind and flung forward against the balcony railing.

Whoever said lightning never struck twice clearly didn't know Jurassic George!

For the second time that day Joe found himself staring down at the area of paving seven floors below which was likely to be the last resting place of his scattered brains.

One part of his mind was thinking, no misnomer calling George lightning, speed he'd got here. The guy couldn't be human!

But the other and larger part, that devoted to self-interest and survival, was instructing his voice to scream, 'George, George, my man, no need for this, I thought we got it all settled, you seen my girl, you seen my Beryl, I got eyes for nobody else, man!'

In view of his recent lascivious fantasy about Mimi, this wasn't strictly true, but while Jurassic might have superhuman physical powers, not all the hard training in the world could make him telepathic.

The one improvement on his earlier experience was that this time, rather than being dangled over the balcony, he was folded across the rail on his stomach and he had instinctively taken a vice-like grip of the metal bar. Also his attacker seemed more interested in dragging him back than pushing him over; but as his preferred method of doing this was to heave at Joe's personal parts while simultaneously punching him in the kidneys, it did not appear that his motives were altogether benevolent, and now Joe found himself hanging on to prevent being dumped on the balcony floor rather then being dropped to the entrance paving stones.

The hand between his legs twisted viciously and Joe, who'd always envied the ability of the solo tenor in the Boyling Corner Chapel Choir to soar effortlessly towards his top-C's, now found himself hitting notes even a coloratura soprano might have balked at. Just as the agony brought him to the point of fainting, there was some kind of disturbance behind him and suddenly the grip on his testicles relaxed. But this blessed relief seemed likely to be counterproductive. Weakened and barely conscious, he slumped over the rail like a sack of potatoes and hardly registered that gravity was pulling him inexorably down towards the waiting paving stone.

Too late he recognized his peril. His fingers clawed once more at the balcony railings but he could draw on no strength to get a grip. Then he was falling . . . falling . . .

Then something grasped his legs and dragged him upwards and backwards and bore him through the balcony door and deposited him on his own sofa.

He opened his eyes, blinking away the tears which the pain had started there, and as his sight cleared he saw looming over him the terrifying features of Jurassic George.

Now to the sound range which he'd never expected to reach was added a whimper. He would have declared with some force that whatever else he might be he wasn't the whimpering type, but there was no other word to describe the noise he heard himself make in anticipation of George's renewed assault.

And now that monstrous face was coming closer, so close that he could feel the hot breath as the boxer uttered words Joe could not understand but which he knew must be his death knell.

21

Frozen Broccoli

In his detective career Joe had formulated many a hypothesis which proved so far from the truth that it would have taken a fully equipped inter-galactic space expedition to traverse the distance between. This time he felt he understood the truth beyond hypothesizing. George had made such a ham-fisted effort at reconciliation with Eloise that he'd provoked her into saying something like, *Yeah, that Joe's quite tasty and you're dead right, he really fancies me and I wouldn't mind getting something going there.*

The only problem was, as the sounds issuing from the boxer's mouth stretched into syllables and then joined together to form words, something was going wrong with the script.

What he seemed to be hearing was, 'Hey, Joe, my man,

are you OK? Take your time, man. Breathe deep. Here, try to sit up, get your head between your legs, long breaths, that's it, yeah, you keep doing that, I'll get you some water . . .'

Then George vanished into the kitchen.

Persuaded that he was orally hallucinating, Joe glanced desperately towards the door. What he saw there drained any little strength he had remaining. The frame around the lock was splintered like matchwood . . . the wooden chair he'd wedged under the handle had snapped in half like a breadstick . . .

In any case George was back.

'Drink this. Hey man, how are your goolies? Thought that bastard was going to pull them right off. My corner man say, anything an ice-pack can't cure, you need surgery, so let's try this.'

Joe found himself looking at a packet of frozen broccoli as, with remarkably delicacy, Jurassic's banana-bunch fingers unfastened his trouser belt, slid down the fly zip and pressed the packet against his crotch.

After the initial cold shock, it felt great, and as his injured parts stopped demanding ninety-nine per cent of his attention, it started getting through to him that either George had a serious schizoid condition, or he wasn't in fact the attacker.

He gasped, 'George . . . why you here, man?'

'Came to say I'm sorry,' said George. 'For this morning, you know . . . the misunderstanding . . .'

'Like when you tried to kill me, you mean?' said Joe.

'Hey, no, I was never gonna let you go,' said the boxer earnestly. 'Just give you a fright, shake the truth out of you.'

'And now you know the truth?'

'Yeah. That Beryl girl, she convinced me. Then when I saw Eloise later at the garage . . . well, she really bad-mouthed me for even dreaming she'd pick you over me – no disrespect meant, man . . .'

'None taken,' Joe assured him, feeling better by the second. 'So things are OK between you two?'

'Just great!' said George, his face lighting up. 'But she says I gotta apologize to you, which I want to do anyways. So I come round here and there you are getting into the lift, only you don't wait. So I come up after you and I reach your door and I hear this noise of yelling inside. First, I think maybe you and your girl are having a domestic, then you start screaming and I know it ain't no family row. So I push open the door and there's you hanging over the balcony and this guy pummelling you and trying to pull your goolies off. So I give him a tap and he hits the deck, and I'm just going to make sure he don't get up again when I notice you're slipping away. So I've got to grab you and meanwhile the guy has got to his feet and hightailed it out of the door. Sorry about that, Joe, should have hit him harder, then he'd still be here for you to give him a kicking.'

'George, don't be sorry, you made the right decision and I'm truly grateful.'

'That's OK. You must be really burning up, this pack's beginning to thaw. Think I saw some prawns in the freezer, how about I try them?'

It occurred to Joe that lovely little Mimi, who'd jumped to the wrong conclusions this morning when she burst in on him standing starkers over a nurse with her legs in the air, would really mark him down as a Number One weirdo if she could see him now having his crotch massaged by Jurassic with a packet of broccoli.

He took control of the pack himself and said, 'No thanks, George, this will be fine.'

But the thought of Mimi brought to mind the conversation he'd just had with her on the phone. King Rat knew he hadn't gone to Spain. Didn't need a Sudoku whiz to work out it must have been Colin Rowe who told him.

And what was King's likely reaction . . .?

'George, my friend, this guy trying to kill me, you get a good look at him?'

'Yeah. Didn't know him, but I'll know him again. Real mean-looking bastard, got them hard eyes, know what I'm saying? Like some guys in the ring who try to stare you down while the ref's doing the intro. Me, I let my fists do the fighting. What you been doing, Joe, to get him so pissed with you?'

'Don't think it was him that was pissed,' said Joe.

Had to be Hardman, the Rat's personal minder, who'd been sent round to take care of him. Not kill him, which was a small comfort. Getting knocked about a bit was regarded as an occupational hazard for a PI. Indeed, Joe had heard Sergeant Chivers, his arch-enemy in Luton's Finest, opine that a day in which Sixsmith got a good kicking could never be said to have been altogether wasted. But not even Chivers would have been able to turn a blind eye if Joe's body had been found splattered on the paving stones under the Rasselas tower. No, Hardman's mission had been to put him out of the picture by terrifying and disabling him.

Which he'd got at least half right. But what he'd also done was confirm that King Rat was definitely involved, and the only thing that got the Rat's nose twitching was the ripe smell of filthy lucre. Lots and lots of it. A multi-million deal. Which, together with Mimi's hint that something big was brewing between ProtoVision and the supermarket chain, put Wright-Price in the frame, dead centre.

It was beginning to look like Butcher's obsessive belief that Sir Monty was involved was more than just political prejudice.

But Joe found it hard to accept that a man so selflessly devoted to the wellbeing of Luton City FC could be party to any form of physical violence that took place off the field. He was ruthless in business, yes. He would cut so many corners in a deal he could turn a polygon into a straight line. But he was at heart a sportsman. Would he underwrite beating up a fellow Luton fan? Or framing an honest golfer for cheating?

Joe found it hard to believe. Which meant nothing. He'd been absolutely certain the Lutes were going to stuff Spurs last time they went to White Hart Lane, and look what happened then.

But he only knew one way to find out.

With a sigh, he started to push himself upright.

'Hey, you take it easy now,' advised George. 'You want I should call that girl of yours? She's a nurse, right? Maybe she could give you a massage or something.'

'Think that would probably finish me off right now, George,' he said. 'Look, I got things to do. Thanks a bunch for helping me out here. Don't know what I'd have done else. Except maybe die.'

'My pleasure,' said the big boxer. 'Listen, man, you get any more trouble, you give me a call, right?'

'You'll be first on my wish-list,' Joe assured him.

As George left, he paused and looked at the splintered door frame.

'Sorry about that,' he said. 'You'd best get that fixed afore some of them Hermsprong brothers come across to borrow your TV and hi-fi. You got anyone you can ring?'

'Yeah, but it will probably be the weekend before he gets here.'

'Then leave it to me. I know this guy owes me a favour. He'll be round this afternoon, right?'

'Right,' said Joe, thinking, the Prince of Wales would probably be round this afternoon if Jurassic George asked him. 'Tell him I'll leave the door open.'

It took George a full thirty seconds to work this one out, but when he did, he really appreciated it, and Joe heard his deep bass laugh echoing all the way down the corridor.

When it died away, he felt suddenly lonely.

In the bedroom he stripped naked and examined his assaulted parts in a mirror. Apart from being a rather fetching shade of red and feeling very tender, no real damage seemed to have been done, and five minutes under an icy shower completed the good work begun by the frozen broccoli. He got dressed in his loosest fitting boxers and slacks and gingerly made his way down to the Morris.

22

The Right Price

Ten minutes later he was walking into the Supporters' Club. He met Larry Hardwick and one of his staff coming out of the kitchen bearing trays of beer and sandwiches.

'Those for the directors?' Joe asked.

He knew a meeting was scheduled for today.

'Yeah, they just rang down. Must have a lot to talk about.'

'Give Sir Monty a message, will you, Larry? Tell him I'd appreciate a quick word.'

'Now, you mean?' Hardwick looked at him. 'Joe, personally I'd walk a hundred miles for one of your smiles, but I don't think even your rendition of "Mammy" is going to get Sir Monty out of his meeting.'

'Tenner says you're wrong, Larry,' said Joe.

'You're on.'

Joe sat down at the big corner table and hoped he was going to have to pay up. If Monty Wright appeared, it had to mean he really was involved.

A couple of minutes passed. Then the door opened and the club chairman came in.

He made straight for Joe's table and sat down heavily. He carried too much weight, most of it round his waist, and his round face was flushed.

'You've got two minutes,' he said.

'No,' said Joe, determined not to be over-faced. 'You being here means I got as long as I like.'

The man said, 'We'll see. So talk.'

In most of life's transactions there are two possible approaches, the subtle and the direct. By getting Sir Monty to leave his meeting, Joe reckoned he'd scraped the bottom of his subtlety barrel. Time for a dose of directness.

He said, 'You planning to build a hyper-market on the Royal Hoo golf course, right?'

If this came as a shock to Wright, he was too experienced a negotiator to show it.

He said, 'Nice idea. So how am I going to get planning permission?'

'Getting permission's no problem. Specially not with Mr Ratcliffe King on the case,' said Joe. 'It's getting the land that's hard. Mainly because you'd need a majority of the members who are also the shareholders to agree a sale, and the majority shareholder is the Porphyry family, represented by Christian Porphyry.'

'A bastard who loves me so much, he's going to roll over and say, *There you go, Monty, it's all yours for a shilling an acre.* I don't think so!'

This was spoken with real venom.

This isn't just business, this is personal, thought Joe. That was good. Business he'd never really understood, but personal was people and that was his strength.

'You don't like Mr Porphyry much, do you?'

'Hardly know the guy. But from what I've seen, he's not my type, no. Life's been easy for him. When his mother dropped him, he landed right at the top of the pile, didn't have to get dirt under his fingernails dragging himself up there.'

Joe considered this. Social envy played as little part in his own make-up as social ambition. You played the cards life dealt you. Injustice wasn't the deal, it was when some joker cheated. And he didn't really believe Sir Monty had a socialist chip on his shoulder either. If you think you're any man's equal, there's not much space for social resentment.

Suddenly he recalled something Merv had said the other night about his conversation with the club chairman at this very table.

He said, 'This is because you think Chris Porphyry black-balled you, isn't it?'

Sir Monty shook his head perhaps a little too emphatically.

'That's not the way I work,' he growled. 'Business deals are about money and markets. Minute you start letting personalities get into them, you're in trouble. I've got thousands of employees, even more shareholders. You don't think I'd put their wellbeing at risk for the sake of a private grievance, do you?'

He spoke with a dismissive assurance that was completely convincing. But it rang a note Joe recognized. He'd been performing in public, and certainly in public houses, as long as he could remember, and he knew that to take your audience with you, it wasn't enough simply to sing a song, you had to inhabit it. You had to leave people in no doubt that, martial or romantic, melancholy or comic, you really meant those words you were singing.

That was the note his performer's ears were hearing. The note of rehearsal to such a pitch of perfection that Sir Monty probably believed himself when he spoke, the same way Joe could never finish singing 'Mammy' without tears streaming down his cheeks.

He said, 'Don't believe you. I think you're so pissed off with Porphyry that when Ratcliffe King contacted you to say there could be a chance the Royal Hoo was coming on the market, you didn't ask questions.'

Wright said, 'I always ask questions.'

'But maybe this time you didn't ask enough. And when you found out it all depended on Chris being stripped of his membership 'cos he'd been found guilty of cheating, bet you didn't ask questions then? Bet you were just over the moon to hear he was going to be disgraced?'

'No, I didn't ask questions then because it didn't surprise

me,' said Wright aggressively. 'That type, they think they've such a God-given right to be on top, the usual rules don't apply to them.'

'Yeah? So why'd you start asking yourself questions the other night when you heard Porphyry had hired me? I think you started wondering why the shoot would someone like Porphyry hire someone like me to prove he was innocent? Bet you thought, a guy would have to be really desperate to do that. And then you got to thinking, or maybe he'd have to be really innocent.'

Wright leaned forward so that his round perspiring face was close to Joe's.

'OK, mind-reader, so here's a question for you. Have you proved he's innocent, Sixsmith?'

Joe didn't flinch but said, 'No, I've not proved it. But I know!'

'You've not proved anything, but you *know*?' Wright echoed mockingly. 'And this is what I've missed my beer and sandwiches for? Sixsmith, I'd always heard you were a better singer than a detective. My advice is, get yourself a pitch down the underpass and start busking.'

He began to rise. Joe tried to think of something that might hold him, but nothing came. Running out of ideas rarely involved him in a marathon, but this hadn't even been middle distance.

Then his phone rang.

He took it out, glanced at the caller display and said, 'Hi, Christian.'

Sir Monty froze.

'Joe, glad I got you. I'm sorry to disturb you when you're away on another case . . .'

'No, that's OK,' interrupted Joe. 'Change of plan. I'm still here.'

'Thank God for that! Listen, something's happened.'

There was an edge of desperation in the YFG's voice which made Joe's heart sink. It was like hearing Callas reaching for the notes after her ill-advised come-back.

He said, 'What?'

Sir Monty had sat down again and was watching him like a cat who sees his dinner slowly approaching through the long grass.

Porphyry said, 'Have you seen the *Crier*?'

'Yeah, but that's nothing . . .'

'Yes, it is. I hadn't mentioned any of this to Tiffy, that's my fiancée, but now she's seen it and her father Bruce has seen it and he's furious about that crack about the *Bugle* and furious that I hadn't told him what was going on . . .'

'Chris, this is all irrelevant,' urged Joe. 'Newspapers print so much crap, no one even notices the smell any more. Tomorrow it will be forgotten.'

'Don't think so, Joe,' said Porphyry gloomily. 'Tomorrow it looks like they'll have an even better headline. I've just been talking to Tom Latimer. He said the Four Just Men had been worried about my hearing because the next round of the Vardon has to be played by the end of next week and it depends on the outcome whether Syd or myself goes into the draw. Then this thing in the *Crier* made up their minds for them. As long as it was kept inside the club, that was fine, but now it's in the open, it isn't something the Hoo needs to have hanging over it. The upshot is they've brought their meeting forward to this evening. God, Joe, I thought we had a fortnight and now there's only a few hours. What do you think, Joe? Is there any hope?'

No wonder King was happy to get me out of the way for a couple of days! thought Joe. The bastard knew this was on the cards. It was probably him who primed the *Crier*! There I was thinking it would make no difference when the truth was I'd have come back to find everything done and dusted! And when he discovered I hadn't gone to Spain, he decided that a few broken bones would do the job just as well.

He said, 'There's always hope, Chris. You at the club now?'

'Yes. I'm in the car park. Had to come out here to ring you, but I'm heading back to the terrace. Mustn't let people think I'm running for cover.'

That's my Young Fair God! thought Joe. Still sticking to the rules even though the bastards were going to chuck him out for breaking them! And determined not to let anyone think he was running scared.

He said, 'I'm following a lead just now but I'll be along later, OK?'

'A lead?' The hope in Porphyry's voice gave him a jolt. 'I knew I could rely on you, Joe.'

He looked at Sir Monty who, though he'd only heard one side of the conversation, had an expression on his face which said, *So that's it, Sixsmith. Give it up. You had your chance to convince me and you blew it.*

Maybe if I got him to talk to Chris, thought Joe. No, there was no way forward there. What could they say to each other? Sir Monty would only be rudely triumphant and Christian would be completely bewildered.

On the other hand . . .

He said, 'Hold on, Chris,' and put his hand over the mouthpiece.

'Sir Monty,' he said, 'I'm going to ask Mr Porphyry a question and I want you to listen to his answer, OK?'

Wright shrugged indifferently.

'Chris,' said Joe. 'Just to clear something up, Sir Monty Wright was up for membership recently and he got blackballed. Was it you who put the blackball in?'

He shuffled his chair round alongside Wright's and held the phone between them.

'Good Lord, no,' said Porphyry in a surprised tone. 'I thought he was an excellent candidate. I met him when his sponsor brought him round to look over the place. Very nice chap, and I heard he could hit the ball a mile. I was really knocked back when he didn't get elected.'

'Yeah? Any idea who might have blackballed him?'

'No. Whole idea is that nobody ever knows, you see. Though I did hear . . . but no, idle gossip causes nothing but trouble, I should know that!'

Thinks he's being disloyal to his beloved club, thought Joe. Dear God! How could anyone believe this guy was a cheat?

He said, 'Nothing you tell me is gossip, Chris. Client confidentiality, right?'

He felt bad about that, sitting here with his phone held up so Sir Monty could hear the reply.

'Well, if you're sure,' said Porphyry reluctantly. 'The only person who might get a glimpse of who puts what ball in is Bert Symonds, our steward, who carries the bag round when the vote is taken. That evening after Sir Monty got blackballed, I went round to the service area to have a word with Bert about some catering matter and I overheard him say something about the vote to another member of staff. Well, when I got him by himself, I really tore into him. Firstly because I hate gossip, and secondly because I knew in this case it must be untrue.'

'What was it he said?'

'He reckoned it was Tom Latimer who put the blackball in. But he must have got it wrong. I'm absolutely sure of that because . . . Joe, the pro's waving at me, wants a word. I've got to go. Keep in touch. Please.'

The phone went dead.

Joe switched off and looked at Sir Monty, who shook his head violently and said, 'No!'

'No? Hey, listen, this wasn't something I set up . . .' began Joe indignantly.

'No, it can't be true,' said Wright, ignoring him. 'He

got that right at least. No way it could have been Tom Latimer . . . no way!'

He was shaking his head, but to Joe it seemed he was shaking it to dislodge an idea rather than deny it.

It took Joe his usual ten-second delay to get there. And then . . .

'It was Tom Latimer who proposed you! Wasn't it?'

'Yes, of course it was,' snarled Wright. 'And Latimer's a smart guy, he knows which side his bread's buttered on. So tell me, smartypants. why the hell would he want to put the black in?'

This time Joe didn't need ten seconds.

'Maybe because if you'd just got elected to the Royal Hoo, you were hardly likely to be interested in knocking the place about and building a hyper-mart on the site, were you?' he said.

He saw Wright taking this on board and pressed his advantage.

'Who was it told you it was Christian who blackballed you?'

Wright didn't answer. He didn't need to.

'And how long was it afterwards that King Rat said he'd got a whisper that the Hoo might be up for grabs?' Joe went on.

Now Sir Monty spoke.

'About a fortnight.'

Joe did some working out.

'That would be a good week or more before the Porphyry cheating thing came up,' he said.

He didn't need to say more. He had a great respect for people whose minds left his standing when it came to working things out, and it wasn't for nothing that Sir Monty watched the beautiful game from the Directors' Box while Joe's season ticket placed him high behind the south goal with the sun straight in his eyes.

Larry approached the table looking a bit nervous.

'Sir Monty,' he said. 'They're asking about you upstairs . . .'

'Yeah, yeah, I'm coming,' said the chairman. 'You done here, Sixsmith? I got a *really* important meeting to attend.'

Joe found the stress offensive. If the guy didn't think what they'd been talking about was important, he'd been wasting his time.

'Just one more thing,' he said, letting his irritation show. 'Woman called Bradshaw got fired from your Luton store a while back. You probably never heard of her . . .'

'Betty Bradshaw? Yes, I know her. Nobody gets fired from my stores without I know, Sixsmith. What's your point?'

'She says she got made redundant to make way for cheaper labour.'

'She's right. The amount of stuff she was lifting from the store, anyone would have been cheaper!'

'She got fired for thieving?' Joe was disconcerted. He tried to think like Butcher and heard himself saying, 'Well, maybe you weren't paying her enough to feed her family and she thought you wouldn't miss a few tins and stuff . . .'

'She wasn't stealing food, Sixsmith,' grated Wright. 'It was top-quality Scotch and cognac mainly. About five hundred quid's worth a week. Nice little scam, undetectable if she hadn't got greedy. Only reason I didn't charge her was it might have given some other people the same idea. I take care of my staff. All I expect in return is honesty. You might find it hard to believe, Sixsmith, grubbing around in the muck where you spend your working days, but being a businessman doesn't mean being a crook. You make hard decisions but there's a line you don't step over.'

'Does Ratcliffe King live on the same side of the line as you?' asked Joe.

The supermarket magnate stood up and glowered down at him.

'Interesting talking to you, Sixsmith. But at the end of the day, you've proved nothing.'

'Maybe not,' said Joe. 'But I know. And the difference is, now you know too, don't you?'

He watched the man make his exit. What he might do now, Joe couldn't guess. Probably nothing. *The Wright Price is the right price.* What effect did having that printed on your notepaper have on a guy? He said he was an honest businessman. Joe wanted to believe him. He'd kept Luton City afloat in the bad times, which meant there was certainly something he loved more than money.

Let's hope his reputation was another thing.

Sir Monty had certainly got one thing right. Though he was beginning to see the shape of the conspiracy more and more clearly, Joe still felt as far away as ever from getting his hands on firm proof of Porphyry's innocence.

So what next? Joe asked himself.

He needed help from above.

A ten-pound note came fluttering down in front of him.

'There you go, Joe,' said Larry. 'Like the good Lord, I always pay my debts.'

Joe picked up the note and took it to the bar where there was a coin-filled appeal jar for Save the Children.

He tucked the note into the jar, saying, 'Yeah, I know you do, Larry. You and Him both.'

23

Pillow Talk

One of Joe's strengths was knowing when he needed help.

And another of his strengths was knowing what sort of help it was he needed.

Give half a dozen people the same information and you get half a dozen different interpretations, all equally valid and probably not even mutually contradictory in any significant way, but each of them will bear the style of the individual interpreter.

Butcher's interpretation would be sharp, incisive, intellectually rigorous, and indelibly marked with her law training on the one hand and her political philosophy on the other.

Merv Golightly's response would be direct and pragmatic, almost you might say simplistic, and marked with a taxi driver's cynicism about the purity of human motives which had left him so ready to believe the worst that it tended to be the first thing he looked for.

Beryl Boddington, on the other hand, was the personification of common sense. Her job as a nurse had given her the ability to recognize when someone was terrified either because of what their body was doing to them or what they thought their doctor might be about to do to them, and the capacity to deal with this. In all other areas she tended to see what was clear and say what was obvious, though in Joe's case the clarity and the obviousness often only became apparent after she'd pointed them out to him.

It was Beryl he needed to talk to.

He headed back to Rasselas and took the lift up to her floor.

After ringing her bell twice he began to think she must be out. Then the door opened on the security chain and she peered through the crack at him.

'Joe, what do you want?'

'Hi, Beryl,' he said. 'Can I come in and have a talk?'

The eye he could see regarded him dubiously, then she said, 'I suppose.'

When he got into the flat he saw why she'd taken so long. Nurses work odd hours and catch their sleep when they can. His detective expertise put together the clues of her mussed-up hair, the dressing gown she was wearing and the fact she kept on yawning and arrived at the conclusion that she must have not long arrived home from her shift and he'd woken her up.

Normally he would have been full of apology, but his sense of urgency was such that he just plunked himself down on a chair and started filling her in on what had happened since their last encounter early that morning.

She stretched out on the sofa opposite him. The dressing gown had fallen open above her knees revealing enough leg to have set Joe's blood bubbling through his veins at a dizzying speed normally, but today he had other concerns, or maybe the damage Hardman had done to his nether region had been more serious than he'd realized.

He went on talking, but not even his sense of urgency or his possible injury could prevent him registering when the dressing gown slipped down her left shoulder revealing the upper curve of her full and darkly smooth breast.

But that wasn't what he'd come here in hope of today. In any case, having forced his way in more and less and woken her from sleep after her hard labours, it would be unmannerly to try to take advantage. And besides, Beryl was a woman well able to take care of herself.

So he carried on and it wasn't until she closed her eyes and her breathing became regular and her grip slackened altogether on her dressing gown, letting it fall apart to reveal beyond all doubt that she was quite naked underneath it, that his sense of professional urgency diminished at the same rate as his feeling of incapacity, and he began to lose the thread of his talk and eventually stuttered to silence.

It was Beryl who broke it.

'Well,' she said in a low husky voice, 'you just gonna look, or are you gonna do something about it?'

It occurred to Joe to wonder as he approached the high point of doing something about it whether he would have got Beryl into bed if his reaction to getting her out of it had been grovelling apology and averted eyes, rather than apparent indifference to her deshabille. Perhaps inadvertently he'd hit upon the perfect scoring technique! But he was far too clever to even dream of suggesting this and in any case as he spiralled towards the aforementioned high point, all his expressive baritone could produce as counterpoint to her coloratura trills was an increasingly atonal series of rumbling, roaring, profundo groans.

Finally there was silence.

They rolled over so that they lay side by side, face to face.

And Beryl said, 'So now we've established what's important, what was it you wanted to tell me?'

He told her everything, in order and in detail, and she never interrupted once, which roused in him the suspicion that he'd bored her to sleep.

But when he raised his head so that he could see her face clearly, her eyes were wide open and she was looking at him so lovingly he would have been happy to forget his professional responsibilities for a second time.

She said, 'This Christian, he's a lucky guy to have someone like you working for him, Joe.'

'You reckon?' said Joe, his heart ready to burst with pride at getting praise from this most precious of sources.

'I do,' she said, then spoilt things by adding, 'not that you've been able to help him, of course.'

'Eh?'

'He hired you to prove he didn't cheat. Can you prove it?'

'No, but I can show what's really going on here . . .'

'Can you, Joe? Have you got one tiny little bit of hard evidence to back up this theory you've got?'

'Well, no, but I've got lots of circumstantial . . . quite a lot anyway . . . some . . .'

'Yeah. So you've got nothing to prove Chris is innocent and even less to prove there's some complicated plot going on. Right?'

'Right,' he admitted glumly. Here was where he'd been able to get by himself. On the one hand (which was caressing her left buttock), it was disappointing that Beryl's common sense and clear vision wasn't going to take him any further. On the other hand (which was cupping her right breast), no way the visit had been wasted!

'Joe, you forget about that for the time being,' she commanded. 'And don't look so downhearted. What you got to ask yourself is this. If you're getting nowhere with proving the cheating was a set-up, why are they so keen to get you off the job? I mean, why not just let you go bumbling around in full view of everyone so they can say, Look at how Christian Porphyry even smuggled a private detective into the club to try to find a way out of his trouble, but what did he come up with? Nothing! No. Trying to bounce you off the case one way or another was a bad move, an unnecessary move, but they still did it. So you gotta ask, Why?'

'I'm asking, I'm asking,' said Joe. 'What do you think I'm doing here?'

'Don't know what you call it, but you did it well enough for me to wonder where you're getting the practice. Listen, Joe, it's obvious. You go to the Hoo to meet Christian. Those three guys – what did you call them . . . ?'

'The Bermuda Triangle.'

'Right. The Triangle's waiting for you. They chat you up, check you out, probably decide you're no problem . . .'

'Hold on. How did they know I was coming?'

'Sir Monty,' she said in exasperation. 'You said Merv was shooting his mouth off at the Supporters', right? And Sir Monty took an interest. Don't matter if he knows the cheating is a set-up or not, he'd be straight on the phone to King Rat asking, What's going off here? This going to make any difference to our deal? The Rat says, No way. Be still. I'll sort it, and gets on to this Latimer guy and warns him to look out for you. Not that you were going to be hard to spot. But Porphyry might have got away with it if it hadn't been for Merv's mouth. I mean, no one's going to think Christian's so stupid as to hire a black PI who knows nothing about golf to go undercover at the Hoo!'

She laughed so heartily at the notion that her breast

joggled interestingly beneath his hand. But he forced himself to concentrate on what she was saying.

'So you have an ice coffee with them, and they have a bit of a laugh with you. Then you go on a walkabout with Chris. You visit the guy with the pool . . .'

'Jimmy Postgate.'

'No trouble there. Either he knows nothing or they've got him all tied up.'

Joe shook his head.

'Knows nothing, I'd say,' he said. 'That's what makes the case so strong. He's such a big admirer of Chris, for him to give evidence against him is a real big strike.'

'Whatever. So nothing here to make them worry. But there was something else during your visit, wasn't there?'

'Was there?'

'Yes, you told me!' she cried in exasperation. 'You talked to this greenkeeper, Davie.'

'Chris did most of the talking,' said Joe.

'Yes, and what about? He was asking about the lad who'd gone missing, Steve Waring, right? Then you say when you got back on the terrace, Christian actually mentioned him to one of the Triangle . . .'

'Rowe, yeah, he's in charge of the Greens Committee or something.'

'Never mind that stuff. Did you say anything about him then?'

'Might have done. Just protecting my cover.'

'Cover!' she snorted. 'Then while Chip, the assistant pro,

changed your wheel, you talked to him too about Waring, right?'

'Just passing the time,' said Joe.

'Yeah, and someone probably passed the time with Chip after you'd gone and heard what you'd been saying and reminded the boy he should be discreet when talking about club matters with non-members.'

Joe nodded and said, 'Rowe came into the car park to make a call from his car phone while Chip was changing the wheel. Went off with him later. That could explain why Chip got so uptight with Eloise about me coming to the Hole.'

'Good! You do have a brain as well as . . . other things. So someone, probably this Rowe, passed all this on to King Rat and he thought, This guy's a no-hoper but better not to take chances, let's get him out of town for a few days. So he calls you in and makes you an offer you couldn't refuse. And if Jurassic George hadn't got the wrong idea about you and that Eloise – it *was* the wrong idea, wasn't it, Joe . . . ?'

Her grip tightened on a part of his body which put him in mind of Hardman's assault that morning.

'Yeah, definitely wrong.'

'Good. But if George hadn't got so jealous, you'd have been sipping pina coladas in sunny Spain with that Mimi this moment, and Christian would be facing them Four Just Men with no help pending.'

'Oh yeah. Jesus, the poor bastard. I said I'd see him at

the club before the meeting . . . but what can I tell him, Beryl?'

Now she did give a painful tug and said, 'Joe Sixsmith, don't you listen? You ask questions about this kid, Waring. You've no idea why you're asking questions, but they don't know how stupid you are. So they decided to ship you off to Spain. Only you don't go. Instead you go round to Waring's lodgings and ask questions there . . .'

'Hold on. How they know that?'

'You said this Rowe's car was pulling away as you arrived. That old tank of yours is going to get you recognized, isn't it?'

Joe was hurt by *old tank,* but couldn't fault her logic.

'Yeah, right.'

'So now they decide to break your legs or something. Only George gets in the way again. Look, it's obvious. This is what's bothering them. You being interested in Steve Waring!'

'Yeah, yeah, I've got that,' said Joe. 'But what I haven't got is why? You're so clever, tell me that, why don't you?'

This was less gracious than a man in his position who'd just received such favours both physical and detective ought to have been, but the playful twist she'd given him had been more painful than she realized. And besides, for all her admittedly clever analysis he didn't feel any further forward.

She said, 'Way I see it from what you told me, Waring must have seen something.'

'Like what?'

'Maybe he'd been working round there somewhere and heard Christian's ball clatter among the trees. Goes to look for it and next thing he sees this Rowe guy placing a ball nice and handy on the edge of the fairway.'

'Wouldn't he have said something?'

'To one member helping another out? None of his business. He'd tiptoe away and forget all about it till later he hears that his friend Mr Porphyry has been accused of cheating on that self-same hole. Now he's interested. He buttonholes Rowe and asks him what's going on. Rowe realizes the whole scheme could unravel completely if Waring starts talking to anyone else. He doesn't know what to do. So he tells Waring to hang around a couple of minutes and he'll explain everything. Then he goes off and rings King Rat.'

'Who says what?'

'What do you think? This is the Rat we're talking about. Everyone's got his price. Bribe him. Rowe says it may not work, he knows how much Waring respects Porphyry. So Rowe goes to plan B. If money doesn't get what you want, add a bit of sheer bloody terror. But he knows that's probably beyond Rowe so he sends reinforcements.'

'Hardman.'

'I'd bet on it. Rowe offers young Steve a ride home. Somewhere en route, this hard case Stephen is standing by the roadside. Rowe pulls over to give him a lift. Young Steve's probably already made it clear he's not interested in money. One look at Stephen tells him that this is something else and he decides that getting things out in the open is the safest option so he tries to ring Christian. When the hard man realizes what he's doing he takes the phone off him.'

'And then?'

'I don't know, do I?' said Beryl. 'I'm just making up a story here. Maybe they really did make young Steve an offer he couldn't refuse. He's just a kid, right. OK, he wasn't about to accept money to keep quiet about something that would affect Christian, but when the hard man made it clear that the alternative was several months in traction, he thought, What the hell. Grab the money and run. So next morning that's what he did: got up, ate his breakfast, and took off. Didn't need to take anything with him 'cos he had enough money coming to buy him all he needed brand new.'

'Couldn't buy his Frank Lampard picture,' said Joe.

'Sorry?'

'Doesn't matter. Beryl, I gotta go. Thanks a bundle. You've been a great help.'

'That what you call the best lay you've ever had, a great help?' said Beryl, pouting.

Pouting lips are made to be kissed and Joe obliged.

'You know what I mean. As for the other, some things go way beyond thanks.'

'Tell me about it,' she said invitingly.

'Oh, I will, I will. But not now.'

He dressed quickly before he could change his mind.

As he left, she called after him, 'Joe, don't know what you're going to do, but it will be the right thing. Be sure you come back and tell me all about that too.'

His heart was singing as he drove away.

Suddenly he had a feeling it was all going to be all right.

24

A Saving Bell

Joe's joy slowly evaporated as he drove into Upleck.

It wasn't a bad suburb as suburbs go. The houses were spick and span, the well-tended gardens brandished a rich variety of bold coloured summer flowers at the sun, the streets were relatively litter free, and in daylight at least it looked like a place where a man could go for a stroll and expect to come back with his pocket and his person intact.

But the cord of memory which linked him to Beryl's lovely body stretched more and more tautly till finally it snapped as he turned into Lock-keeper's Lane.

As he approached No 15, he recalled his visit this morning when the silver Audi 8 had pulled out ahead of him and he'd gratefully turned into the vacated space.

Now most of the parked cars had gone and there was

ample room to stop. But he drove on past 15, following the route the Audi must have taken that morning.

Soon the houses had petered out and the road grew narrower as it ran into an area of scrubby countryside. A couple of lane ends made him slow down but they were so overgrown that it was plain no vehicle had forced a way through there recently, and in any case the brambles would have left their mark on the silver paintwork.

Finally the road came to the end promised by the sign two miles back which read *No Thoroughfare,* but he kept going after the tarmac ended, following a track that at first was broad and not too rough, but gradually became muddy and bumpy as it ran into a copse of sun-stealing alder and willow where eventually further progress was barred by a high rusting metal fence.

This was the area known as Leck's Bottom.

In *The Lost Traveller's Guide* (the best-selling series devoted to places you were unlikely to visit on purpose) it merited a single paragraph.

Leck's Bottom is a stretch of boggy land covering approximately five hectares and acting as a sink for all the waste moisture of the surrounding area. Its unattractive ambience and noisome effluvia did not, however, daunt the Victorian engineers creating the Luton–Bedford Canal and for a while this useful waterway ran through the Bottom. Indeed, one of its most important locks was situated here. But such a situation required high maintenance and once the canal had outlived its usefulness the Bottom rapidly reverted to what it had been, or perhaps, because of the unsavoury traces of man's interference, something rather worse. A man would have to be a psychopath or a social historian to want to linger here. Certainly to find an example of the non-picturesque rural ruin more dreary and depressing than the old lock would be difficult, even in central Iraq.

Joe got out of the Morris. It was clear now where the mud on the Audi's tyres and Rowe's shoes had come from. Not even the week-long heatwave had been able to suck all the moisture out of this ground, and though the air was warm it still had a clammy feel that made your skin crawl.

Ahead behind the fence he could see what remained of the lock-keeper's cottage. There was no history of any dreadful event having taken place here, nothing to hang a ghost story on, but Joe recalled that according to Aunt Mirabelle, who had a great store of spine-chilling bedtime tales, some places could be haunted by their futures as well as their pasts. 'Like Mrs Orlando's bungalow in Brook Street. Even when she was cutting me a slice of her cherry cake and chattering away merrily about that doctor brother of hers in Freetown, I could feel she was haunting her own life, and that was five years or more before that psycho on early release broke in and slit her throat with the cake knife.'

On the fence was a sign, *Fly Tippers Will Be Prosecuted.* The good people of Luton like the good people of most other towns in England cannot see a hollow of any size from a ditch to a canyon without wanting to chuck their unwanted household rubbish into it. Joe sometimes felt that if ever he reached the end of the world and looked over, the first thing he'd see would be an old fridge. A few years ago, tipping at Leck's Bottom had become such a health hazard that the Council had moved in, cleared all the rubbish out and erected the fence and the warning sign. But there is nothing your true-Brit fly-tipper likes more than a challenge, and despite the fact that the Council had its own efficient bulk-waste collection service and easily accessible landfill site, and though the fence was kept in good repair, hardly a week passed without some devotee of the sport hacking his way through with a pair of wire cutters, then dragging his defunct TV or washing machine twenty yards or so across rough boggy ground in order to drop it into the old lock basin.

Joe found such a hole now and made his way through it.

As well as being a great dumper, your true-Brit is a great scavenger, which explains the Empire, both what got taken out and what got left behind. Everything removable from the lock machinery had long since vanished, leaving only the huge basin which Nature herself had filled with murky water of a consistency somewhere between gumbo and grits, with none of the nutritional values of either.

Joe stood on the crumbling concrete edge and looked down. The surface was black and gave no reflection. He knew what he was looking for but didn't have much hope of finding it. The Audi had come down here, of that he was almost certain. And when it reached the Hoo car park, nothing remained in its boot. Except a patch of oil, which suggested to Joe that before coming to collect Steve Waring's belongings, Colin Rowe and his companion had already picked up the foldaway scooter.

Something as heavy as that would probably have been sucked into these dismal depths within minutes. But a bin bag with its fairly broad surface area, containing what Joe guessed would be the relatively lightweight contents of Waring's wardrobe and drawers, might stay close to the surface for some time.

He almost didn't spot it because the black plastic so closely matched the colour of the water. But there it was. At least he guessed that there it was. The only way of confirming the contents was to fish it out and there was no way he was going to attempt that. The sides of the basin were vertical and slimy. Man on his own who fell in there might as well sing 'Goodnight Vienna!', exhale his last breath and dive deep to get it over with quickly.

But it wouldn't be much of a problem to return with some kind of grappling iron and haul it out, then take its contents along to Mrs Tremayne and get that formidable lady to confirm they belonged to her errant lodger.

On second thoughts, that might not be so easy without official backing. Mrs Tremayne didn't strike him as a natural-born witness.

In any case, a witness to what? Suppose he even managed to get her to identify Colin Rowe, what did that prove? With King Rat in the background, and that ingenious lawyer, Arthur Surtees at his side, Rowe would probably be able to come up with some tale to explain his behaviour.

Whereas he, Joe Sixsmith, the People's gumshoe, couldn't come up with anything to positively link Waring doing a bunk to the case against Chris Porphyry. Should have spent more time trying to trace Waring, he told himself. Station, airport. But you needed more clout than he had to do that kind of thing properly. Besides, he'd only been on the case since yesterday!

And you spent most of that time reckoning it was going to take a miracle to rescue the YFG! he accused himself.

Well, way things stood, that seemed about right. With the Rules Committee meeting only hours away, things were as bad as they could get.

A noise behind him made him turn, and he saw that yet again he'd been wrong.

Things had just got worse.

Coming through the hole in the wire fence was Stephen Hardman.

'Afternoon, Joe,' said the man. 'All alone? What happened to your pet gorilla?'

'He's around, never you mind,' said Joe. Then he called out, even to his own ears not very convincingly, 'George, my man! You there?'

Hardman laughed.

'Good try. But he's not coming. I followed him down to Sullivan's Gym and saw him start on a training session which looked likely to keep him occupied for a good few hours. Nice mover for a big guy.'

He sounded laid back, but Joe registered that Jurassic had scared him enough to make him want to be sure he was out of the picture before coming after his prey once more.

But how did he know where I'd be? he wondered.

One way to find out.

'How'd you know where I'd be?' he asked.

'Sat at the top of Lock-keeper's Lane till I saw you drive by,' said Hardman.

That signified . . . something. Man should be able to work out what if he had time to sit and have a good ponder.

But pondering was for a comfy chair with a pint of

Guinness in your hand. Standing here in Leck's Bottom with the lock basin behind you and in front of you a guy who'd tried to pull your goolies off last time you met, pondering anything but how the shoot you were going to get out of here wasn't on the agenda.

Hardman, who'd been slowly approaching, had halted only a few feet away. One leap forward, one hard push, and Joe could feel himself toppling over backwards into the foul depths of the basin.

Except all the guy wants to do is put me on my back for a few days, he reminded himself. Didn't push me over the balcony rail when he had the chance but pulled me back to safety. OK, he did it by grabbing my goolies, but as Aunt Mirabelle always says, it's the thought that counts.

Then he recalled his own subsequent analysis along the lines: PI getting a kicking, no one's fussed; PI's brains splattering over the pavement, even DS Chivers would take notice.

But PI vanishing without a trace . . .

He knew from experience that when someone goes missing without any immediate evidence of foul play, it takes the cops forever to take an interest.

But what was there in this affair that would make offing Joseph Gaylord Sixsmith Esquire a possible option?

'So what are you doing here, Joe?' the man asked, sounding almost friendly.

How to answer? Lying wasn't his strong suit. He didn't have the O-levels. To sound really convincing he had to tell the truth, which in this case, he concluded hopefully, might just set him free.

'Don't rightly know,' he said. 'Got this idea this is where you and Mr Rowe must have come this morning after you drove off from Mrs Tremayne's.'

'And why should we do that?'

'Thought maybe it was to get rid of Steve Waring's things you'd just picked up.'

'Yeah? And why would we want to pick his things up? And if we did, why would we want to get rid of them?'

What was it with all the questions? wondered Joe. Hardman didn't strike him as the conversational type. Action first, ask questions later, if at all, that was more his line. Which meant maybe the questions were someone else's line.

No prizes for guessing whose.

And if King Rat was asking the questions, Joe had an uneasy feeling that his future wellbeing might depend on the kind of answers he gave.

He couldn't think of a lie better than the truth, so he stuck with it.

He said, 'I reckoned, maybe you paid him off or frightened him off and you didn't want anything left lying around to make people start asking, where's he gone then? So you paid him up to date at Mrs Tremayne's and put his gear in a bag and came down here to dump it.'

It was funny. It was the truth he was speaking, but somehow hearing himself say it out loud made him see how feeble it was.

Other possibilities began to swirl around in his mind. Like, what if Waring was a loose end they'd thought they'd got tied up till he'd come bumbling along? And when it looked like he was taking an interest, they wouldn't know it was only because he couldn't see anything else to take an interest in. No, they'd think he must have a reason, and suddenly they started thinking maybe they'd better tie up their loose end a bit tighter.

He quickly put the lid on such speculations.

Keep it simple, Joe, he urged himself. Play it dumb. You're a poor, over-stretched PI who don't know shoot! Which was the truth of it because you couldn't call some foolish idea slowly rolling over in the murky basin of his subconscious *knowing*.

But those cold eyes, focused unblinkingly on his face, felt as if they had the power to penetrate beyond the bewildered openness of his expression into those dark depths he was trying to ignore.

The wise words of his guru, Endo Venera, came into his mind.

You find yourself on the wrong end of a gun, you gotta put yourself one step ahead of the guy holding it, which means seeing where he is going and letting him think he's one step ahead of you.

No gun here, but there might as well be one. Best he could hope if Hardman tried to push him over the edge was to delay matters by grabbing hold of the guy so that if he went, they both went. But he didn't doubt that Hardman had a dozen easy moves to dislodge an overweight underfit middling-aged PI.

But playing it dumb didn't mean you had to come on like the village idiot. If, as he thought, he was in the situation because King Rat thought he was smart, then he had to act smart, but not so smart as they were!

He said, 'Hey, I was wondering, this guy in Spain I was meant to be watching, he wouldn't be Waring using another name, would he? All fits: get him out of the country, then get me out there to watch him. Kind of neat trick I can see Mr King pulling.'

Hardman stared for a moment then laughed.

'Joe, it's true what they say about you. You're a lot smarter than you look.'

Was this mockery because he'd been fooled? Or was it a genuine compliment, meaning *Good try, but now I'm going to kill you?*

A few more seconds should tell.

Then a phone rang. Not the *Hallelujah* chorus but the theme from *Star Wars,* for God's sake!

Hardman took out a phone, glanced at the display then said, 'Yeah?'

He listened, looked at Joe, said, 'Yeah, that's right.'

He listened again for some time, then said a third and final, 'Yeah, I think so.'

A final period of listening, and he said, 'OK. Will do,' and switched off.

'Joe,' he said. 'Nice talking to you. That was Mr King.

Needs me elsewhere so I've got to love you and leave you, Joe. Listen, I wanted to say, sorry about that business in your flat earlier. Mr King was pissed at you letting him down about the Spanish job, so he asked me to go round and make it clear, and I got a bit carried away. But he's over it now. He says if I see you to tell you, no hard feelings. But he'd like his stuff back, you know, the tickets and the euros. You got them with you?'

'In the car,' said Joe.

'I'll pick them up now then.'

Together they walked back towards the fence. With every step Joe took away from the lock basin, Leck's Bottom assumed a different aspect and began to feel like a very good place to be alive in.

When they reached the Morris, Joe dug out the green file and handed it over.

'Thanks,' said Hardman. 'One thing more, Joe. Don't know what it means myself, but Mr King says he'd heard on the grapevine that some little job you were doing out at the Royal Hoo Golf Club was going to turn out OK for your client. So all's well that ends well. Mr King says he's really impressed by what he's heard about the way you handled things there, and he looks forward to employing your services again some time in the future. Could mean you're a made man if Mr King puts the word around, *capisce?*'

Capisce? and *Star Wars* as his ring tone? This guy was a joke, thought Joe. But he decided to laugh later.

'Tell him I'm truly grateful,' said Joe. 'Truly, truly.'

He didn't have to try and fake it. His gratitude was real. But it was limited to that phone call which had taken the decision away from Hardman.

Who clearly took it as going a lot further.

'Glad to have you on board again, Joe,' he said. 'Live well.'

He walked away towards his own car, a Mazda RX-8, bright red naturally, parked twenty yards further back.

Now would have been a good time to ponder. Better still would have been to ponder in the company of Butcher, and of Beryl, and even of Merv, and see how much their disparate views overlapped with his own assessment of what all this meant.

But this was one of those dreadful times in a PI's life when time didn't permit him to spread the burden. He had to act as if he was absolutely certain, which to a man whose genuine absolute certainties often turned out to be completely wrong was not a pleasant prospect.

As the Mazda drove away, he took out his mobile.

His first call was to Directory Enquiries. He asked for the number of the Royal Hoo and a few moments later he heard Bert Symonds' voice say, 'Royal Hoo Golf Club' in a tone that would have got him a butler's job anywhere.

'Bert,' he said. 'This is Joe Sixsmith. Listen, are the Bermuda Triangle there?'

The steward didn't pretend not to know who he meant.

'Yes, out on the terrace with everybody else. It's another scorcher.'

'Not where I am,' said Joe, glancing round at the dank shades of the Bottom. 'Bert, I need a favour. Any phone calls come through for the Triangle, like someone asking one of them to ring back urgently, don't pass it on.'

There was a long silence.

'Just had a call for Mr Latimer,' said Bert finally. 'Was on my way to give the message when you rang.'

'Don't. Specially if the message is to give Mr King a bell.'

Another silence.

'How'd you know that?'

'Never mind. Will you help me?'

'It's my job if Mr Latimer finds out,' said the steward.

'Who'd you rather rely on for your job, Tom Latimer or Chris Porphyry? Is he there, by the way?'

'Oh yes. Toughing it out. You know the Rules Committee are meeting tonight?'

'Yeah, no problem. That's all fixed.'

'You mean . . .'

'Never mind that. I'll explain everything later. Will you help?'

'OK, but I . . .'

'Good. Is Mr Postgate on the terrace?'

'No. Too hot for him. I imagine he's at home in the shade.'

'You got his number handy?'

'Sure.'

After Joe had noted it down he said, 'One last thing. Can you tell Mr Porphyry discreetly that I'll be on my way shortly? See him in the car park in say half an hour. OK?'

'OK. But if this goes wrong, Joe, you'd better be able to afford a well-paid assistant, because I'll be on your payroll, believe me!'

Joe switched off. That had been close. If the Triangle hadn't been on the terrace, held incommunicado by the Hoo rules on mobiles, or if Bert had already delivered King Rat's message, then his plan would be worthless. On the other hand, he'd have had plenty of time to try to put some flesh on the very skimpy bones of his theory before he made a call to the one man in Luton he really didn't want to piss off.

But needs must when the devil drives, and rehearsing in his mind the tones of absolute certainty, he turned to his phone again.

He didn't need to ask Enquiries for the number this time.

When the phone was answered he said, 'Hi. My name's Joe Sixsmith. I'd like to speak to Detective Superintendent Woodbine, please.'

25

Last Breakfast

Joe stood outside No 15 Lock-keeper's Lane and rang the doorbell with some trepidation.

To his relief it was the boy Liam who opened the door.

Joe glanced at his watch. It was half past three.

Joe said, 'Hi, Liam. Back from school already?'

'Exams,' said the boy lugubriously. 'You want to see Mum?'

Not if I don't have to, thought Joe.

He said, 'Just wondered, that morning Steve left, did he actually eat his breakfast.'

'Yeah, Steve always ate his breakfast,' said Liam wonderingly. 'He really liked Mum's cooking!'

Recalling the burnt offering he'd seen on his previous visit, Joe understood Liam's wonderment, but he wasn't sure the boy had fully understood the question.

'Don't mean generally,' he said. 'I mean, that specific Wednesday morning, did he definitely have breakfast before he went?'

Now the boy understood him.

He turned away and yelled, 'Mum! It's for you!'

Then he vanished up the stairs.

Oh shoot! thought Joe, his heart sinking not only at the prospect of renewing acquaintance with Mrs Tremayne but because he already had his answer.

She emerged from the kitchen in a puff of vegetable steam. Presumably she was preparing her returning lodgers' evening meal. It did not surprise Joe that she belonged to that old-fashioned school of landladies who thought that vegetables could never be boiled too much.

Her face was already flushed from the heat of the kitchen, but irritation at the sight of Joe slapped on another coat of puce.

'What?' she demanded.

'Mrs Tremayne, quick question then I'm out of here. Did you cook breakfast for Mr Waring the morning he left?'

She hesitated, obviously debating whether an answer or a slam of the door would get rid of Joe quickest.

Then she glanced up the stairs and said, 'What's he been saying?'

'Nothing,' said Joe. 'He's a good lad. I can see that.'

'He says you're a private detective.'

'That's right. And all I'm doing is asking a question that the police might want to ask.'

‘The police?’ she said, outraged and anxious at the same time.

‘Nothing for you to worry about,’ he assured her. ‘Only, please, in your own interest, answer me the same as you’d answer them, so there’s no contradiction.’

As an argument it didn’t feel all that weighty to Joe, but it worked for Mrs Tremayne.

‘Yes, I started cooking it, but no he didn’t eat it, if that’s what you’re getting at. Two eggs, three rashers, half a pound of pork sausage, mushrooms, tomatoes and a slice of fried bread. No use to me when it’s cooked, is it? So I didn’t see why your friends shouldn’t pay for it.’

‘Ain’t no friends of mine,’ Joe assured her. ‘So when Mr Waring didn’t appear for his breakfast, what did you do?’

‘I yelled up the stairs, then I went to his room and knocked, then I opened the door.’

‘Did his bed look like it had been slept in?’

‘It looked like it always looked,’ she snapped. ‘A tip! I told him, Mr Waring, I said, if you want your room cleaned and your bed made, you had better start leaving it halfway decent. Till you do that, I’m not going in there!’

‘But you went in that morning and he wasn’t there?’

‘No.’

‘And when Mr Waring’s brother was settling his bill this morning, he didn’t make any fuss about exactly when Mr Waring had left?’

‘No. He was most accommodating. He said, “Mrs Tremayne, no problem, I’m perfectly happy to accept that my brother was here till the morning of the Wednesday the twelfth and left after eating his usual hearty breakfast," and he insisted on me putting that down on the receipt.'

'I bet he did,' said Joe. 'Thank you very much, Mrs Tremayne.'

'Is that all I get? What about some explanation?' demanded the woman switching back to aggrieved-party mode. 'I'm entitled to know what's going on in my house.'

Joe sniffed. The steam seemed to be darkening and the boiling smell was being overtaken by the odour of burning.

'Think what's going on is your veggies have boiled over,' he said.

With a scream of rage, she turned and rushed back into the kitchen.

Joe made his escape. As he headed up along Plunkett Avenue, he felt his sense of relief at escaping from Mrs Tremayne evaporate like the nourishment from her overcooked vegetables.

He was bearing news to rejoice and news to dismay the Young Fair God, and by now he felt he knew his man well enough to be sure which would prevail.

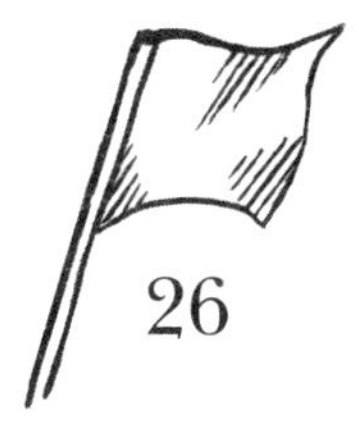

26

Pain

The Young Fair God was pacing up and down the Hoo car park in a state which came close to mortal agitation. Even the capsule of coolth in which he moved seemed to have shrunk to a mere aureola.

Joe opened his passenger door and said, 'Get in.'

Human anxieties of course are no match for divine good breeding and, as he settled into his seat, Porphyry looked around with interest and said, 'What a nice car. And a lot more comfortable than my sardine tin.'

'Swap you,' said Joe.

'You bring me good news, Joe, and it's a deal,' said Porphyry fervently.

Anyone else, Joe might have asked for this on paper, but somehow with the YFG that would have been really offensive.

He said, 'Chris, I got news and some of it's good and some of it's bad, and a lot of it's guess work and, like the man said, sometimes my theories make them Harry Potter movies seem like documentaries.'

The man in question being Willie Woodbine, but he saw no need to name names.

He took a breath and began.

'Don't know what order most of this stuff is in, but here's what I think happened. I'd guess it really started after you'd let Arthur Surtees take a look at the foundation document before the AGM in the spring. Having a drink later with his mates, Rowe and Latimer, talking about their favourite subject, money, he probably said something like, if you ever lost your membership, they should move quickly to buy up your shares as the Hoo site was worth a bundle. Now they knew that already, of course. What they probably hadn't realized till Surtees spotted it was that the rule about giving up shares applied just as much to you as any other member. Expect you knew that already?'

Porphyry shook his head.

'Never really thought about it,' he said, clearly struggling with the implications of what he was hearing.

'Why would you?' said Joe. 'The only difference is that your shares go to your successor on death whereas with everyone else the share merely returns to the pool. You still with me, Chris?'

Porphyry had got there and didn't much care for where he found himself.

'Joe, if you're suggesting that Arthur or either of the other two may be involved in this business, then really I think you're barking up the wrong tree,' he said almost indignantly. 'They've been members forever, and good members too. I mean, Tom's vice this year, he'll be captain next . . .'

This had been a foreseeable problem. Joe had guessed that getting Porphyry to believe ill of anyone of his acquaintance was going to be hard.

He said, 'Chris, just listen, will you? You don't like my theory, that's fine. Should know pretty soon if there's any facts to support it, but, just in case, you gotta listen, OK?'

'Yes, of course. Sorry, Joe. Go on.'

'Right. Then Latimer probably mentioned this to Ratcliffe King – you know Ratcliffe King?'

'Not personally, but I've heard of him. Little good, I'm afraid. He's not involved, I hope?'

Welcome to the real world, thought Joe.

'I think he is,' he said. 'King Rat – that's what his friends call him – thought about it a bit, then saw a way that this could be turned into really big money, with himself getting a fat slice, coming and going. It involved getting Sir Monty Wright fired up to throw huge sums of money into acquiring the site to build a new branch of Wright-Price on.'

'But why on earth would anyone want to build a supermarket here? Couldn't do it anyway. This is Green Belt. And what about access? Even some of our members complain about these little country lanes. Building new access roads alone would cost a fortune, and they'd never get planning permission . . .'

'Chris, you'd better believe me, everyone knows – everyone 'cept you maybe – that King Rat's got hold of enough people's strings to get permission to put up a massage parlour in the town cemetery if that's what he wants. As for the roads, I reckon he's been quietly buying up a lot of the land they'll have to cross, at agricultural prices, natch. No, the Rat only needed two things to make this work. First was to get Sir Monty fired up enough to make him ignore the fact that the Hoo's a really stupid place to build a new hyper-mart. That was easy. Latimer proposed Sir Monty for membership and then blackballed him.'

'You mean Bert was right and it really was Tom? But that's . . .'

'Not playing the game? Yeah, these guys aren't playing the game, get your head round that, Chris. And the real clever thing was that Latimer made it personal to Sir Monty by letting him think it was you did the blackballing. Second part of the plot was harder. You had to lose your membership of the club. The only way they could see of doing this was getting you caught cheating. Like you said, the rule here's absolutely clear. You get found guilty of cheating, you're out, no appeal, right?'

Porphyry was still in denial.

He shook his head and said, 'Joe, this really is crazy . . . I mean, the Sir Monty thing was nothing to do with me;

unfortunate, but these things happen, and as for catching me cheating . . .'

'Chris, when you're King Rat, you plan things carefully, you take your time. I'd guess that the Triangle worked out half a dozen schemes that would put you in the frame for cheating. Some of them probably involved Latimer or Surtees or Rowe or all three giving evidence. At its simplest, it just needed two of them to testify they'd seen you do something dodgy, and what's the Rules Committee to do, specially as two of them are on it? But best of all would be if they could keep right out of it and someone no one would suspect of having an axe to grind pointed the finger. Some old chum of yours, like Jimmy Postgate.'

'You're not saying Jimmy . . . ?'

'No way! He was conned like everyone else. I bet they had half a dozen possible schemes, but this was the one that worked out first. Lucky for them, unlucky for you. I guess everyone in the club knows about you being such a long hitter that you usually tried to carry the corner on the sixteenth. Jimmy Postgate told me you were one of the few people who'd ever put a ball in his pool. Every time you played that hole for the past few weeks, I bet one of the Triangle was lurking in that bit of wood. Then, during your Vardon Cup match, it all fell perfect. You clattered one into the trees and Colin Rowe saw his chance.'

'Colin . . . how can you be sure it was Colin?'

''Cos I had another word with Mr Postgate and he

recalled that just after the ball plopped into his pool, Rowe turned up at his house. Said that committee he's chair of . . .'

'The Greens Committee.'

'That's the one. Said they were thinking of relocating a couple of bunkers and he wanted to sound Jimmy out. I reckon Rowe heard your ball hit the tree, maybe even saw where it finished, so he picked it up, and placed it nice and handy right at the edge of the fairway then took off into the woods and lobbed another ball into Postgate's pool.'

'But he'd have needed one of my own personalized balls . . .'

Joe was getting a bit exasperated.

'Chris, you gotta get it into your head these people aren't playing around. They'd been planning this for months. They probably got more of your personal balls than you have!'

'That's monstrous!' exclaimed the YFG.

'Yeah, that's right,' said Joe, gentle now as he remembered the real pain that was still to come. 'Monstrous. That's what they are. So Rowe showed up, which stopped Jimmy wandering off into the wood looking for you, which would have ruined everything. Also, after chatting for three-quarters of an hour or so, Rowe suggested they went up to the clubhouse for a drink and even reminded Jimmy to bring your ball along so he could return it to you. They timed it perfect. Maybe Latimer or Surtees belled Rowe and told him you and the guy you beat were in the bar and he was telling the tale of how you came from behind and took the game from him. Like I say, perfect. Except for one thing. Someone had seen Rowe placing your ball at the edge of the fairway.'

Hope lit up Porphyry's face.

'You mean you've found a witness? Joe, you are a marvel!'

'Hold it there, Chris,' said Joe. 'Said I *think* there was a witness, didn't say I'd found him. I think it was Steve Waring.'

'Steve? But if it were Steve . . . then why hasn't he . . . ?'

'That's the question, Chris,' said Joe. 'Why hasn't he come forward? I think he was working somewhere round there, maybe he'd dipped into the woods to have a quick fag where Davie wouldn't see him. He heard the ball hit the trees, saw Rowe pick it up and place it, then disappear. Bit later he probably saw you come along and play it.'

'But surely he'd have spoken to me?'

'To say what? "Hey, Mr Porphyry, that friend of yours, Mr Rowe, he just done you a favour by really improving the position of your ball." No, Steve liked you, he knew how you'd helped him and his mum. If someone wanted to give you a helping hand, that was OK by him. He took off and it wasn't till he was talking to Bert, the steward, later, that he heard about all the fuss there'd been when Postgate turned up in the bar.'

'So why didn't he say something then?'

'Wanted to talk to Rowe first, make sure he'd got things

right. Got Bert to tell Rowe that he wanted a word, urgent. Rowe came out to see him. Must have nearly squittered himself when he heard what the lad had to say. Laughed it off and said, Oh yes, I can explain that. Just hang on here a few minutes while I sort out some stuff I got to do in the clubhouse, then I'll explain to you exactly what's been going off. Went somewhere quiet and belled Ratcliffe King.'

'Why King? Why not talk to Latimer or Surtees?'

''Cos in a real emergency, the Rat's the man you turn to to get things fixed. King wasn't going to rely on Rowe to sort it. He said he'd send out one of his own guys to make Waring an offer he couldn't refuse. There's this guy called Hardman that the Rat uses when he wants to persuade people to co-operate.'

'Sorry? Co-operate?'

'When he wants bribes paid or arms twisted,' said Joe. 'The Rat probably told Rowe that Hardman would be waiting for him somewhere along the road to Upleck. All Rowe had to do was get Waring in his car and bring him along. So Rowe wanders back and says to young Steve, Why don't I give you a lift home while we talk? Steve's got his scooter here but likes the thought of getting a ride in a comfortable posh car, and kids never worry about what they'll do tomorrow, do they?'

'No,' said Porphyry. 'Steve lives very much day by day. Are you saying they bribed him to keep quiet? Oh God. Poor devil. He always dreamt of being rich, you know. That would explain why he took off like that. His conscience wouldn't let him face me. Poor Steve. Can't really blame him. I've always had money. Not having it must be a terrible trial.'

It broke Joe's heart to hear the YFG talking like this. Even if the boy he'd helped so much had let him down, he would find excuses, never dream of condemning him.

He said, 'I think it could be worse than that, Chris. I think that Hardman got into the car and told Steve something like, You get a lot of money if you keep your mouth shut; you get a lot of pain if you don't. Usually works. Only this time, I don't think it does, 'cos Steve reckons he owes you. They're getting close to his lodgings now and he probably feels safe. Anyway, he's in Mr Rowe's car, and Mr Rowe's a member at the Hoo, a gent, so no real problem there. He says he thinks he'll just check things out with you, see if all this really is no problem like they say. He pulls out his phone and hits the speed dial . . .'

'That's right! I told you there was a call from him that night . . .'

'Yeah,' said Joe, wanting to get the next bit over quick. 'And when he hits that button, I think Hardman, sitting in the back, hits him.'

'Good Lord! The bastard. Would he do something like that?'

'Oh yes. Probably didn't mean to hit him too hard. Or maybe Steve tried to fight back, so he thought he'd give him a bit of a bang. Doesn't matter. Steve keels over. Rowe thinks he's been knocked unconscious. They're near the lodgings in Lock-keeper's Lane now. Hardman tells him to keep going, not to stop. He feels for a pulse in Steve's neck. Can't find one. The car gets to the end of the road. Keep going, he tells Rowe. Finally he has to stop 'cos he's reached the fence in front of the old lock. And now Hardman gets the boy out of the car and tries to revive him. But it's no good. He's dead.'

There, he'd said it. Whatever shocks to the YFG's system he'd administered before, this was the big one. This was reality wake-up time.

'Dead? You're saying Steve might be dead?'

His tone was incredulous.

'Can't be absolute sure, but yeah, I think it's likely.'

'But surely for something like this . . . I mean, why would they kill him for something like this?'

'Don't think it was meant,' said Joe. 'You recall telling me his dad had this thin skull condition so that, when he fell over, a bang that would just have given someone else a headache killed him? Well, seems it can be inherited. I think Hardman gave him a tap with some sort of cosh maybe and it fractured his skull. There'd be bleeding in the brain. That would kill him.'

Probably not instantly. Still hope with rapid treatment. But even if the lad had been alive when they stopped in Leck's Bottom, even if Rowe had wanted to call up help, by the time he and Hardman were through arguing, it would be too late, and Hardman would be able to say, He's gone, you want to call up help now and explain all this?

But he didn't want to load Porphyry with the possibility that Steve might have been saved. He was having difficulty enough accepting the possibility of the boy's death.

'Joe, this is terrible . . . but it's just theory, right? I mean, what makes you think this is more likely than that he accepted a pay-off and headed out somewhere?'

'Because I got a message from Ratcliffe King saying that the pressure was off you, that this cheating thing was going to go away.'

This should have been the news that brought a sunburst of relief to Porphyry's face, but he remained sombre.

'I don't understand – what's this got to do with Steve? Unless he's decided to give evidence . . . Couldn't that be it? Steve's told them he's going to come forward and tell the truth?'

'No, Chris. I'm sorry. I told Monty Wright what I thought had happened. When I got through to him that it wasn't you but Latimer who'd blackballed him and that it was probably the Triangle who framed you for cheating, I reckon he just wanted to step right away from the whole business. Probably didn't make much commercial sense for Wright-Price anyway. So I think this afternoon he rang King Rat, told him what I'd told him, and asked him to confirm or deny it. Whatever King Rat replied, it was enough for Sir Monty to realize I was telling the truth. Then he probably told King Rat he was pulling out. Not only that, if these accusations against you weren't made to go away, he'd make a public stink about it. He's a very sporting guy, Sir Monty.'

'And that was enough for King to scrap the whole deal, despite all the money he must already have put into it, buying land and such?'

'I think it would be a close call. I think that King Rat would know very well that, with regard to you, they were in the clear. What proof did Sir Monty have? What proof did I have? There was a good chance they could still get you out and get their hands on your shares. Worth a fight anyway. Except . . .'

'Except for Steve!' cried Porphyry triumphantly. 'If they knew Steve was going to tell the truth . . .'

'No, forget that, Chris,' said Joe urgently. 'They'd taken his gear and his scooter and dumped them in Leck's Bottom. They'd got his landlady to say he was still around on the Wednesday morning. But he wasn't. I think that the previous night, when they realized he was dead, Hardman put him in Rowe's big golf-bag carrier that he had in his boot, plus a few rocks maybe, zipped it up and dropped it in the lock basin. That's what tipped the balance with King Rat. When it comes to financial deals, and regulations, and legal trickery, he can run rings round anyone. Bodies are different. Bodies can't be explained away with figures. All you can do is hide them and hope they never show.'

Pain was sharpening the YFG's perceptions.

'And he begins to fear your enquiries might reveal what had happened to poor . . .'

His voice broke on the boy's name.

'Right,' said Joe. 'He does his best to tidy things up. But

it's not working. Getting me out of the way one way or another is a definite option. Then Sir Monty backs out and threatens to cry foul! Suddenly it's all unravelling. So King decides to cut his losses, press the restore button, and get everything back to where it was. You're in the clear, the Hoo is safe, everyone's happy.'

Porphyry considered this for a moment then said, 'But I'm not in the clear, Joe. Latimer's been here all afternoon and he's not said a word about me being in the clear . . . Perhaps that means you've got it wrong and Steve's alive after all . . .'

His willingness to be labelled a cheat if it meant that Waring was still living confirmed everything Joe felt about the man. He hated to remove even this dry crumb of comfort but it had to be done.

'No, Chris,' he said. 'Latimer's not said anything because he doesn't know that things have changed yet. This has all just happened in the last hour. King Rat's trying to get in touch with the Triangle, but they're all here with their mobiles in their cars. And I've persuaded Bert not to pass on any messages.'

Porphyry stared at him for a moment, then his expression hardened from hope to resolve.

'Right!' he exclaimed. 'Let's go and give those bastards a nasty surprise.'

He started to get out of the car. He had the look of an avenging angel.

Joe held him back.

'Chris, no. All you'll do is warn them, give them time to get their story straight and tidy away any evidence that might be lying around in their homes or offices. King will be squeaky clean by now. The only way to him is to get those three so terrified they start singing like Rev Pot's choir. No way we can do that. That needs special training. The kind of training Willie Woodbine's had.'

'Then let's call Willie.'

'Done it,' said Joe. 'But even Willie needs evidence. He should be down at Leck's Bottom by now with a bunch of police divers.'

This reminder of what the evidence might consist of drained the light of avenging fury from the YFG's face.

'Poor Steve . . .' he murmured. 'Poor Steve . . .'

Joe assumed what he hoped was the reassuring briskness of a man in complete charge of events.

'Listen, Chris, I asked Willie to ring me soon as he found . . . anything. You take my mobile and stay here. Soon as Willie rings, you come up to the clubhouse to let me know. Tell Willie to get his ass over here quick as he can. I'll go up to the terrace now and check on the Triangle. If they look at all restless, I'll find a way to keep them occupied. This sound OK to you?'

The YFG nodded and with an unconvincing attempt at brightness said, 'Joe, as usual you're spot on. You should be top man at the Yard.'

'Great,' said Joe. 'Then I'll see you soon.'

He got out of the Morris and walked away.

Just before he entered the alley through the shrubs he turned and looked back.

Porphyry was slumped forward over the dashboard, his head in his hands, his shoulders shaking with the force of the sobs that had finally broken to the surface now he was alone.

Joe turned away.

The bastards who could cause so much pain to his Young Fair God deserved everything they had coming to them.

He went on his way to play his part in making sure they got it.

27

End of Play

The terrace was crowded.

Joe took in the scene as he approached. The elegantly dressed members and their guests lounging beneath huge sunshades striped in the club colours of crimson, green and blue, the sound of chattering voices and laughter and ice cubes clinking against glass, the swift but unobtrusive movement among them of Bert Symonds and his white-coated assistants, the sense that all was for the best in the best of possible worlds. But he knew it now for a world in which butterflies roared and you couldn't tell by looking who was playing gotchas.

He glanced at his watch. Five o'clock. How time flew when you weren't enjoying yourself. He tried to remind himself that most of the people here had worked hard to earn their place in the sun, but he couldn't help wondering how many of them had decided to make an evening of it at the club because they knew the Four Just Men were sitting in judgement on Chris at eight o'clock.

He recalled reading somewhere that public hangings way back had always drawn huge crowds. It wasn't every day you got the chance to view the death of a Young Fair God.

He spotted the Triangle at the same table they'd occupied when first he met them. Perhaps, like Sir Monty's table at the Supporters', it had an invisible reserved sign on it. He advanced, looking to right and left as if in search of someone.

'Good day, Mr Sixsmith, nice to see you again.'

It was Bert, the steward, who'd contrived to cross his path. The reason why became apparent when in a rapid whisper which didn't trouble the deferential expression on his face, he said, '*King's getting really pissed no one's returning his calls. Can't keep this going much longer, Joe.*'

Joe didn't blame him. He knew from experience that being on the wrong end of King Rat's anger was not a pleasant experience.

He smiled and said, 'Nice to see you too, Bert. Is Mr Porphyry here? *Won't be long now, promise.*'

'*Better not be.* No, sir, I haven't seen him.'

Joe moved on to Latimer's table.

'Joe, good to see you again!' said the vice-captain.

The guy should be in movies. He really looked and sounded like he meant it.

'Hi, Tom. I was just asking Bert if Chris was around. I'm supposed to be meeting him.'

'Story of your life, waiting for Chris, it seems. Like waiting for Godot. He was here earlier, I think. Pull up a chair till he shows.'

'Thanks. Don't mind if I do.'

He sat down and nodded a greeting at Rowe and Surtees, both of whom regarded him narrowly, but there was nothing about them which suggested the jitters. He guessed that after Rowe had reported that, contrary to expectation, Sixsmith was still sniffing around this morning, King Rat had assured them there was nothing to worry about, he'd now make absolutely sure that any potential problem was nipped in the bud. Way their minds worked, seeing him here not walking on crutches probably meant he must have accepted a sackful of banknotes from the ProtoVision petty cash.

He decided to encourage this misconception. Dipping into his back pocket, he pulled out the YFG's notes, which still managed to retain some of their crispness.

'Buy you gents a drink?' he offered.

'Thanks, Joe, but not allowed, not till you're a member,' said Latimer. 'But let me get you one. Bert!'

The steward materialized at the table.

'Joe?'

'Thanks. I'll have one of them ice coffees.'

'Wise man. Alcohol and sun don't mix. Thank you, Bert.'

'You not having any more?' said Joe as the steward moved away.

'No, these will do us. Such a lovely evening we thought we'd play a few holes shortly. Can't do a full round, more's the pity. Arthur and I have a meeting at eight.'

Now he felt their eyes hard on him, looking for his reaction.

He said negligently, 'This that discipline thing? Chris mentioned it. Shame, but rules is rules, that's what I say.'

He almost felt Latimer and Rowe relax, but Surtees with his lawyer's cynicism liked his judgements handed down signed, sealed and bound with scarlet ribbon. He emptied his glass and said, 'Better get going or it's not going to be worth it.'

He wants to get away from here and as soon as he's out on the golf course with no one in earshot but the other two, he'll get his mobile out and check with King that I've been truly nobbled, thought Joe.

By then it probably wouldn't matter. If Woodbine had got his finger out, they'd be trawling through the lock basin now, and once they found Waring's body in Rowe's bag Willie would be all over them like galloping shingles. Surtees' legal nimbleness might keep him clear for a while, but Joe would have put his own money on Rowe crumbling like meringue and spreading the blame like runny butter.

On the other hand, if the police didn't find Waring . . .

But they would find the body, Joe assured himself. What else could the evidence possibly mean?

He pushed aside all the previous examples of fatal misinterpretation which came swimming out of his past. No time for a faint heart now. He had to be true to himself. And when this bunch of bastards got what was coming to them, he wanted to be there and he wanted it to be in public. Had to think of a way of delaying them here, certainly of keeping them in sight.

Latimer said, 'You're right, Arthur. Joe, what about you? Why don't you keep Chris waiting for a change and join us for a few holes?'

He was taking the piss, like they'd all done from the start. In their eyes he was a sad little snoop who'd probably let himself be bought off for what in their eyes was a pittance. Joe didn't mind. The brightest and the best had often discovered the price of justice was humiliation. And in any case he'd made it clear from the start he was a crap golfer with a zero handicap.

He said, 'Sure, why not?'

They looked at him in amazement which rapidly turned to amusement.

He added, 'But I don't have any gear. Last time you said you could kit me out. That still on?'

His thinking was that he could probably drag out the process of being kitted out long enough for Woodbine to get in touch.

Latimer said, 'No problem. In fact, it might give the rest of us a bit of a chance if you have to play with borrowed clubs, eh?'

They all laughed. There was malice in their laughter.

The bastards are really enjoying themselves, thought Joe.

It made him uneasy. Seeing a bad golfer play badly couldn't be all that funny, could it?

In any case, he had no intention of actually trying to hit a ball!

He glanced around the terrace, hoping to see Porphyry with the look on his face that said Woodbine had rung to say their search had turned up a body. But there was no sign of him.

Latimer was urging him to his feet and next moment they were walking down the steps from the terrace in the direction of the pro's shop.

It was now that Joe began to feel his will and muscle power melting. All he had to do of course was say, Hey, let's end this farce; you know who I am and what I'm doing here, and before very long you are going to be in deep doo-doo.

But somehow he couldn't utter the words. No great gambler himself, he recalled Merv Golightly, who would bet on the next bit of bird crap to hit his windscreen, saying, Never show your hand till the last card's dealt. Did that really apply here? Maybe, maybe not. All he knew was that his thoughts were flitting like a bat in a cellar trying to find a way out and coming up against stone walls and locked doors in every direction.

In the shop, Chip Harvey looked slightly puzzled to see Joe in Latimer's company, and even more puzzled when the vice-captain explained what was happening.

Latimer said, 'Joe, I'm just going to go and get my own gear together. Chip, don't go digging out any fancy clubs for Mr Sixsmith. He's scratch, you know, so we want to give him every disadvantage.'

He moved away, laughing.

Joe looked after him with a distaste that unusually for him bordered on loathing.

'Real funny guy,' he said. 'Why do they say "scratch" anyway? Because guys like me would be better off not starting? Or maybe because the way we play looks like scratching around?'

Chip ignored the question and said anxiously, 'Joe, what's going on?'

'It's OK, Chip,' said Joe, feeling sorry for the boy. 'Really, everything's going to be sorted soon. Nothing for you to worry about. You just do as Latimer said, get me kitted out, but you needn't rush the job, OK?'

The assistant pro brought him a selection of golf shoes which he tried on, some of them twice, till he found a pair that felt more comfortable than his own slip-ons.

He stomped around the shop in them, then selected a club at random from a display rack and waggled it about.

Chip said, 'You're left handed then. That'll make things a bit harder.'

'No,' said Joe. 'I ain't a leftie.'

'You're not? Well, that's a left-handed club you've got.'

'Is it? Thought it felt kind of funny.'

He picked up one with the head facing the other way. It felt only slightly less funny.

Chip had been watching him with growing unease.

Now he burst out, 'Joe, are you really scratch?'

'Yeah, unless you can get worse than scratch, in which case, that's me.'

The young man let out a pained sigh and looked heavenward like a curate who's just been told that the ten commandments only apply where there's an F in the month.

He said urgently, 'Joe, you've got it so wrong. Being scratch means you're a very good golfer indeed. The worse you are, the bigger your handicap. So if your handicap's, say, eighteen, it means that a scratch golfer would give you a shot start on every hole!'

'No, that can't be right,' said Joe with confidence.

The door opened and Tom Latimer called, 'You about ready, Joe?'

'Coming,' Joe replied. 'Just choosing my clubs.'

'OK.'

The door closed and Joe repeated, with less confidence this time, 'That can't be right. Can it?'

'You'd better believe it,' said Chip in a low voice as he set a couple of golf bags before Joe. 'You ever play golf before? Ever?'

'Once went on a putting green in the park,' said Joe, adding as he sought desperately for evidence that he was misinterpreting the young man, 'You trying to tell me that scratch means you're good?'

'It means you're very good. Very very good. Very very very good.'

There's no arguing with three verys.

'Oh shoot,' said Joe.

'Never mind,' said Chip, unhappy to see the distress he had caused. 'It's really not a difficult game if you stick to the basics. Eye on the ball, head still, swing easy. Piece of cake.'

It was clearly well intentioned, but to Joe it sounded like telling a man bound to a stake before a firing squad to watch out for flying bullets. He picked up the golf bag. It weighed a ton, but that didn't make much difference when your legs felt they were anchored in lead. Suddenly his determination not to get anywhere near the first tee blotted out everything else in his mind.

He emerged into the bright sunlight. He worked out that if he turned left and moved quick, he could be back at his car and using his phone to ring Woodbine and ask him what the shoot was holding him up before the Triangle noticed his disappearance.

But Tom Latimer was waiting for him just outside the door.

'This way, Joe,' he said. 'Thought we'd play the first two then cut through the woods by Jimmy Postgate's house and play ourselves in over the last three. See if you can carry the corner on the sixteenth like Chris sometimes does.'

The mockery was almost open now.

Bastard! thought Joe.

The adrenalin surge of the hatred gave him strength to move forward with the man down a steep pathway towards what he guessed was the first tee. Surtees and Rowe were there already. They watched his approach with smiling bonhomie. It should have been a comfort to think that soon they'd be getting their comeuppance, but somehow he'd lost all confidence in his theories. He suspected that the only reason Willie Woodbine was going to make contact with him was to vent his fury.

'Now how shall we do this?' said Latimer as they reached the tee. 'High-low takes, that all right with you, Joe? Means you'll have to carry me, but that's the penalty of excellence. OK by you?'

Joe didn't answer. He was staring down the tree-lined fairway which stretched away to a green so distant, he had to screw up his eyes to make out the flag.

Then he heard a murmur of voices and a ripple of laughter and, looking up, he saw to his horror that their path had taken them round the side of the clubhouse and the first tee was positioned right beneath one end of the terrace where so recently he'd been sitting sipping iced coffee. Directly above him, the ornate balustrade was lined with spectators, drinks in hand, like Romans in the Emperor's box, waiting for the gladiators to start the slaughter.

'By rights it should be low man's honour,' said Latimer. 'But as it's your first time here, Joe, we'll let these bandits show us the way, shall we?'

Joe looked at him blankly. Now was the time to have his heart attack, but somehow the presence of all these people looking down from above, while making it even more imperative that he put a stop to this farce, made it even harder to do so.

Rowe was on the tee. He placed a ball at his feet, then

without ceremony and with very little evidence of effort, sent it soaring greenwards. It took one mighty bounce, a couple of skips, then rolled for ever and finally came to a halt right in the middle of the fairway at a distance which Joe's good eye reckoned as two eighty or two ninety yards.

There was a ripple of applause from above.

Surtees took his turn. More methodical than Rowe, he had three studied practice swings before cracking his ball away to finish some fifteen yards behind his partner.

Now it was Latimer. He was a real fusspot, standing behind his ball as if taking very precise aim, before doing some stretching exercises followed by half a dozen practice swings. Above someone yawned audibly and there was a snort of quickly stifled laughter. Finally he addressed the ball and after staring at it for what even to Joe, who was happy to wait forever, seemed a hell of a long time, he swung.

It wasn't a bad hit; a bit misdirected, so that at first it looked like it was heading towards the left-hand trees, then it curved back into the fairway, bounced, ran to the right-hand edge, and came to a halt some thirty yards back from Rowe's ball.

'Sorry about that, Joe,' said Latimer, shaking his head in rather stagy disappointment. 'Lucky I've got you to put things straight.'

Joe advanced on to the tee. Each step was the last before his dodgy knee buckled beneath him. Each second was the one before he had his seizure. But somehow he kept taking the steps and somehow the seconds kept ticking by. Perhaps it was his certainty that he physically couldn't do this that kept him going. Why fake illness when any moment now you really were going to collapse in a heap?

But the collapse never came and finally here he was, adrift in space, looking down at that little white orb so many light years away, and waiting in vain for a black hole to open and swallow him up.

The silence was absolute. Not a sound from the terrace above. His three companions stood behind the tee still as statues. Even the birds had stopped singing.

But there was sound in that silence. Now he could hear it, though he doubted if anyone else could. The sound that Porphyry had told him about, the sound that was less intrusive than the music of the spheres to normal human hearing but disruptively cacophonous to the golfer, destroying all his powers of concentration and co-ordination.

He could hear the roar of the butterflies in the adjacent meadow.

Time for the farce to end. All he had to do was step back and say in front of everybody, Listen, you bastards, you may have stitched poor Chris Porphyry up, but you ain't going to make a fool out of me.

He took a deep breath and tried to persuade his feet to take that step back. Nothing happened. Oh shoot. Collapse was one thing, petrifaction was another. Maybe they'd all just tiptoe away and leave him be. Maybe in years to come people would pay cash money to come and see the famous statue of the man who turned to stone at Royal Hoo.

Maybe . . .

He said a prayer, but he doubted if it could be heard beyond the stars, so loud now were the butterflies.

But somehow it got through, for from high above he heard a voice reply.

'Joe!' the voice called. 'JOE!'

He looked up and wouldn't have been surprised to see a circling dove or two.

There were no doves, but he beheld an infinitely more welcome sight.

It was indeed the voice of god, a Young Fair God, holding up a mobile phone.

Yes, still young and fair, but now Christian's face was the face of a very vengeful deity.

'They found him, Joe. They found him. They're on their way.'

Even as he spoke, Joe realized that the faraway sound that had so paralysed him wasn't a roar of butterflies or anything else. It was the high-pitched, rhythmic wail of sirens, still a long way away but approaching fast, and now detectable by the terrace spectators, who broke their own expectant silence with speculative chatter.

Joe turned his head and looked at the Triangle. They too had heard and their faces were twisted in fearful speculation.

He smiled at them. Now at last his muscles unlocked and he felt he had the strength to step away.

On the other hand, there was a YFG above him, and Joe knew from his upbringing that while God might not dish out His grace too frequently, when He did, there was no stinting and a wise man filled his boots.

He brought to mind what Chip Harvey had said.

Eye on the ball, head still, swing easy.

He swung so easy, without any sense of contact, that for a second he was convinced he must have missed. Except that the ball that the eye in his perfectly still head was on wasn't there.

On the terrace the spectators forgot about the sirens and fell silent again, a silence quickly broken by the hiss of in-drawn breath. Of many in-drawn breaths.

He looked up and saw his ball. At least he saw someone's ball, though it was so distant and receding so fast he couldn't really believe it was his.

It was still high in the air when it passed over Latimer's, it made first contact with the ground a yard or so beyond Surtees', its first bounce took it past Rowe's, and it continued for a good fifty yards before finally coming to rest in the middle of the fairway.

From the terrace above came a rattle of applause, a rumble of cheers, and even, despite the fact that this was the Royal Hoo, a skirl of appreciative whistles which turned into gasps of horror as the first police car appeared, making directly for the clubhouse straight up the sacred fairway.

One thing about Willie Woodbine, he knew how to make an entrance.

Joe turned and walked off the tee.

Chip had been right. It was an easy game. And the roar